The Library of Scandinavian Literature

IN THE DAYS OF THE COUNCILLOR

IN THE DAYS OF THE COUNCILLOR

TRYGGVE ANDERSEN

TRANSLATED FROM THE NORWEGIAN BY
BEATRICE H. STROUP AND STEIN MATHISEN

INTRODUCTION BY
EDVARD BEYER

TWAYNE PUBLISHERS, INC., NEW YORK
&
THE AMERICAN-SCANDINAVIAN FOUNDATION

The Library of Scandinavian Literature
Erik J. Friis, *General Editor*
Volume 4
In the Days of the Councillor, by Tryggve Andersen

Library of Congress catalogue card number: 71-99537

MANUFACTURED IN THE UNITED STATES OF AMERICA

Contents

Introduction 1
The Wife of the Councillor 9
The Parson's Family 41
The Perjurers 91
Captain Tebetmann's Daughter 113
Autumn Assizes 145
Anne Cathrine Bühring 177
In the Councillor's Kitchen 193
The Sermon 211
Miss Nannestad 221
Famine 231

Introduction

NORWAY is a comparatively large country with a very small and scattered population. In regard to travel and communications, it was until recently quite far removed from the European Continent, and its history as an independent nation is a short one.

From the end of the fourteenth century until 1814 Norway was united with Denmark, and from 1814 until 1905 it was in a union with Sweden, again as the weaker partner. During the latter period the Norwegians were at the same time groping their way toward a cultural identity of their own after centuries of Danish predominance, and fighting for an extension of self-government and equal rights within the new political union. Both aspirations implied opposition to the conservative elements within the population and a striving for democracy.

Like the writers of the "new" nations today, the leading Norwegian writers of the time played an important part in the realization of these aspirations. They turned to account the newfound ore of balladry and popular tales, and broke the ascendancy of the Danish language by giving pith and marrow to no less than two written Norwegian languages. Later on, about 1870, they took to writing plays and novels of severe social criticism.

The 1870's and 80's, a golden age for Norwegian literature, were dominated by a strong current of realism and naturalism, characterized by vehement and relentless criticism of the established order of society in the name of truth and liberty and the rights of the individual. It was the period of *Pillars of Society, A Doll's House, An Enemy of the People,* and *Ghosts* by Henrik Ibsen, of a number of novels and plays in the same vein by Björnstjerne Björnson, Jonas Lie, Alexander Kielland, and other talented writers.

A reaction set in about the year 1890. The younger generation—Knut Hamsun and others—wanted to liberate literature from its social obligations. They advocated and created a more subjective and introspective literature, they wrote poetry or poetical short stories and novels rather than problem plays and naturalistic novels, they were more interested in the complex life and longings of the mind than in the conflicting forces of society. Whereas the literature of the 1880's had mainly been a literature dealing with the people in the towns, the "neoromantics" of the 1890's to a great extent preferred the country as a setting for their work, and regional literature was in vogue. And whereas "the eighties" had been engrossed by the present, the poets of "the nineties" made new approaches to popular tradition and history. Like the old romanticists some of the young writers cherished the memories and living relics of the past. Unlike them, however, they treated these matters realistically, as means to a franker and fuller understanding of the national character. Most important of these authors were Hans E. Kinck, whose imposing literary production covers all genres, and Tryggve Andersen, whose fame rests almost exclusively on *I Cancelliraadens dage—In the Days of the Councillor.*

Tryggve Andersen was born near Hamar, in the southeastern, inland part of the country, in 1866. His father was a civil servant, his mother of peasant stock, and from his early years the boy steeped himself in local lore and traditions. He also acquainted himself with the poets of German romanticism, and about 1890 he was one of the most ardent spokesmen of the neoromantic revival. He was a student of Egyptology, and a brilliant scholar's career seemed to lie before him when in 1892 a trifling episode caused his dismissal from the university.

Andersen never completely recovered from this blow, but after a couple of years he returned to his native district, where propitious circumstances brought him into close contact with the old public archives of the city of Hamar. His perusal of these records extended his familiarity with and further aroused his interest in the local traditions. Episodes and characters of the past took shape before his eyes and on paper, and in 1897 he published *In the Days of the Councillor,* his first book and his masterpiece. It was followed by a very interesting—and very modern—novel called *Mod kvæld* ("Toward Evening") and a number of exquisite short stories, some of which are among the best in Norwegian literature.

A discerning critic, Tryggve Andersen tutored his younger colleagues generously and wrote brilliant newspaper articles. But personal disasters and excessive self-criticism paralyzed his creative powers for the greater part of the years left him. *Diary from a Sea Voyage,* published posthumously, gives moving glimpses of a mind harrowed by misfortune and despair. He died in 1920.

In the Days of the Councillor takes place in the inland district of Ringsaker, near Lake Mjösa, north of Oslo (or Christiania, as the city was then called). The time is the period 1798 to 1812, i.e., the last years of the Danish-Norwegian dual monarchy, when the Napoleonic Wars and the

British blockade of the European coasts broke off communication and trade between the two countries. Historical events—the suicide in 1808 of Enevold Falsen, a leading member of the administrative council of Norway, and the great famine of 1812—influence the action, and the peculiar social and cultural conditions of the period make up the general background.

The feudalism of the Middle Ages had largely bypassed Norway, and by 1814, the old native aristocracy of the country had long ago died out; its role had been taken over by the civil servants, including the clergy. Due to the superior role of Denmark in the Dano-Norwegian union, these officials were often Danes by birth and had at any rate been educated in Copenhagen, the common capital of the two countries. Appointment in Norway was often considered a banishment from a center of civilization to a barren country with a barbarous and hostile population. What they did not see was the fact that the people had a cultural tradition of their own, and they did not seriously attempt to bridge the gap. At all events, this is the case with most of the officials as depicted in this book, and their isolated and rootless position is the underlying reason for their individual tragedies or decay.

However, the chief character in the book, Councillor and Judge Weydahl, gradually realizes the predicament and the responsibility of his class, and in the central chapter, "Autumn Assizes," he looks prophetically into the future of his country.

In his great work Tryggve Andersen has succeeded in combining realistic and romantic qualities in a very harmonious way. He is a realist in his fidelity to fact and his sober and straightforward style. But he is a romanticist in his devotion to the past, in his intimate sense of atmosphere, and in the way in which he has imbued the work with his own personality.

Most of the characters in the book are molded on models known in local tradition. Andersen himself has carefully listed them, and scholarly investigation has confirmed that he has treated factual circumstances with a high degree of fidelity. But research has also made clear to what extent his characters are, after all, of his own creation. Many of them share his own melancholia; in fact, they carry "my own burdens" as he once put it. And they are all colored by a unifying poetic vision of the past, and of life in general.

This vision turns the book into something more than a collection of short stories. Each of the chapters is complete in itself and testifies to the author's mastership as a storyteller. But the stories are also bound together, not only by a set of recurring characters, but—what is more important—by a unity of theme and atmosphere approaching that of a novel.

When first published, *In the Days of the Councillor* was an immediate success. It took the public by storm and was very favorably received by the critics, adherents of realism and spokesmen of neoromanticism alike. It was hailed for its truthful and intimate rendering of the past as well as for its artistic qualities, its balance of composition and precision of style. Björnstjerne Björnson warmly applauded it, and Henrik Ibsen, who was never lavish with his praise, recommended the book, admitting that he had been impressed by the young author. Tryggve Andersen's first work has become one of the great classics of Norwegian literature.

It has also had a lasting influence. Its terse and vigorous style made it a model of modern Norwegian prose. "He is, after all, the foundation," wrote his contemporary Hans E.

Kinck. As a prose writer Andersen is generally recognized as one of Norway's greatest; indeed, his prose has been a paragon to many young authors and a counterbalance to Hamsun-like lyricism and whimsicality.

Many writers of historical fiction have derived a special inspiration from Andersen's work. Among them was Johan Falkberget, the outstanding narrator of the last few decades. In the structure of Falkberget's magnificent historical novels, Andersen's work is seen to have been a vital influence.

EDVARD BEYER

The University of Oslo

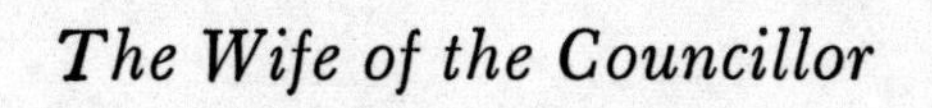

The Wife of the Councillor

I

DURING one of the last years of the eighteenth century, on an evening in the middle of summer, Judge Weydahl, the new Councillor of Chancery, came to the district. For a long time before he and his wife arrived, they had been talked about and discussed among the better families of the neighborhood.

Parson Lind had asked questions about the new judge over a glass of homebrew at the home of Attorney Höegh, an old lawyer officiating during the interim, but he didn't know much about the new councillor. Then the parson had visited the major at Emilienberg and the major's wife had told him confidentially, as they sat drinking their liqueur (which she herself had made) that the name of the judge's wife had been Catharina von Zehren before she was married, but that she didn't know anything about the councillor. In fact, when she was in Christiania three years ago, she had never heard him mentioned. This was strange, of course, because he already had been a judge then, and she knew everyone who was of any consequence in the entire country. Apparently his name was not Danish. She had, by the way, received all of her information from Mr. Vamberg, the curate, who had heard about the family as he was coming home from Copenhagen last Christmas. "You know the good curate goes down to Copenhagen to apply for a new post as often as he can afford to! Why not ask him about the new judge?" she continued.

The parson lowered his thin eyelids and with a tight little smile assured her that the curate probably knew next to nothing. Obviously, Curate Vamberg was not in the good graces of his parson.

Pastor Lind made no further inquiries until he happened to hear a remark made by Mr. Jespersen, the bailiff. It was the third day of the spring assizes, and Mr. Jespersen, standing by the punch bowl, said in his rather broad dialect that he would be damned if they were going to have cringing courtiers and petticoat government in the district again.

The bailiff was already befuddled and couldn't remember any more details. By now the parson's sharp little nose had already caught the scent of gossip, so the next day he pocketed his pride and sought out his curate, Mr. Vamberg, anyway. He smoked a peace pipe of cheap tobacco with him, praised his last sermon about unnecessary extravagances and the wasting of God's gifts, telling him the sermon was very appropriate in this parish where there was so much lavishness. In return, he heard the tall, sallow curate's quiet bilious malice about the new judge. It was certainly petticoat influence and not, he dared say, the man's qualifications or any regard for the welfare of the country that had given the new judge his office and title. He was sorry to say that there had been injustice done again, because several other persons had better reasons for being appointed to the post. It was the people around His Majesty who were continually hoodwinking the sovereign and urging him to push the wrong man into the wrong place. It was too bad, yes, too bad.

As for the councillor's wife, one heard that she had various connections and that these connections, though not very respectable, had been instrumental, according to the gossip he had heard, in sending to the district the new judge that they had to put up with. Evidently, it had been more or less a setback for him. He had been secretary to some very high-ranking person in Copenhagen, but had been completely disgraced because, one guessed, he had taken part in some intrigue. Then he had married and immediately after his marriage to this Mademoiselle von Zehren, he had received the appointment. The curate was sorry to say one could draw one's own conclusions from such an appointment.

The curate obviously did not know anything more, so the parson warned him rather gently about too hasty judgment of one's neighbor. After humbly enduring this admonition, Mr. Vamberg hissed a quiet thank-you to his superior for his well-meaning advice. He said, "Indeed, it is easy to err, not only in word and thought but also in deed . . ."

Pastor Lind left rather quickly, as he intended to call on Lieutenant Juell at Romstad on his way home. One never looked in vain there for a bowl of good strong punch and a game of cards. The lieutenant's uncle, old Justice Hammer, lived with him and could still make a third at cards, half-witted though he was.

The lieutenant met the parson in the courtyard and helped him from the cariole. Everything was out of repair at Romstad. Only the lower parts of the large, two-story building seemed to be habitable. The roofs of the barn and the cow shed were saddle-backed and caving in, and, in the garden, lilac bushes and wild cherry trees grew with abandon. Old apple trees stretched their crooked branches to the sky as if praying for air and space.

Lieutenant Juell was a tall, well-built, rather pale man, between thirty and forty, with lean features and sleepy eyes. His right arm had become paralyzed as the result of an accident sustained during the campaign of 1788 against Sweden. Because of his injury he had left His Majesty's service and retired to this, the only farm left of the vast property that had formerly belonged to his family.

Of necessity he took things as they came, and tried to keep what was left of the estate. His wife had died some years before, and he was left with two children, a boy and a girl. Except for lessons by the parish clerk, or an occasional itinerant teacher, they grew up unchecked and as best they could.

Hardly was the parson seated in the parlor and orders given to bring hot punch, before he told his news. When he mentioned the maiden name of the councillor's wife, Catharina von Zehren, the sleepy eyes of the lieutenant lit up for a second. Yes, he knew her. Yes, he had known her ever since he had been in the king's service in Copenhagen, but he had known her better in Christiania, where he had met her during the happy days when the Crown Prince and the commander-in-chief of the Norwegian army, Prince Carl of Hesse, stayed there following the victory at Kvistrum Bridge.

Even though the lieutenant was not willing to say much about her, he did admit that it might be possible that the former Miss von Zehren had helped her husband to advance, perhaps even get out of a serious difficulty. She *was* a wonderful woman—and she was exceptionally lovely in those days.

That was all the parson could get out of him. His old uncle, the justice, who spent most of his time sleeping in his room, was not sent for. Card playing was not mentioned, and the host did not ask his guest to stay after the punch bowl was emptied. The parson had no sooner left than the widowed and retired Lieutenant of the Royal Dragoons,

Lemmich von Juell of Romstad, who was still entitled to wear His Majesty's uniform, saddled his fastest horse and rode for hours through the fields and meadows, not noticing the spring rain splattering his face. The name of Catharina von Zehren had brought back memories of the exciting days of his youth, not so very long ago—only ten years—but still so far, far in the past—.

The recollection of Catharina von Zehren's coquettish manner and girlish figure made him think of the elegant parties and balls in the capital of the dual monarchy. Once more he danced by her side in the beautiful ballrooms of the Christiania aristocracy—then she had been more ardent, more strong and intense, and still more beautiful and lovely—

For a long time he rode, daydreaming, until his horse began to falter from the unusually fast pace, and he, wet as a crow, decided to stop at Emilienberg to see Major Brager. The two ex-soldiers reminisced about their past love affairs, while they sang and drank far into the night, when the major's wife and a maid had to help them up to bed.

Late one midsummer evening Judge Weydahl arrived.

The carriage left the highway and went creaking and bouncing along under the maple trees toward the old residence. The leaves of the big trees rustled in the night wind. In the twilight the buildings stood dark and shadowy, bordering the road and blotting out the view to the lake; the windows of the main building reflected the yellow gleam of the setting sun.

On the front seat, the coachman quietly cracked his whip. Behind him sat the councillor, tall and massive, in a traveling cloak and broad-brimmed hat. Behind the coach rumbled two ordinary wagons; in one rode a boy and a couple of carpenters, brought from town to make the necessary repairs to the houses before the arrival of the mistress, the second wagon was loaded with all kinds of tools they would need for their work.

Past the goose pond and the bleaching hut, the driver turned into the courtyard. On one side stood the stable and the byre and, at right angles to them the barn lay directly opposite the main building. On the fourth side was a ramshackle old house, used by the servants. Between this and the barn one could catch a glimpse of the lake and the mountain ridges in the distance.

No one came out to meet them, for no message had been sent to tell the time of their arrival, and the family of the former judge had already moved away. The councillor got out of the coach and tried to open the door, but it was locked. He knocked loudly, but no one answered. Finally, he ordered one of his men to the cow-barn to see if someone was there. But then he heard sounds inside, and the door opened.

A buxom woman in a night shift appeared in the doorway. At first she seemed a little scared of the tall man, but realizing that he was the new judge she curtsied several times and explained that she was Ma'am Nannestad and was taking care of the house until his arrival. After the councillor had identified himself, she made repeated curtsies and left the room.

The councillor hung up his cloak and hat and went into the sitting room. It was empty except for a large gateleg table and some wooden chairs. Wearily, he sat down and waited for the housekeeper's return.

In the courtyard he heard sleepy voices talking to the drivers and workmen. The cottagers evidently were helping them unharness and stable the horses. Later he heard heavy footsteps as his trunks were carried into the house. Voices coming from the kitchen indicated that the workmen were already entertaining the maids.

In a short time Ma'am Nannestad returned, still curtsying, with a candle in each hand and a white tablecloth over her arm. A girl not more than ten or twelve years old followed her, carrying a tray with a plate and a glass. They whispered discreetly to each other as they moved quietly between the kitchen and the sitting room, setting the table. All the while they stole stealthy glances at the stranger, who sat so still that he appeared to be asleep.

He was a large man, with broad shoulders, dressed in a dark suit buttoned to the neck by mother-of-pearl buttons. Strong hands rested on his knees, and a ring with precious stones glittered on his right hand.

He sat bent forward with his head drooping a little. In the late twilight of the summer night, his face shone pale and sallow and the flickering candles gave him an eerie look. High cheekbones jutted out over a large mouth with full lips, and under his bushy eyebrows and high forehead was a broad prominent nose. His dark blond hair was touched with gray at the temples. His lean face did not harmonize with the large features; he might be about fifty years old, but perhaps he looked older than he was.

Mrs. Nannestad asked timidly if the councillor would like something to eat and added that a bed was made for him in the adjoining room. Was there anything else she could do for him? He nodded and thanked her in a husky voice. He wanted nothing else, so the housekeeper and the little girl left him alone again.

The councillor helped himself to the food on the table.

He was hungry and thirsty. He tasted the home-brewed beer with some misgivings, then satisfied, emptied the wooden cup.

After he had finished eating, he went to have a look at the rest of the house. Upstairs he walked through several empty rooms before coming to a large hall that seemed to take up most of the second floor. On both sides of the room were large windows divided into small panes. He stopped and lingered before the one that had a clear view of the lake. For a long time he gazed out over the landscape.

The afterglow in the western sky had turned gray and pale; it looked like rain. Looking southward across the lane, he saw a ridge outlined by dark firs with lighter birch trees between them. The wooded ridge ended in a promontory, with beaches below. The sloping green fields in front of the house and courtyard were intersected by a row of maple trees, a continuation of the avenue of maples in front of the building. To the north, the fields became slopes covered with birches. Behind them he saw the spire of the church, silhouetted against the gray sky. On the far side of the smooth, placid lake lay farm houses with pastures and woods. The councillor stood for a long time looking at the landscape. Suddenly he shook his fist at it. He made a wry face and ground his teeth, quivering with fury. As he stood there in the quiet of the night, the realization that here in this desolate spot he would have to stay till the end of his days, nearly overwhelmed him. Only a few months ago he had dreamt of a greater and more glorious future. He had hoped to be something more important than a country judge in Norway. He bowed his head in agony at the very thought of the idle, empty years he was condemned to pass here.

Then he laughed hoarsely in suppressed anger. But after all, shouldn't he, the son of a poor sexton from Romerike, be content to have come so far? Didn't he hold one of the best positions in his native country? He ought to be happy and thankful—yes, thankful to her, who had saved his honor when he had been indiscreet in a delicate situation.

He laughed again.

Somewhere in the house a clock struck. The tones resounded through the empty rooms. The councillor turned and went back to the sitting room. He put out the candles on the table and opened the door to the bedroom. It was stuffy and close in there. Mrs. Nannestad had apparently given him her own bedroom.

II

The councillor did not stay long this time. He called at Gihle, for Attorney Höegh had been taking care of the official duties in the district until his arrival. Then, after staying hardly a week in the district, he traveled south to the city. They did say, however, that he stopped to see the district governor and the bailiff, but had talked with no one else.

The carpenters remained, however, and made a great many changes in the house. The neighbors, and not merely the old women, were very curious, wondering what the workmen were doing. The office was moved to the servants' building, and all the rooms in the main building were made to look festive indeed; from the kitchen to the drawing room they were repaired and redecorated. All the rooms were painted, some green, some blue. Most beautiful of all was the large drawing room which was hung with yellow damask wallpaper. The fireplace was taken down and replaced by big iron stoves brought from the Bærum Ironworks. All this expensive redecorating was being done to please the lady of the house who was accustomed to the best, for it was said she had frequently been to the Royal Palace. The cultured people smiled at one another and shook their heads at such extravagance, but they were secretly a little proud of having such a lady come to their community. Not until autumn, when the rye was ripe and yellow, did the councillor return. He paid off the workmen without any haggling and sent them back to town, much to the regret of the kitchen maids.

At the same time a ship from Eidsvold anchored down by the shore, and all six of the cottagers were ordered to help with the unloading. They pushed and pulled and carried, working hard from sunrise to sunset. One crate after another was unloaded and taken to the house; that which had not been packed in cases had been wrapped in straw and jute. In the courtyard the councillor, flushed and soaked with perspiration, stood in his shirt-sleeves directing the unpacking. And the things they saw unpacked that day the men would never forget. There were beechwood chairs with carved arms, sofas covered with velvets that stood on elaborate legs twisted and turned like roots, gilt-framed mirrors as large as doors, chests of drawers and desks with the most wonderful curves, tables with white marble tops and gilt decorations all over. The strangest thing of all was a heavy piece of furniture with five legs, not unlike a table, that needed six strong men to move it. The councillor showed them where to put it, and as it was placed on the floor, he went over to it, lifted the lid, and touched the inside; it made a strange sound. No doubt, a kind of musical instrument.

Mrs. Nannestad went from room to room, followed by her little daughter and half a dozen maids. They arranged everything neatly in rows along the walls as she thought they should be placed.

Only one accident occurred during the day when Matjas

Nordsveen pushed a mirror against a chair rail and cracked it. He swore, terrified. The councillor was there in a second. He didn't say anything, but white with anger, he took the mirror and threw it to the floor, smashing the frame and glass into a thousand pieces, even though the frame had not been damaged, and the rest of the glass could have been made into two smaller mirrors. Then he shook his fist at Matjas and damned his carelessness. Matjas was afraid that the councillor was going to hit him, so that he would have to hit back, but the councillor didn't go that far.

About an hour later he was as controlled as ever and quietly told the housekeeper to pour drams of brandy for everyone, including Matjas.

As the men went home that night, they all agreed that the new judge was a fine fellow, a little hotheaded perhaps, but not anywhere nearly so difficult as parsons and other aristocrats usually were. In that respect he was much like Attorney Höegh—

Two nights after the councillor's arrival, white curtains had been drawn across all of the windows except those in the drawing room; there, red ones with white tassels had been hung. The house was ablaze with candlelight.

That night the councillor's wife arrived by coach. He stood waiting to greet her, and lifting her from the coach, kissed her on both cheeks and took her into the house. A young girl with slender ankles and unbelievably tiny shoes showing from beneath her short skirt, followed her mistress from the coach.

Mrs. Nannestad stood in the doorway looking very dressed-up in her starched ribbon-cap. She made repeated curtsies to her new mistress, a tall pale lady about thirty, who nodded graciously with lowered eyelids. Mrs. Weydahl asked a question in Danish that the housekeeper didn't understand, so the councillor answered for her. The mistress nodded again and, without shaking hands with Mrs. Nannestad, accompanied her husband to her room, followed by her maid.

Ten minutes later the maid announced something in Danish, from the top of the stairs, intimating that the master and the mistress would not want supper, just a cup of tea in the mistress' chamber. From this, Ma'am Nannestad understood that the girl was Mrs. Weydahl's maid. Disappointed and with a heavy heart, she took all of her splendid supper back to the kitchen. She had taken such pains and had used all her skill on this supper, from the delicious mutton chops à la Maintenon to the almond pudding.

What transpired at the councillor's house were the most talked-about events in the district that autumn. During the corn husking, people stopped in the midst of their work and started gossiping about them, and if a young girl had a new jacket, or a cottage woman a new head-scarf, they said: she is finer than the councillor's wife. They were most deeply impressed by the lady's maid. There had been only two others that they knew of, one at Governor Winterfeldt's, and the other at the home of Major General de Place. This maid at the councillor's was the third. Ma'am Nannestad became very popular and was asked to visit one after another of the best families. The women asked so many questions that at last she was completely worn out with telling about the councillor's household. One night after supper at Höegh's, the attorney went into the kitchen to have his beer-mug filled. All the women of the household were there at their spinning wheels; even his wife sat listening to little Julie Nannestad, who was visiting there. Just as they would resume their work, the wheels would stop or the thread fly off, because they all were more interested in what little Julie was saying than in paying attention to their own work. Julie was all excited. Without pausing for breath, she told them about life at the judge's house; about the councillor and his wife, about the varnished coach, and the yellow damask in the drawing room. Off to himself by the fireplace sat an old man with a gray beard. He was the poor pensioner in the attorney's household. He pretended not to listen to the women talking, just went on carding wool and making lots of dust. But the attorney leaned against the fireplace and listened to the girls gossip. Turning to the old man, he said, "It seems as though you must have heard of greater luxury before, Otto; perhaps you even remember when King Christian VI passed through these parts?"

"Indeed I do," the old man answered, "such happenings as these I have heard of from time to time, I guess."

"You old men can tell a lot of stories, but wasn't that tale you used to tell about the English Court and not about this country?" the attorney asked.

"It could have taken place here just as well," said the old man and went on carding wool. Nevertheless, given his cue, he continued: "The new judge and his wife drive in a coach, but the young lady of Græfsum rode to church in a carriage and six with servants on horseback before and behind. She owned farms everywhere, so many that she could attend church services only once a year in each parish. On that Sunday the common people came to greet her and look at her finery."

"Who told you that story, you old fool?" asked the cook.

The old man put down his carding tools and with a faraway look said: "You see, my grandfather told me that his grandfather used to sit on the coach seat beside the young lady of Græfsum in those days."

The attorney laughed, tore off a big quid of chewing tobacco and handed it over to the old man who took it and thanked him. "You are pretty sharp, old man," he said. "It's not for nothing that your name is the good old Norwegian one of Otto Valdemarssön Skaktavl."

III

It was a long time before the former Lieutenant of Dragoons Juell and the former Catharina von Zehren met. He shunned the social life that the arrival of the new judge had created in the district; as a matter of fact, his finances had for years been so bad that he could not afford to take part in any social gatherings except for small drinking parties with the major and the attorney and perhaps some other good friends and neighbors. Besides, Mrs. Weydahl was not very well. According to Dr. Müller she suffered from anemia and had to live in Christiania most of the winter. Life in the country already seemed much too monotonous and depressing to her, and the councillor in this respect bent to her wishes and lived patiently as a widower, since there was nothing else for it.

Thus, it was not until spring at the annual child-christening feast at the major's, that she and Lieutenant Juell met. He had long since forgotten his old dream about Catharina von Zehren. Actually, it had evaporated together with the hangover from the drinking bout he and the major had had when he first heard the rumor of her coming. Dreams and serious thoughts never stayed long with Lemmich Juell—the dreams because there were so many and were put to flight by new dreams; the serious thoughts because they were hopeless and useless torments, which had to be driven away either by some grand schemes that he didn't really believe in himself—conceived, as it were, only to be forgotten —or by some wild revel. In the latter instance he showed his carousing companions, only too often, both his thoughts and decisions in all of their contemptible misery and laughingly followed them to the door. Ten empty years had day by day dug the pit that separated him from the time when he had really lived, when his dreams had really given birth to purpose and his thoughts to achievement. When he so fancied, he let, even when drunk, his former life and the shadows of the future, the memories of his merry youth, and the discouraging sight of his and his family's actual situation, all pass in a gay and mocking review before his drunken friends. In short, he was the wittiest and the most happy-go-lucky fellow for ten miles around; besides he did everything with such a supercilious elegance that even his companions were touched by his grace and charm, and though his military and landowner friends might be the roughest drunkards of the district, when they were with Lieutenant Juell they all felt like refined gentlemen.

The major introduced Lieutenant von Juell to Mrs. Weydahl, adding that it was probably unnecessary, as he understood they were already acquainted. Mrs. Weydahl was very gracious, and said she remembered Lieutenant von Juell very well. She went on to mention several homes in Copenhagen and Christiania where they had met; unfortunately, she happened to remember the wrong places, but Lemmich Juell never noticed it. The sight of her made him feel as if he were facing the very incarnation of the most splendid memories from his short and wasted youth. Her soft, sweet Danish accent, her elegant movements, that little expressive smile, her exquisitely fashionable dress—everything was like a caress to his starved senses. She wore rouge, which offended the other ladies, for here in the country they made a virtue of the unfortunate fact that they were unable to have such luxuries. He, however, could have blessed her for it. It was so wonderful and refreshing to him to see once again this charming touch of color in a lady's cheeks.

He knew that she was over thirty and noticed at once a few wrinkles at the corners of her eyes and observed that her bosom was rather small; but he forgot these things immediately and did not think of them again. He was charmed and delighted to stand beside this perfect lady and to talk to her, and as usual Juell's feelings influenced everything he said and did.

The tall, slim gentleman with the embroidered waistcoat and well-cut but slightly old-fashioned blue frock coat with frilled shirt, had immediately attracted Mrs. Weydahl as a very pleasant contrast to the others, a rather rustic-looking group. Earlier she had noticed with some satisfaction how even the heavy-handed correctness of her husband was a pleasant contrast to the manners of the others. Lieutenant von Juell belonged to the same society that she herself had left, and she listened to him with the pleasure that a banished man feels when suddenly he hears in his exile the song of a bird from his native country. He interested her and she thought he might be a pleasant acquaintance. As their conversation became more animated, the buxom wife of the attorney, who had been entertaining "the lady of the court," as they called her, took the opportunity to walk over and have a cozy little chat with Madame Müller, who, out in the entry, had whispered to her something amusing about the latest escapade of the crazy Lieutenant Wallace.

Before she left the party, Mrs. Weydahl had asked Juell to pay them a visit soon, so that they could renew their acquaintance. The councillor had also urged him very politely not to wait too long to give his wife the pleasure of his visit—

she did not have much chance to meet her old friends. With a courtly bow, Lieutenant von Juell assured them that he would be honored and pleased.

Thus, Catharina von Zehren and Lemmich Juell renewed their acquaintance. But before the end of the following year they were both dead and buried, and this is the way it happened.

All during the spring and summer Juell was a frequent guest at the councillor's. His half-witted uncle remained at home at Romstad, bored and alone, wondering what had happened to his nephew. The lieutenant, who had never paid much attention to his children anyway, left them alone more than ever to play in the green fields and woods and associate with the servants.

In the autumn Mrs. Weydahl told the lieutenant that she had canceled her winter stay in the city and hoped she would not be bored by staying here. That night Lemmick Juell asked the attorney for a loan of five hundred dalers. It was the first time that he had borrowed money from his friends. He didn't tell why he wanted the money and offered no security, but Mr. Höegh gave it to him anyway. Juell had already mortgaged all of his property to a wealthy man in Christiania, and it was only because Mr. Orre, the country merchant, was giving him credit that he had been able to keep afloat this far.

But it was soon apparent why he had borrowed the money. Mrs. Nannestad was sent for; she was the widow of a curate, who had been known in the parish as a gourmet. After his death, her small widow's pension was not enough for her and her daughter to live on, so she used the culinary skill she had acquired during her marriage to cater for large parties and feasts in the neighborhood. She was given complete charge of everything concerning the food for the grand feast that Lieutenant Juell was to give at Romstad in three weeks. In the meantime, preparations went on from morning until night; the whole house was turned upside down. Every nook and corner was scrubbed and cleaned, and loads of shabby furniture were stowed away in the outbuildings. The garden, under the strict supervision of the old uncle, was tidied up and the walks sanded. He said he intended to make the inevitable shortcomings of the arrangement a little more forgivable and would fix things like a garden party. Thus, of his own accord, he told the man whom the lieutenant had sent especially to Christiania for wine and other things to bring back with him a few dozen paper lanterns to hang in the garden. He especially took great pains to rebuild a broken-down old summer-house made of interwoven roots and branches of trees. The foolish old gentleman hinted rather romantically at how convenient and agreeable it would be to have such a trysting place in the garden; the pious hermit could not object to having a pair of lovers seek shelter in his hut. The uncle knew all about this kind of thing from his younger days, before riotous living had broken him and made him the wretched old fool he was now.

At last all the preparations were finished and invitations sent to the military officers, officials, and highly respected landowners in four districts asking them to come to the party at Romstad. When the parents of Lieutenant Juell were alive, such invitations had frequently been sent out from Romstad; such occasions had eagerly been anticipated both by young and old of the districts. But that was long ago, and the young people now hardly understood what was meant when their parents wondered whether Lemmick Juell was really capable of living up to the proud traditions of his house.

However, everyone came to the feast. Once again the old mansion shone in all of its former splendor; once again the formal dining hall with its ornamented stucco ceiling and small green windowpanes housed elaborate dining tables. The light of the tall candles flickered and glowed against the soft patina of the decorated walls; on them, the curious guests could still see the outlines of the white-bosomed nymphs playing their frivolous games with fawns and satyrs. Once again the gleam of fine porcelain and massive family silver covered the damask cloths, embroidered with the Juell coat of arms, and once again beautifully dressed people danced in the great ballroom known far and wide for its size and beauty.

No expense had been spared to make the feast perfect. The best musicians of the district had been sent for, others had come from a distance, and they fiddled and played on their violins, bass fiddles and clarinets with a zest that was due as much to a good advance payment as to many glasses of brandy. Outside, the garden was lit up by the colored lanterns. In a far corner of the garden a solitary torch burned in front of the summer-house.

Within the house the gentlemen played cards when they were not dancing. In this pleasant, gay atmosphere the stakes ran high and a great deal of money changed hands. But Lemmich Juell did not take part in the cardplaying. He had already given his last thirty dalers to his uncle, and he watched the old man lose them in a most grand and dignified manner to the bailiff and the major general. The old gentleman was in high spirits. Dressed in a magnificent orange-colored frock coat and wearing a pigtail peruke fashionable twenty years before, he looked like a *grand seigneur*—perhaps a little too condescending towards the bailiff, whom he considered a parvenu. This evening he did not show his peculiar foibles, so that, if one did not know, one would hardly suspect that this distinguished man of the world in his attacks of madness burned his clothes if they had been touched by servants or that he always got up on the front stairs of storehouses and other high places to make water.

His restoration of the summer-house proved not at all to be one of his useless foibles, for it was here that Lemmich Juell told the councillor's wife that he loved her, and it was in the seclusion of the little house that she let him know that her marriage had been a dreadful mistake. In a moment of excitement she had thought she was in love, and now she was so miserable, yes, so very lonely and miserable. She would have been lost in this wretched country if she had not happened to find him. Certainly this deep sympathy between them was God-given, consequently it could not be wrong! Lieutenant Juell was her only friend here, the only one who sympathized with her in her anguish. She told him so, as they held each other, and she kissed him tenderly. In return she received a thousand words of love, but she was careful all the while not to muss or disarrange her dress and quickly wiped away those tears that might damage the rouge on her cheeks.

Meanwhile, the councillor sat at the card table and discussed the political situation with solemn indifference. The party lasted until the gray light of dawn, and the host beamed with delight over its success.

Even after most of the guests had left or gone to bed in some of the half hundred beds of the house, the attorney, Pastor Lind, the major, and Lieutenant Wallace still sat at cards. Bids were raised and finessed; there was a strange undercurrent of excitement in their play. They did not talk; they only laughed when the cards were shown; all of them were worn out, red-eyed, and half drunk. They did not notice the sunrise nor the light of early day shining on the burned-out garden lanterns. Pale rays of sunlight filtered into the dusty, disordered room through the windowpanes. The light made an incongruous halo of the parson's thin, bristly hair. None of them noticed it, nor did they pay any attention to the ten-year-old boy who, awkward in his new clothes, stood near the card table watching them play. He was Lemmich Juell's young son. The child, forgotten by everyone, had fallen asleep on a pile of blankets and traveling-rugs in the next room. The early morning light had awakened him and he had gone in search of the voices that had drifted to him through the door.

Finally, Attorney Höegh got up from the card table, and toasted his three companions as he emptied his glass. He paused, and looking around at the disordered room, said: "Do you remember, Lind, what the priest from Toten said when he had been ill and arrived two days late for the wedding-feast? 'When I saw the remains of the party, I could have cried.' "

They all laughed, gathered up their money and departed. The boy, still tired and sleepy, sat down, laid his arms on the card table, and fell asleep again.

* * *

Soon the whole district knew that Lieutenant Juell and Mrs. Weydahl were lovers. Everyone talked about it, everyone except her husband, of course. Some one had seen Mrs. Weydahl go out for a walk in the woods to meet her lover; others had noticed them exchanging intimate words and glances. The councillor's house-servants hinted broadly at what they might see if the two were taken by surprise in the drawing room during one of Lemmich Juell's visits. The mistress was often alone with him because the councillor was always busy in his office across the courtyard. Even there the clerks would smirk at each other and fall silent if the councillor entered unexpectedly.

No one dared to speak of the affair; only the servants would make allusions to it, for in that district people felt that the shame of it reflected on the entire household if the lady of the house had a lover. For that reason they became grumpy and fresh to her and openly insulted the lady's maid, whom they blamed for being her accomplice. More than once during the absence of the councillor, Juell had to tie up his own horse when he visited Mrs. Weydahl; even the groom would not help him. The lieutenant understood this and put up with it; the mistress, because of the difficult situation, conveniently forgot to complain to her husband of the impudent behavior of the natives of this boorish country.

So the winter passed. Toward the end of March, the councillor returned home after a week of traveling for the spring assizes.

On a bright sunny day he drove down the lane. The snow was melting; it dropped off the trees and roofs, but it was still possible to drive a sleigh. As he sat there, warm in his fur coat, happy to be home again, he had a feeling of contentment; he felt he was almost at the point of being able to relax and reconcile himself to his situation; perhaps he could forget about his former dreams and ambitions. His was a position important enough to occupy most of his energies, he had a house and a home, and a beautiful piece of land. As he looked over the wide fields, his feeling for the land, which was such a part of his heritage, came to life again. Yes, there was a lot of work to be done here. He would turn his estate into a model farm. These broad fields and pastures were public property, and he wanted his farming to be an example to the Norwegian farmers, an example worthy of imitation.

But as he drove into the courtyard, no one came to meet him or to put the horse in the stable. There was a sinister stillness about the house, as if everyone was keeping out of the way, and he noticed that white sheets covered the drawing room windows.

He went into the entry and flung off his heavy fur coat. There on the floor was a spot, a blood stain, which someone had washed and scrubbed in a vain effort to remove it.

The councillor stopped and looked around him with an uneasy feeling that something had happened.

The chambermaid curtsied as she tiptoed past him on her way upstairs from the kitchen.

"Has something happened, Annette?"

"Hush, Sir, the mistress is ill and not to be disturbed. Dr. Müller's orders. Lieutenant von Juell had an accident and is dead." And with that she disappeared.

The councillor kicked off his big boots and went into the kitchen. One of the maids was washing dishes, and another was on her knees stirring up the fire. At the table Lars, the groom, was having his breakfast with two of the cottagers, Gudbrand Sveum and Matjas Nordsveen. They had heard the judge enter the courtyard and looked up shyly as he came in, but said nothing.

"What is going on here?" No one answered.

"I am asking, what is going on here? Is Lieutenant Juell dead?"

"He is, Councillor," Lars said.

"When and how did it happen?—Was it in the entry?"

"It was, Councillor."

"When and how did it happen?"—No one answered.

"I am asking how did it happen and when?" They gazed

at one another. The maid in front of the fireplace backed away.

" What the devil is wrong? Answer me!" he shouted. "When and how did it happen?"

Matjas Nordsveen, pale and frightened, stood up. "The lieutenant fell down the stairs . . . last night," he said hoarsely.

"Last night!" The councillor's face turned yellow, the veins in his temples swelled and became purple, his voice rasped in his throat. "What was Lieutenant Juell doing here last night, and upstairs? When did he come?"

"He came day before yesterday." It was Matjas who answered.

"And at what time did he fall?"

"It was about five o'clock this morning, sir, just as he was going to leave." Matjas kept his eyes on the councillor, expecting to be hit.

But the councillor turned and went out of the room. They remained silent as he stood for a short time on the other side of the door before he dropped the door handle with a bang.

Weydahl opened the door from the entry into the drawing room. Through the white sheets covering the windows the softened sunlight made streaks across the floor and gleamed on the gilt furniture. In the middle of the room, under the chandelier, the servants had placed a bed, and on it lay Lieutenant von Juell in his elaborate red dress uniform. Weydahl had never seen him in uniform before and was a little startled by it. The face was pale with a big reddish-blue bruise across the forehead, and the hair on one side was matted with blood. His thin Roman nose jutted out from his face. His chin had sunk down; the jaw was held up by the high stiff collar, so that the mouth was only half open. Regular white teeth were visible between the colorless lips. The eyelids were shut and the hands folded on the regimental coat.

Weydahl went up to the bed and looked at him. The window covers moved a little in the wind from the entry; the dead face seemed to quiver. The councillor leaned over and placed a finger on the forehead of the dead man. It was already ice cold. He pressed harder; it gave way, and he felt the crunch of broken bones.

Then he went upstairs. The chambermaid, frightened, slipped out of the bedroom as he entered. The bed curtains hung down around the four-poster bed; behind the curtains his wife lay moaning. He drew the curtains apart so violently that they were torn. She crouched in bed half-dressed, looking up at him with terrified eyes, all the while biting her handkerchief to stifle her wailing. Without a word he took her by the arm and pulled her out of bed across the floor and out into the hall. Powerless to resist, she followed barefoot down the stairs and into the parlor and over to the corpse.

He pointed to the dead man: "You and he—you and he—what was there between you two?"

He let go of her, and she fell whimpering to the floor in front of him, her hands convulsively clutching her long disheveled black hair. Her eyes seemed glued to him in despair.

He lifted his hand to strike, but her eyes gleamed, in desperate defiance of the strong, broad-shouldered man with the furious, distorted face. She whispered rapidly: "Have you something to thank me for, Christopher? Do you remember what I did for you when you were in great trouble?"

His arm fell. "I wish you had never done it," he said, "I wish you had never cared for me or helped me. One should never help another in that way unless it is for life. It makes for ingratitude and heavy demands . . ."

She slipped to the floor again and, leaning her head against the bed, started to cough. He went away with quick, heavy steps, and she was left alone. She pulled herself up by the bed-post, tired out, broken. She did not notice the dead man, she no longer remembered Juell or her husband or anything. Coughing, she dragged herself upstairs to her bedroom.

A little later, Lars the groom was summoned to the office. The councillor stood looking out the window with his back to him. Very abruptly Weydahl said: "Drive the body of Lieutenant Juell to Romstad." Lars waited for further instruction . . . "What are you waiting for?" the councillor said gruffly.

"What shall I take? The two-seated sleigh?"

"Take the flat sleigh, and throw a cover over the corpse."

And so it was done.

Slowly, step by step, Lars the groom drove the lifeless body of Lieutenant Lemmich von Juell to Romstad. He was not very eager to reach there, because he knew that there was only a half-witted old man and two young children to receive the dead.

IV

The judge's household soon returned to the monotony of everyday life. Nothing more of importance happened. The councillor went over to the office every morning and stayed there all day, absorbed in his work. He was silent and morose, hardly speaking to the clerks who, when he was there, moved as little and as quietly as possible. They looked at each other furtively now and then when his quill pen scratched the paper too loudly.

The councillor had dismissed Annette, paid her the remainder of the year's wages and sent her back to town.

The lady of the house never again left her bedroom, nor did her husband ever see her again or inquire about her.

Once in a while the fat, good-natured district doctor came to see her. He had been one of the councillor's favorite acquaintances, but now he did not speak to him. The councillor let him come and go as he pleased, and treated him to food and drink in the best parlor, but the doctor always left without having spoken to the councillor.

The details of Lieutenant Juell's death and the happenings at the judge's were talked about in the district for some time. It was said at first that the councillor himself might have had something to do with it, but the servants soon put the gossips right about that, and the whole story was interesting enough without adding anything.

At length the gossip stopped, for as the major phrased it, "the leading characters" of the tragedy seldom appeared in public. The three-day auction which the creditors announced would be held at Romstad of the farm and all its belongings also passed off quietly and without much of a sensation. It had been more or less expected. The auction, however, lasted a whole week, because after sorting out everything, furniture, farm implements, and all the property, there was a great deal to be sold.

At first, it had been decided that the old gentleman and the children of Lemmich Juell were to be sent to board with some of their wealthy relatives in a district farther south, and Mr. Orre, the district tradesman, had them driven there in his best carriage. Both the children were seated next to the driver. Haughty as a prince, old Justice Hammer sat proudly alone in the back seat. A shabby and bent old man with a white beard, standing by the side of the road, took off his hat mockingly as they drove by. He was Otto Valdemarssön Skaktavl, who stood there meditating on the fact that a hundred years ago the great-grandfather of Lieutenant Juell had driven his own ancestors from Romstad. Thus the last of the Juell family left this part of the country.

* * *

Mrs. Catharina lay in her room upstairs. The heavy red curtains were drawn so tightly that light could scarcely come through, and even those few rays which twinkled dimly among the bottles on the table had been further reduced by the high green folding screen in front of the bed. Behind the curtains of the four-poster there was hardly any light at all.

Between the screen and the bed there was a chair where Curate Vamberg sat nearly every day talking to her for an hour or so. Lying like this night and day for weeks on end, coughing and in great pain, numbness slowly disappeared. Memories and thoughts of her past life, as well as the knowledge of the terrible moment of death, haunted her for the first time in her life. They surged about her, coming out of the dusk like ghosts which refused to flee. She sent for the preacher.

The parson, Mr. Lind, arrived smiling politely and bringing with him the aroma of French brandy. He spoke officiously about the sorrows of life which overtake us all and about the infinite mercy of God. Furthermore, thanks to the enlightenment of human beings and their increased comprehension, they should no longer despair. His shrill voice and affected manners tortured her. His words did not reach her.

His visits increased her disquiet, and so the parson had to accept the humiliation of having the curate visit her in his place.

The tall, sallow curate was at a loss as to what to do as he sat down in front of her. He greeted her. She scarcely nodded, merely folded her thin, sensitive hands on the coverlet and looked at him with burning eyes, eyes bloodshot and puffed from coughing and weeping. He asked her what she preferred to talk to him about. She murmured that her one desire was to have peace, peace. Suddenly, something strange took place within the curate. It had been a long time since anyone in such deep anguish had tried seriously to communicate with him. Compassionately, he tried to forget what he knew about this woman's past life and sinful deeds. In a faltering whisper he started to talk to her about a comfort that he hardly believed in himself.

What at other sick beds had often been just an official duty, in this case was changed and became the effort of one unhappy human being to express understanding and sympathy to another, still more unhappy. He talked on and on for a long time, until his hoarse, strained voice seemed to give up. As he wiped his narrow, moist forehead, he suddenly caught himself wondering what he really had been saying. Worried, he put his hands in his vest pocket for his snuff box, but stopped. After all, it wouldn't be decent to have a pinch in the presence of the councillor's lady, and he gave up the idea.

She lay with her eyes closed. At last, she held out her hand to him, and as he took it, she thanked him and asked him to call again soon. He did often, not only for her sake but for his own. He longed for and loved these hours at her bedside, for then he was able to speak of all sorts of things, things that were soothing and good for both of them.

Homeward bound, he would let the reins fall loose and the horse would amble along at will while he indulged in vague daydreams. The shriveled, middle-aged, unmarried curate felt his eyes grow moist as he thought of such details as the fact that this former lady of the court, now dying and in great pain, actually fixed herself up in a freshly starched night-cap and beautiful lace around her wrists when she expected his visits.

During these weeks he became more gentle at home, easier to get along with and less stingy in his dealings with the farmers.

Mrs. Catharina fell into a gentle sleep following the visits of the curate. But one evening in the middle of August it happened that she did not awake when Beata, the housemaid, noisily came into her room with the supper. The mistress could not be wakened. She was dead.

As wife of the Councillor of Chancery, Judge Weydahl, Mrs. Catharina was given a magnificent funeral. The magistrate and the major general attended and the parson, Mr. Lind, officiated in a highly creditable manner.

A month or two later the councillor had his office moved back to the main building, and about the same time he resumed his visits to the major and to Attorney Höegh, who would call upon him in return. He no longer seemed as reserved and formal as he had been even though he would always keep friends and acquaintances at arm's length.

Judge Weydahl certainly seemed more at ease now. There was about him a new air of friendliness as he, confident and self-assured, sat at the card table, master in his own house.

The Parson's Family

I

FOOTHILLS of the great forest-covered mountain range reached down to the valley and ended in steep spurs beneath the high, tapering ridges; the undulating fields and deep green meadows sloped down to the lake. On the bank, not far from the shore, stood the centuries-old church.

Its present form was in the shape of a cross with white plastered walls and a pointed, elegant spire, but in the old days it had been an oblong building with a squat, defiant steeple straddling the roof. In those early days, it was said, dense fir forests covered most of the region. Farms were few and far apart. There were people living on these farms who not only were the descendants of long-forgotten local chieftains, but had also inherited their ancestors' power.

The church had been added to and altered over the centuries. Both the church and the district had undergone many changes; now at last it stood completed. The several layers of plaster and whitewash were not sufficient to hide the different kinds of stone and brick, for one could still see that the nave was of fine workmanship, and that it had been built of huge sandstone blocks. The transept had been added by later generations which had not felt strongly about long-lasting values and were content with inferior work and materials in order to have a larger and more pretentious building.

Close to the church, and separated from it only by the

churchyard and a row of giant maple trees, stood the parsonage. The group of houses surrounding the courtyard was not very different from those of any other farm of its size, except for the long one-story main building with hip roof and black Dutch tiles. The buildings of the parsonage farm had certainly been more spacious and numerous in earlier years, for according to the local stories, it had been able to accommodate a great many people, and so had become a popular stopping-place for travelers, especially for pilgrims on their way to Trondheim.

The story went that in order to maintain the church properly and to pay for the hospitality for all of these travelers an entire valley on the other side of the lake had been added to the parish. About 1700, however, this very complex establishment had burned to the ground and the pastor who rebuilt the parsonage had done it on his own account and had consequently planned only for the needs of his own family. His successors had followed his example, patching and repairing where it was urgently needed, but not wasting their own money on property which did not belong to them. The ancient arched cellars of the original Catholic vicarage remained as the only tangible sign of its past size and grandeur.

There were few other remains from the Catholic era left in the district. The churches and private chapels which in those days rich and pious men had been accustomed to build for their own use, had all disappeared. People still spoke rather vaguely about wars and battles and pointed out the burial mounds of local chieftains and notorious villains, but mostly even their names were forgotten. The people knew that at that time the priests taught popish doctrine, which was certainly dangerous and led the soul toward damnation rather than toward salvation. In addition, these men had pledged themselves to celibacy and never to marry, but in spite of that, they were often guilty of breaking their holy vows with regard to women. Since they were able to give themselves indulgences, it is easy to see that conditions in the parish could be rather bad, when those who were supposed to chastise the people were the most ungodly.—These solitary Catholic priests had had few ties with the local families and consequently had not become part of the traditions of the district. Neither had they tilled their soil and farmed their lands, and they had soon been forgotten in the district.

It was quite different following the Reformation. Most of the tales and stories told over the centuries were centered around the parsonage and the different vicars, for the Lutheran clergymen had moved into the district as heads of families, bringing their wives and children with them. They farmed the land, and their servants were sent to fish in the lake. The living was so rich and pleasant that a parson seldom left the parish once he had settled there. When he died, his sons and daughters inherited his property, and they usually stayed in the district, often having married into the best families, so that his name and his deeds were well-remembered over the years. By this time the nobility, the natural leaders of the district, had gradually disappeared. They seemed to have become worn-out physically and intellectually, and had no progeny. Or, impoverished, they left to try their fortune elsewhere. Some had even sunk down into the peasantry. These great landowners had been replaced by the Lutheran pastors, whose way of life fitted them to mingle with the rich farmers. Thus because of their knowledge and education, as well as the authority which their position as spiritual heads of the parish gave them, they also had become the temporal leaders of the district.

Everyone came to them for advice and help, and the parson was wanted at every family event and important occasion, such as a marriage, baptism or death. It was natural then that the parson and the vicarage became the center of a living local history, handed down by word of mouth from generation to generation.

Many of the important events in the region might be forgotten; flood, plague, and even war and invasion were only vaguely remembered. Yet, on the great farms, which were entailed from one generation to another, it was very well known which of the parsons had married the parents of the owners' great grandfather or christened the children. Sometimes those who could write put these things down in family records for the benefit of their descendants.

Most people of the district divided their history into different eras by the dates of their parsons' tenures, much as ancient peoples divided theirs according to the dynasties of their kings.

This long line of dead parsons was a queer lot, living as ghosts in the memories of the people. Most of them were regarded with sympathy and with an odd kind of local pride. No one could tell the farmers that their parsons had not been the best to be had in the country. The more eccentric, the more inconsiderate and violent the parsons had proven to be, the more their conduct had seemed to contradict their peaceful office, that much more important they became in the stories and tales of the district.

* * *

About 1795, Pastor Lind and his family came to live in the vicarage. He came from one of the poorer parishes on the south coast of Norway, which was also his home. He didn't bring much furniture with him, not only because of the great distance and the cost of transport, and what he had was worn and shabby.

He was a comparatively young man, small and stout, with a florid face and sandy hair. He was vivacious and active, especially amiable and talkative with his rich neighbors, whom he met with effusive friendliness. He told them he was completely happy and satisfied at having left the out-of-the-way place on the coast in order to work among so many enlightened and educated people.

It was said by one of his colleagues that it would take several generations to repair the damage he brought about in the moral and religious life of his parish.

True, he began his tenure with the best of intentions; he wanted to administer the parish wisely and well. Unfortunately, however, he was one of those people who insist upon being the center of attention, always enjoying the commotion that he could stir up. His vanity had gradually changed to foolishness, because of the domineering attitude he had acquired in his former poor and isolated parish by the sea. Being an adherent of Rationalism, Mr. Lind had at first worked for public education and other kinds of progress. But, imprudent in his methods and ignorant of local affairs, he soon offended the well-to-do farmers. In his former parish he had been accustomed to travel about and tell the uneducated fishermen what to do and how to do it, and they had received his advice with respect, regarding him as a superior being. Here, the people of the parish did not like their parson to go dashing about telling them what they should do, and dropping in on them any time he chose to do so. They just wanted him to attend to his official duties with dignity, to correct their faults with solemn severity, and to bring the Word and the Commandments of God to them with the proper authority—for which they were willing to pay him well. For the rest, they expected him to remain quiet and solemnly wait for his parishioners to call upon him if they wished to. They found his pushing friendliness patronizing and responded by being rude and gruff. On his part, he was dismayed to find his efforts received with constant suspicion, and his overtures met with reserve whenever he tried, to the best of his ability, to be friendly and kind. He remembered with regret how much more he had been appreciated by the poor sailors and fishermen, and he recalled with some bitterness the advice the Reverend Bishop had given him when he was transferred to this parish. His superior had warned him about the difficulties of the task that he, Mr. Lind, would have as he worked among the landed proprietors and rich farmers and other inhabitants of this parish, because they had, unfortunately, retained so very little of the genuine and unspoiled characteristics of the Norwegian peasants.

Mr. Lind was the *first* Rationalist and enlightened parson to be sent to the district. The cynicism and the questioning attitude of the times had already found willing converts among the rich landowners, all of which suited their own sentiments perfectly. Modern ideas had crept in and grown strong and fanatical, in spite of the efforts of the orthodox clergy. Indeed these new sentiments were joined with the old hatred of priests. Even the most radical of these rustic free-thinkers were actually of the opinion that the duty of the parson, the one for which he was paid, was to scold and force them back to obedience within the church. It wasn't much sport to make fun of the dogmas and miracles when the clergyman was indifferent. It gave the mockery a dangerous air of effrontery.—Nor were the common people satisfied with Mr. Lind's preaching, for his explanations seemed to turn both the Holy Scriptures and Martin

Luther's catechism upside down. His friendship with Hans Orre, the country tradesman, was another reason for their disapproval, for Mr. Orre had been considered by the former parson to be an atheist, hardly worthy of being buried in the churchyard.

Before Lind realized how it had really happened, he had to admit to himself that he and his parish were at odds. Tired from his futile attempts to obtain the confidence of the farmers he finally gave in and only associated with those he considered his equals. The rich people in the district laughed slyly and made fun of the defeated reformer, but appreciated his easy friendliness and sociability. They were glad to welcome him into their small circle. By their hospitality they helped this weak, amiable man to forget many restrictions imposed by his clerical gown and collar. Lind was not accustomed to this kind of life and let go all moderation; he soon became engulfed in the wild social life indulged in by the upper classes of the region. The gay parties went around and around from one house to the next in turn: from the major at Emilienberg to the attorney at Gihle, from the chamberlain at Stav to Juell at Romstad, and from there to Captain Tebetmann at Kjelsrud with sometimes a detour to many places outside the district. Card playing, heavy drinking and drunken singing were the main ingredients of every party.

In this social whirlpool Mr. Lind suffered more than any of the others. He ruined himself economically and soon destroyed his physical and spiritual health by his carousing and late hours, and it wasn't long before Lind lost his dignity and prestige in the community. His parishioners thought he was carrying this kind of life too far, since he was a clergyman. Unwittingly he came to be regarded as a fool and a buffoon, and soon the group of old impoverished officers and other hangers-on of the rich families in the community felt quite free to make fun of him, just as their own benefactors and their children showed their contempt and poked fun at them. Sometimes these jibes provoked him to a state of fury, and in these fits of anger he wrote scathing articles in the local newspapers about the corrupt civil servants in the district or about the careless and lax behavior of the military men. After this had happened a few times, and much trouble had been caused, he was no longer a popular guest and only tolerated, since one just could not avoid meeting him.

All over the parish, people spoke of their parson as a gambler and drunkard, one moreover who did not believe in the Word he preached. It was also rumored that he was cruel and mean in his own household, to his wife and children. Mr. Lind became the object of general contempt, and no one paid him any more attention than the law demanded. In the time of Mr. Lind the power and prestige of the parsons were completely undermined in the district.

The one who suffered most from the sins and follies of the parson was his wife. It was inconvenient when he suddenly told her he was going to entertain a great many guests who were to be wined and dined in spite of her not having enough food for the children and herself; and she spent tortured, miserable hours sitting up waiting, shuddering at the thought of his return, when he had been losing at cards, he vented his anger and irritation on her. Those nights when he was helped inside by the coachman, so blind drunk he was unable to utter a single word, were almost a relief to her.—Worst of all was the daily life with him. He either locked himself up in his study where he sat drowsily speculating on his complicated affairs and broke into a rage if disturbed, or confused and cross, possessed with the idea that the household expenses were too high, he would wander about the kitchen and dining room, upsetting and frightening everyone. At such times he screamed and scolded in his excitement, complaining particularly of his wife's extravagance.

Sometimes when she was alone, and the children had been taken care of, and the immediate problems put aside for a little while, she would sit for hours in the drawing room indulging in memories of the good days in their seaside parish where they had been happy. In spite of being poor, her husband had been content then and kind to her, but now—that it should come to this!—She wept and longed for the return of those other days. She hated her new home and surroundings, for they had robbed her of her husband, changing him into a household tyrant and an evil person. She cooled her forehead against the windowpanes and dreamed of the view from their former home that had looked out on the blue waters of the sea. How she hated this dull gray inland water lying like lead down there in the lake.

She dreamed and wept until she heard footsteps approaching, and the old confused feeling that something was wrong suddenly returned.

She had her children to live for, but illness and death had already added to her sorrows, for several of them had died as babies. There was thus a ten years' difference in age between Nicolai and his younger twin brothers. They had no daughters.

Nicolai was both her pride and joy; it was for him she worked and contrived, suffering all the privations and humiliations in order to send him to school in Christiania. The two little boys did not worry her overly much—they were so young—for in her own mind she felt that if Nicolai succeeded, if he behaved himself and got a good education, certainly it would be possible to manage for the others also. With many little tricks, she tried to get Nicolai the things he needed. She put aside one half of the winter's butchering and gave it to one of the neighbors to sell for her, and she deprived herself of every shilling that might have gone for a few clothes and a little finery for herself. She even went so far as to let the little twins go barefoot in the summertime like beggars' children. When Nicolai came home for the holidays, she told him about her efforts, always adding that when he was able to make his fortune, there would be better times for all of them. Even the parson contributed a little from time to time and finally Nicolai graduated and went to Copenhagen. That year she begrudged herself and the little boys even dry bread to eat. Mr. Lind, of course, had to be taken care of properly; he should never lack for anything.

The years went by, and in Copenhagen Nicolai fought his way alone with occasionally a little help from his father. He didn't write home very often, for postage was too expensive. There was little contact between him and his mother now, and since she could not reach him with her loving care, she seemed to have little to keep her going. She grew old and dull; her strength, as well as the will to cope with the situation and make the best of it, was gone.

In the spring of 1804 she revived a little for she had received the good news that Nicolai was going to come home for a visit that summer. Secretly she sold two barrels of barley and had new suits made for the twins. Mr. Orre, the country tradesman, had given her credit for the material, but more than likely he never even entered it in his books.

II

It had been raining hard all night. The heavy downpour had slackened at daybreak and had then stopped, but banks of clouds still hung over the bluish gray lake, and the morning sun was not strong enough to force its way through. To the south, however, the landscape was suffused by the sun's gleaming and white light.

Small and elegantly dressed, Nicolai Lind stood leaning against the palings of the garden fence in the vicarage courtyard. He kept looking at the hills on the other side of the lake. Usually the mountains looked like a continuous range, but today wisps of fog filled every cleft and ravine and gave new shape and form to the hills. He stretched, feeling grumpy and lazy as he bent his handsome, well-trimmed head back to look at the church spire, shining black and wet, as it towered above the green leaves of the maple trees. The wind had shifted to the northwest. He smiled to himself as he remembered this as a favorable weather forecast. It was good to know that during his stay in Copenhagen he hadn't forgotten all these little things about his native country life. But the swallows didn't trust to the wind. Swift and straight as arrows, they flung themselves downward from their nests in the eaves, spiraling silently through the air and close to the ground in their restless search for food. Only when they were back, secure under the roof tiles, did they give busy little screams.

At the other side of the house, between it and the barn, he saw some youngsters in their early teens gathered around the kitchen door. They were boys and girls who were candidates for confirmation. Every so often, two or three of them left the group and went silently up the steps and into the house; the parson's study was next to the kitchen, and Mr. Lind had told them to come see him, two or three at a time. The others could wait outside as he didn't want them all in his office at once.

Two men, with their backs to Nicolai, were sitting on the big level salt stone in the middle of the courtyard. One of them was old, with long gray hair hanging from under his hat; the other, a hunchback, wore a cap.

Nicolai knew them. The old one, who called himself Palmström, was a Swede, and somewhat of an ignoramus, who, it was said, had run away from his own country to escape punishment for some crime he had committed.

He had lived in this district ever since Nicolai could remember, supporting himself as a jack-of-all-trades, quite capable of doing anything he was asked to. He was equally good as carpenter, quack doctor, barber or blacksmith. However, given his choice, he really preferred to be a gardener, to graft trees and plant gardens. Nevertheless, he was not at all well-thought-of; in fact, he was considered a bit of a wizard, perhaps even practiced black-magic. If he didn't, at any rate he associated with Finlanders and all sorts of itinerant beggars, especially his own immigrant countrymen. He had rented a little place up in the Vestby hills, the worst gypsy hang-out in the country, and it was only his ability to make himself useful to the gentry that saved him from being thoroughly investigated by the authorities. This, Palmström probably wouldn't have liked at all.

The hunchback was the village organist, a poor creature whom the late parson had protected and encouraged to give music lessons to earn a living.

Nicolai strolled over to them and said: "Hello, Palmström, how is everything?"

Palmström got up hurriedly, and pulling off his hat, bowed low: "Well, well, it's young Mr. Lind, isn't it? Is the young gentleman back? How very kind and courteous to remember an old acquaintance! Heigh-ho, its a long time since we met last. I do thank you so much for your inquiry and, yes, I am all right, or at least as well as one could expect in my poor circumstances."

He tried to twist his wrinkled face into a smile as he spoke rapidly with a slight Swedish accent, but since his little eyes blinked incessantly and the big hawk-nose jutted out so forbiddingly, he only succeeded in producing a wheedling smirk. While he spoke he kept waving his right hand, which was covered with queer red and blue tattoo marks.

The organist in the meantime had stood quietly, holding his cap modestly in his hand.

"Good morning, Nyeberg. Put on your cap, man; I'm not royalty," Nicolai said. "Did you want to see the parson this morning?"

It was Palmström who answered: "I'm going to have a look at the organ with my good friend Peder Nyeberg—he thinks it needs a few repairs and adjustments—and at the same time I wanted to register myself for next communion," he put his hat on and crossed his hands piously.

Nicolai laughed. "I'm happy to see you're becoming godfearing in your old age, Palmström—"

"Hm—yes—and, it is that certificate for attending the Lord's Supper," said the Swede slyly and folded his hands in back of him.

The young people crowded around the kitchen steps when a fat blonde girl came out weeping from the parson's office. Sobbing angrily she tried to tell them what had happened, while at the same time the others tried to quiet and console her.

Nicolai turned around and looked at them nervously. Something was wrong; his father had been to a party at the major's the night before, and he was always bad-tempered in the morning after a night of heavy drinking. Nicolai went back to the house without saying anything more to the two men.

The Swede looked after him thoughtfully as he and the organ player sat down again.

"Young Mr. Lind seems to be an educated person," Palmström observed casually with a side-long glance at his companion. "Too bad that I forgot to ask for news from Denmark.—I had the strangest news when I was over at Hans Dahlbye's the other day."

The organist didn't show the slightest interest. He just kept drumming on the stone with his fingers as he watched the young people. Finally he said, "It's the daughter of Gudbrand Nerlien who is crying."

"Really the strangest news," Palmström continued. "A most interesting proof that our magistrates and governors are beginning to show some common sense, even though there certainly will be some people who won't like it very much. Perhaps it would be of some interest to you Nyeberg, to know. . . ."

"What?" asked Nyeberg still not listening. He was much more interested in the weeping girl, who left the group with another girl and disappeared behind the barn. "By Jove! It looks as though the parson has teased Nerlien's daughter, and she is going to run straight home and tell her father."

"Well—if you don't care, I shan't bother telling you," said the Swede crossly. "But I thought I really ought to tell a good friend news that concerns his livelihood, or rather that concerns the livelihood of his superior."

"Of course, you know I care. Is it about a new organ for the church?" he guessed tentatively.

"It has nothing to do with the organ, but a great deal to

do with the organ players," answered Palmström importantly. He continued as though he was reading out of a book: "According to the statement of Hans Dahlbye, some great innovations will soon take place that will change all of the church usages and customs. It has been announced by the government that offerings will no longer be taken during the church service. In the future wedding ceremonies will be abolished, and those who wish to get married will just go to the judge. They will only need to have a couple of witnesses, sign their marriage articles, and it will be recorded and registered. Now, my friend, how do you like that?"

Nyeberg replied rather pompously, "In my opinion, such new government orders would be based on very sound principles."

"Yes, yes," grunted Palmström scratching his chin—"and then people won't have to bother about wedding fees, parson tithes or anything else; it will all be taken care of. But—but what about the offerings? Ha, ha, I don't think the clergymen will get too fat from now on. But—but—"

"Oh, don't bother to pity the parson; his bag won't be empty, he doesn't need any poor help," Nyeberg retorted sharply.

The Swede patted the other's hump in a fatherly way. "I don't have to be concerned about the parson, but I do worry about the worthy parish clerks and organ players. I don't suppose you are able to save very much from the bags of corn and the dalers you get for playing on Sunday, are you? The money you are paid for playing wedding marches is not to be despised, is it? What are you and the sexton going to get in your outstretched hands? I think it will just be a piece of dirt," he concluded, shaking his head.

The organ player's pale face flushed. "I'll tell you one thing, Christian Palmström, you are just making fun of the poverty of your friend."

"No, far from it!—You mustn't think I am doing that, Peder. I'm just glad that at last common sense is about to win out in the rituals of the church, even though I am sorry you will be the one to suffer by it!" As if in protest Palmström raised his tattooed fist. "But look, what is going on over there?"

From the group of youngsters on the other side of the courtyard came sounds of suppressed laughter and excited talk. They huddled together and seemed to be planning something. Palmström got up and started towards them, but Nyeberg caught him by the coat tail and asked again if the news from Hans Dahlbye was really true. But the Swede said he didn't know for sure and was sorry that he hadn't asked the young Mr. Lind about it. Gloomily the organ player trudged across the courtyard after him.

The boys moved aside as the two men approached, but the girls clustered around the stocky blonde girl who was tying a flowered shawl over her head. She looked at the men rather shyly. While the boys were guffawing and the girls tittering, Palmström finally managed to find out that the parson would not allow Berte Nerlien to be confirmed, because there was some trouble between him and her father about the tithe money. The parson had sent her away, saying she was unworthy. But when they noticed that the parson was confused and bleary-eyed—in such a state that he would probably forget tomorrow what he did today—the blonde girl had run home, changed her clothes, and was to return to the parson's office, and to say she was from Overlien where no one was at odds with the parson. The young people weren't afraid to tell this to Palmström, because when he went around to the different farms, he told stories he had read in books about religion and the clergy that seemed even more learned than the catechism and the book of sermons.

The two men made no comment; they just waited until they saw that the girl's trick worked.

Meanwhile Nicolai sat alone in the sitting room. He sat by the window, leaning his elbows on the windowsill and gazed sadly out into the garden where everything was wet: the grass, the stunted apple trees with their moss-covered trunks, and the leaves of the currant bushes, which, shaped like small cups, were filled with sparkling water.

The relationship between his parents seemed indeed to be worse than he had thought. In the two days he had been home his father had behaved decently, but last night he had been drunk when he returned from the major's. Today things were really bad. When Nicolai came down for breakfast about nine o'clock, the bottle of brandy on the table was already half emptied, but, after all, nine o'clock was not so very early according to the custom here in the country. Being a parson, however, he ought to be more careful, especially today when he was to register children for confirmation.

Apparently though, the family finances were not so bad, for his brothers had new boots and good new clothes; before when he had been home during vacations, they had been both ragged and barefoot. Nor had he heard the usual complaints and lamentations about money troubles—at least not as yet.

Still, the furniture was the same—old and shabby. There was the familiar large red gateleg table that was used at mealtime. The sofa behind it was still covered with checkered linsey-woolsey as were the chairs; he recalled that a long time ago they had been covered with dark green linen damask. On the wall above the sofa hung the silhouettes of his father, his mother, himself, and one of his dead brothers. They had been made in Christiansand by a very odd Frenchman. Yes, certainly he had been a Frenchman and very skillful.—The mirror in the carved gilt frame had been bought at the auction after the death of the last parson. The other furniture included a birch-wood card table placed against the opposite wall, a shelf of pipes with silver-covered meerschaum bowls, and a brown escritoire in the corner. The tall white grandfather's clock, which touched the ceiling and was made to show the date and year, as well as to tell the time and to strike the hours, was in a way too precious and beautiful to fit in with the other things in the room. —Nicolai sat there looking at the shiny brass face. At the top, engraved in scroll lettering, was the name Even Hagensen Weelang 1788. The hand that was intended to show the date he had broken off as a child, and he had deserved the whipping he got for doing it. There was still a big hole where the hand had been. Daydreaming drowsily he listened to the quiet tick-tock: "Nothing new, nothing new, not needed, not needed, will do," it tock-tocked.

A big bottle-fly buzzed past his ear and smacked against the windowpane. It woke him. He walked to the window. Indeed there was something new: semi-transparent curtains were hung at every window—he had never seen them before. They were newly starched, certainly in his honor.

The bluebottle flew around again and buzzed irritably under the beams of the ceiling, which he noticed ought to be painted soon, for every year it grew dirtier and more smoke-stained.

In the kitchen, fire blazed on the hearth, for the maids

were already busy preparing dinner. His mother came in quietly and sat down at the table. Nicolai had immediately noticed how much she had changed; now the thought struck him again. She had grown stouter, and though she was not ill, her movements were languid and tired. Her hair had turned much grayer, and the sunken cheeks showed she had lost several of her teeth. Her brown eyes had once been so gay and sparkling and he had been so proud of them because people told him they were like his own; now they seemed to gaze vacantly and appeared exhausted from nervous watching.

She picked up her knitting, and while she automatically counted the stitches, she began in a monotonous voice to ask detailed questions about his life in Copenhagen: how did he manage his food and clothes and what about their family and the acquaintances she had made twenty-two years ago when she had gone there with her husband? She asked about his studies and when he would be finished, about the king —was he still as mad as he used to be?—and much, much more. He had already answered many of the questions several times before but evidently she had forgotten. In a gentle voice he told her over again about all the small happenings, and in between he told her about the more important things.

Gradually he turned the conversation to the people of the district. He inquired about every single one of their friends and neighbors, and asked if any new families had moved to the area. Yes, there was the new judge. New judge? Who was that? It was the councillor, Councillor Weydahl, she corrected herself. Oh yes, but Nicolai knew him before he had gone to Copenhagen. Wasn't it four years now since the councillor had moved here? Then no one had moved to the district lately if he was the last to arrive. They did not meet him very often. Oh, Lind met him from time to time, but since his wife's death he never invited ladies to his parties. Nicolai even remembered when Mrs. Weydahl had died. But what of the Orres at Alm, did she visit them very often? No, she whispered, it was rather awkward, for Lind seemed to owe Orre a lot of money. Nicolai frowned and looked at one of the cracks in the windowsill with a thoughtful expression.

Mr. Orre, she continued, had not been difficult; in fact, she didn't think he had ever asked for the money. Even so, she thought her husband shrank from meeting him.

Evidently, Nicolai said to himself, his mother was not going out very much. She could not even tell him the last time she had gone visiting, but guessed it might have been to the baptism of the major's youngest child, and that was nearly a year ago now.

Nicolai rocked back and forth in the rocking chair. "Mother," he said, "I think it's not good for you to stay at home so much. Will you go with me to visit the Orres this afternoon? You know I ought to go to see them while I am here."

She smiled at him: "You used to be good friends with the girls, Nicolai, and they are both at home now." She hesitated and, at a loss for words, sighed and smoothed her shabby black dress. It was her best dress, and she had put it on for his sake, but it was questionable whether it was good enough to wear visiting.

Nicolai read her thoughts. "You are as elegant as anyone," he said, "and besides we are only going to pay a short visit; it's no party." His mother kept her own counsel and let him persuade her to go, even though it would be a little difficult to get a coach and horses.

The sunshine made the room bright. Outside, it glistened

on the apple trees and currant bushes and sparkled on the grass in the garden. His mother let her knitting fall into her lap, exclaiming, "Oh, how wonderful! It's clearing up." Nicolai opened the door wide into the entrance hall.

The sunshine streamed rich and golden on to the light green fields and on the water curled into little waves by the pleasant breeze. The light fell on the ridges on the west side of the lake where little wisps of fog were being swept away. The distant hills merged again into a connected range of blue mountains. The group of young people had left the courtyard, and only his small brothers were left playing with some of the cotters' children. They were busy trying to destroy a big wasps' nest they had discovered under the eaves of the barn, and went at it with the throwing of stones and wild yells.

The cat cautiously picked her way between the small pools of rainwater in the courtyard. She came to Nicolai and rubbed her arched back against his boots, all the while purring loudly. Then she started to play with a bit of cut-up juniper leaves that were sprinkled on the floor of the entrance hall.

"How beautiful it is here, beautiful, beautiful!" Nicolai thought and meowed to the cat to call her back to him. "It will be fine weather at Alm this afternoon, Pussy."

Just then through the open doors of the sitting room he heard the shrill nasal voice of Mr. Lind. He sounded irritable and displeased. Then his mother replied, apprehensive yet placating, as if defending herself.

Nicolai went in. His father stood beside the corner cupboard. He was pinching his wife's arm and shaking her. "My heart, my heart. I can't find it. It was here this morning, Gine. Now where is it? My dear! Who took it? Haven't I forbidden you to touch it?"

"What is it, Father?" Nicolai asked rather sharply, as he saw his mother wince with pain. Lind released her arm and turned around, surprised and displeased to see his son. His face was flushed, and his eyes were glazed and shiny; obviously he had been drinking.

He forced himself to be affable: "It is only the key to the cupboard, my boy. Someone has taken it."

"You probably left it in your office" his wife interrupted him. "I will run and have a look. . . ." She hurried out as if she did not want to explain further, and her husband followed her.

Nicolai sat down by the window again. He no longer noticed the brilliant sunshine.—Horrible how old his father had grown, his hair so white and thin! And really it was a disgusting habit to call his mother by pet names while he hurt her.

III

During the reign of King Hans there lived in Denmark a nobleman by the name of Jens Orre; he had traveled widely. In the course of his journeys he had embraced many of the modern heretical views regarding religion and, being a very stubborn as well as outspoken man, made no secret of it. Because of these opinions he got into an argument with a clergyman and killed him. Fleeing for his life, he went to Norway with his wife and children. Because he didn't feel safe either on the coast or in the towns, he went inland to the Gudbrandsdal Valley and established himself on the west shore of Lake Mjösen where he carved his coat of arms on the wall of the church as a sign of his desire to stay in that part of the country.

He was the first member of the Orre family known to

history. His grandson moved to the eastern shore and bought the Alm farm, the family seat. He amassed a large fortune, and it was inherited down through several generations, and was kept largely intact, since there were always few heirs.

Even though the Orre family did not succeed in keeping its title of nobility, they were still regarded with great esteem. They never wanted to become great landowners, being content with Alm alone. Their money was invested at reasonable interest; for the rest, they made a good profit from various kinds of trading and in time came to control some of the best mills in the country.

They mostly associated with the farmers and were well liked by them, though they never married into farmer families. It was customary for the sons and daughters to marry into the families of clergymen and civil servants, sometimes even into the rich merchant families in the towns.

They all inherited the heretical ways of their ancestor, and during their youth they were accustomed to travel extensively. An insatiable thirst for knowledge very often caused them to be better informed than was usual among the people of their time. As each returned to Alm from his travels abroad, he brought with him many books, so that gradually the collection grew to be quite a library. But only a few were allowed to use it. The views and opinions of the Orres were of considerable significance in their circles. From the cosmopolitan world outside, they brought back with them a fresh point of view to this quiet secluded part of the Uplands.

At the beginning of the eighteenth century the Orres were at the height of their wealth and power. It was during the reign of Frederik IV that the country was bankrupt because of the war, and the impoverished exchequer had to be refilled through the sale of churches and church property. It was then that Gregers Henrikssön Orre went to Copenhagen and bought the church on behalf of the parish, making a handsome down payment. He was the only one in these parts who had the cash to do such a thing. Later on, the money owed him by the parish was assessed among the farmers and paid back.

In the summer of 1733, it happened that Henrik Gregerssön Orre had the honor of being host at Alm to H. M. King Christian VI and Queen Sophie Magdalene and their retinue. The splendor of his hospitality on the occasion became a legend in the neighborhood. His children certainly never forgot that they had been allowed to pass through the hall and to bow and curtsy to their majesties as they sat at banquet, and to feel the royal gaze rest on them at such close quarters. For some years after the visit, Henrik Orre dreamed of getting his title of nobility again. In anticipation of this he cut a great figure in the society of the district for a while. Then suddenly he died, at which time the family fortune had become much smaller.

His son, however, found a new source of wealth. He became a country tradesman licensed by royal patent, and soon the damage done to the family fortune by his father's hospitality to Christian VI was repaired. There was no other tradesman to be found within scores of miles, and all over the Uplands no one had such an excellent assortment of goods. He had everything in his shop: silks so thick and heavy that dresses made of them could stand alone; blonde laces and colored ribbons; calico and taffeta; velvet and "swansdown"; the finest English cloth; stockings, caps and hats, as well as salt, tobacco, spices, sugar and coffee—yes, even tea, chocolates, and wine for the well-to-do.—It was not without cause that the authorities complained that this business at Alm created the desire for luxuries among the common people and that women and young girls refused to spin and weave because the material sold by Mr. Orre was much prettier than anything they could make themselves and was, moreover, much easier to get. But if the farmers had a good year and were able to sell their crops at a profit, they didn't mind letting their wives spend some money on finery.

At the turn of the century the proprietor of the store was Hans Orre, an eccentric man of fifty or sixty, withered and sallow. As he fussed about the store, his little pigtail bobbed up and down over the collar of his brown coat with the silver buttons. He always carried a tortoise-shell snuff box in his hand. As a young man he had been to London and Paris; he had read a great deal and liked to impress the country people by quoting English or French sayings, which, of course, they did not understand. In addition, Mr. Orre was the most liberal of free-thinkers and a republican. He never went to church and lost no opportunity to speak disrespectfully of both the monarchy and religion, so much so in fact that some people wondered if he would not get into trouble with the authorities.

On even the most serious occasions he had a certain air of formal and sarcastic politeness about him. He was a widower, and the story was told about him that at his wife's deathbed a message was brought to him that a stranger wanted to see him. Orre had asked to be excused for the moment, as his wife was dying, but it was to be hoped he would very soon be at his visitor's service. After a few minutes he came into the drawing room mincing and bowing, "Now I'm at your service, sir—my wife just died."

It was said that in the past he had been a great ladies' man, but now he was a man of regular habits who never drank too much and who detested gambling. Even though he appeared to be hard and unsympathetic, he was really very generous.

His house was run by an unmarried sister. He had two sons; the elder was to take over Alm and the store; the younger was a government official in Jutland. There were also two young daughters.

Alm was about a mile and a half south of the church. The road to it bordered meadows and well-tilled fields, wound around a small outcropping of rock and passed a clump of stunted firs which thrust roots into the poor soil; then suddenly there were the courtyard and the house, almost a mansion, straight ahead. The house, two stories high and surmounted by a clock tower, stood in the center of the group of buildings. The little clock tower placed there by Henrik Orre had a strange history of its own. Mr. Orre had paid an exorbitant price to a clockmaker from Gudbrandsdal to make this four-faced clock for the tower. The clockmaker had been unable to make one clockwork for all four faces, so he had put in separate works for each face. As no two had the same timing and all were constructed to strike on the half hour with a jingling sound, they created such an incessant din during the entire day and night that the master of Alm had to stop three of the mechanical wonders. The fourth continued to chase its hands around and strike persistently, unwilling to accept the authority of the sun as a timekeeper.

Two long one-story wings extended at an angle on each side of the main building. They were used as store rooms and shops and as rooms for the servants. The wing nearest the road was used as the store and was reached by a well-worn flight of narrow stone steps. All of these buildings were painted yellow, but the barn and other buildings on the slope to the lake were gray.

In the courtyard were hustle and bustle of people coming and going from early morning until late at night. Rows of hitching posts had been placed there for the convenience of the customers, who sometimes took hours to finish their errands in the dark and crowded shop. The haughty grumpy salesclerks went about their business behind the counter in such a leisurely way as to suggest they were doing the customer a favor by allowing him to spend his money.

* * *

In the main parlor at Alm the tea table was laid with a white fringed cloth. From the steaming teapot, kind Aunt Birgitte poured tea into the cups of blue-patterned Copenhagen porcelain. Madame Lind was served first, then the daughters of the house, Laurentze and Sophie, and their old great-aunt, who was over eighty and was called the old Miss to distinguish her from Aunt Birgitte. The cake plates were passed around the table. Madame Lind helped herself and after much urging took some more of the dainties. Then came the glass spoon-jar with small spoons on it, followed by bowls of jam. The ladies took each bowl as it was passed and held it for a moment, tasted the jam, and passed it on. After tasting the jam, they put their spoons into a bowl of water in the middle of the table. When another kind of jam was served each took a spoon from the bowl, used it, and put it back into the water.

Bright sunshine filled the room. The beams of light were reflected in the hundreds of glass drops of the chandelier and danced in quivering rainbow colors on the dark wallpaper. It was hot and beads of perspiration stood out on the aristocratic nose of the old Miss as she sat painstakingly knitting. The yarn was encased in a silver filigreed bowl of polished wood which was fastened to a silver cord. She was hard of hearing and her shrill voice frequently interrupted the conversation which flowed quietly around the room.

Laurentze, demure and quiet, sat by her great-aunt, her hands folded in her lap. Like her sister she was dressed in a light flowered-muslin frock with short sleeves and square-cut neck. It was most unbecoming and made her look too big for her age and too fair of hair and complexion.

The door to the library was open, and from where she sat, opposite the mirror over the console, she could watch Nicolai as he stood talking with the other gentlemen. She felt him looking at her and wanted to turn her head and smile at him, but she just didn't dare because Lieutenant Wallace was standing on the doorstep smoking his long pipe and blowing smoke rings into the air. And Wallace—the disgusting old bachelor—always noticed even the tiniest smile or glance, so that he could tease her about it afterwards.

The library was Mr. Orre's favorite room. It was so filled with books that there was hardly enough room for a couch along the long wall or even for the Swedish stove in the corner. There were books all over the place, from floor to ceiling; some had solid brown bindings, and, packed tightly with them on the shelves, were packages of carefully wrapped pamphlets and bundles of newspapers. On the top shelves were rows of old books bound in yellowish parchment; they had been collected one by one by the ancestors of the present owner. Most of them had been bought abroad and brought to Alm by the returning travelers.

Over the couch hung a gilt-framed engraving of Voltaire. Formerly there had been other engravings of famous men, but as the walls had become more and more crowded with books, all the other pictures had been moved to the main parlor. Only the stern old face of Voltaire remained, and he seemed to be peering down at the gentlemen gathered there as though symbolizing the views of the host.

Besides Mr. Orre, Nicolai Lind, and Lieutenant Wallace, there were Major Brager and a well-to-do farmer, who had come to sell his corn to the district tradesman. The major and the lieutenant had just dropped in uninvited to have a strengthening drink after a late party the night before.

Mr. Orre was a hospitable man; even though he himself drank only sugared water, there was a mug of punch brewed from his strong Jamaica rum on the table for his guests.

They kept pressing Nicolai for news from Copenhagen, but he didn't have much to tell, and the conversation soon became a political squabble about the war between France and England. The blunt, unpolished major kept tapping on the oak table with his pipestem, as if to give more weight to his opinions. He swore that this French emperor was a very able soldier—a very able fellow indeed—who was capable of putting down Englishmen as well as Jacobins! Lieutenant Wallace agreed with the major, almost taking the words out of his mouth. He quickly straddled a highbacked chair and began talking a lot of confused nonsense about Jacobins and the king of Sweden, expressing his contempt for both by frowning and knitting his brows so that his black forelock moved back and forth. He was already beginning to feel the effects of the punch, and his thick voice reflected the previous night's drinking.

Mr. Orre gave them a penetrating lecture on the principles of republicanism, and the farmer reached again and again with a thick and clumsy hand for a glass of punch to toast and say "Skaal" to the young student who had been so kind as to address him as Proprietor. Each time he drank, he leaned back in the armchair, pulled both ends of his purple silk necktie, whinnied and laughed so hard that his big paunch shook. Each time the major looked over at the farmer as though to say, "What makes this fellow think that he is among equals?"

From the open window into the garden a continuous streamer of smoke drifted from the pipes of the gentlemen and merged into the afternoon sunshine.

Nicolai was bored. He was embarrassed by the half-drunken familiarity of the farmer and stopped responding to his toasts. He had a strange feeling. This silly madcap of a major whose choppy way of speaking made it seem as if he had forgotten to talk coherently, and this old-fashioned country storekeeper, who was forever talking about the principles underlying a rational order of the state, all the while sprinkling snuff over his clothes, the couch, and the table, were tiresome. Yet once upon a time during his childhood, Nicolai had admired them most among his parents' acquaintances. In his memory there had been a certain glamor about them, and he had thought of them during the years in Copenhagen as the main characters in a rustic Norwegian pastorale. Rather ashamed of his sentimental memories, he looked at them with new eyes, at the dissipated lieutenant and the boorish farmer, whose pretentious behavior now seemed typical of the rude countrymen of the district.

Disgusted, he emptied his glass with one swallow, and as he finished, looked into the parlor; his glance met that of the gay smiling Laurentze, and suddenly he realized that he had suffered an even greater disappointment.

In the early morning hours, during his journey from Denmark, he had known, as he stood on the deck of the little sloop and watched the approaching shores of his own country, that the object of his greatest longing during the three years abroad was only a faint dream. This dream was connected with Alm, and with one wonderful light Whitsunday night in the pine forest. He and his parents had gone with a group of friends to the top of a hill. The party gathered there laughed and sang and made speeches as they built the traditional Whitsuntide bonfire. He remembered seeing a young girl as she had stood by the fire gazing into the flames, just as the tar barrel had fallen from its pole making the flames flare up and sparkle, and the spectators had shouted hurrah. She had been tall and slender, dressed in white, like a gleaming shadow against the darkness of the forest behind her.

As the party broke up, he had gone over to her and had taken her hand, and they had run like two gay children down the hill along the rough forest path, far ahead of the others. Then suddenly he had taken her in his arms and kissed her, saying how fond he was of her and how sorry he was that he had to leave for Copenhagen to go to school. They had kissed and promised each other to be faithful. She had looked pale and pure in the late twilight of the summer night, and they had both felt they were no longer children.

Out of this memory had grown the dream that had sustained him during the three difficult years in Copenhagen. This was the reason his heart had been beating so hard all during the drive to Alm.

And now—he looked at Laurentze, who was still smiling while she emptied the glass that the lieutenant had refilled. He realized there was very little similarity between the girl he had seen in the firelight and the one sitting in the parlor. She had grown larger and too fat; and it wasn't just the dress and her slovenly walk and posture that made her seem so. Her face was freckled and her features poorly defined and uninteresting. The only beautiful thing about her was her blue eyes; they twinkled under her dull blond curls with a gay look that seemed to come from a secret joy. The look tortured him. How different she was from the Laurentze of his dreams! He was still tied to her by the bonds of the mutual memory, which she had apparently kept faithfully.

One thing he was certain of: he no longer felt any attachment to this clumsy girl sitting in the parlor with red hands folded in her lap, however she might regard their relationship. What had caused this change? Was it only because she had become unattractive, or did his more sophisticated point of view about women, since he had been in Copenhagen, cause him to feel this way? In any event she had to understand that now he considered her just an acquaintance, a friend of his childhood, nothing more. He decided to act cautiously and coolly in order to avoid trouble. He recalled her bashful welcome, spoken in such a provincial dialect that it seemed hardly decent language to Copenhagen ears. Without the slightest hesitancy he made the decision to be cool and cautious.

He stuck to his decision until after dinner. The farmer had already left, since no one had asked him to stay, and the other gentlemen had returned to the library and their pipes. Feeling a little hot and dizzy from the punch, Nicolai wandered about in the garden alone. It was laid out in a strange and formal pattern with summer houses and trimmed hedges which turned yellow during the dry summers and were broken by the weight of the winter snows, but it certainly had cost Henrik Orre a great deal of money to make this garden. Laurentze also walked into the garden.

To make conversation Nicolai asked about her brother who had gone to town for a few days. She answered rather awkwardly and then walked silently beside him.

Nicolai could never remember afterwards exactly what happened, for in spite of all his determination he soon found her hands in his. She squeezed his tenderly, and when he looked into her pale blue eyes, he couldn't help speaking of that Whitsunday night. He hesitated, wanting to reminisce about their childhood, but her lips were so red and full that he kissed them and said everything he had decided not to.

The great-aunt was still sitting in her rocking chair when they returned to the parlor together. She nodded to them; they both looked so silly and puzzled. Their comments, as they came into the room, were so unnatural and consciously unconcerned that Madame Lind and Aunt Birgitte looked knowingly at each other, as if they expected some interesting news very soon now. Nicolai caught the significance of the old ladies' glances and felt that the damage had been done. During the twenty minutes in the garden, it had happened. He had bound himself to this girl; his mother and Aunt Birgitte were witnesses to it. Absent-mindedly he ran his fingers through his hair and sighed thoughtfully.

The major said with a raucous laugh: "Look at young Master Lind. How like he is to the parson when the cards aren't running!" Then Wallace started to tell how Attorney Höegh had beaten the parson at cards the night before. But Nicolai squared his shoulders and threw the lieutenant such a look of exasperation and anger that he stopped in the middle of the sentence. Well, of course he never meant to insult young Master Lind. Dismayed at the effect his story had on Nicolai, the lieutenant blurted out an excuse that embarrassed the boy even more.

Fortunately Madame Lind was rising to leave. She was a little uncomfortable at the thought of having come without leaving a message for Mr. Lind, who had been taking his afternoon nap. The officers, however, were in no hurry to depart, so only the mother and son made ready to leave. They were attended to their coach by the entire family, Mr. Orre leading the way and bowing over and over again most politely. They said goodbye with prolonged courtesies on both sides. Nicolai was able to observe Laurentze for quite a while. Aunt Birgitte could not refrain from asking him to return soon, and Laurentze suddenly gave him her hand again, Sophie giggled, and Mr. Orre bowed for the last time as the horses pulled forward and the coach rumbled out of the courtyard.

They passed a couple of customers with heavy bulging birch-bark knapsacks on their backs. The men were just leaving the shop and patiently starting their long walk to the outskirts of the district.

His mother, tired by the unaccustomed trip, sat quietly as they drove along; the son, deep in thought, was glad to be relieved from talking, so they drove in silence through the wonderful warm summer night to the parsonage. The partridge could be heard in the meadows, and the surface of the lake was as smooth as a mirror.

An indolent ragged stable boy came slowly across the yard to unharness the horses. Madame Lind went in the kitchen entrance, while Nicolai helped the boy. After they had finished, Nicolai went in also and unexpectedly met his father groping about in the hall in his shirt-sleeves and with a pipe in his mouth. Behind him in the shadow of the doorway, he caught a glimpse of his mother's dark dress.

"So it's you, my boy! I'm glad to see you. Here I've been sitting alone all evening, waiting for you and your mother to return. It wasn't kind of you to let me stay here by myself and to disappear without telling me where you were going!"

He was drunk and angry but tried to conceal it under a veneer of attempted humor.

"But father—we have not been far, only visiting the Orres. You were asleep after dinner, and we didn't want to disturb you," Nicolai said placatingly.

"Come in, come in, my boy! I have hardly talked to you since you arrived," the parson said, in a kindly but whining voice, and taking him by the arm, pulled Nicolai into the sitting room. The parson pointed to a chair as he sank down on the couch. "Sit down, Nicolai. I want to talk to you. You have been here three days now without talking to me." He threw his pipe on the floor and put both hands into the armholes of his vest. With a sigh he continued, hiccoughing all the while, "Three days under your father's roof without a word of confidence, my son!"

Madame Lind went out quietly, and Nicolai sat down on the chair. On the table in front of him among soiled and crumpled newspapers, stood a beermug, a glass, and a bottle of brandy.

IV

The parson had awakened dull and dizzy in the middle of the afternoon. When the housemaid told him Madame Lind and Nicolai had left for Alm, he became furious and heaped abuse on all the servants in sight, but they were so used to it that they paid no attention, and his two little sons fled from his anger. Finally he went out to the fields and cheered himself with an afternoon brandy with the haymakers. Lind felt better after that, but his disposition was not improved by noticing Major Brager and Lieutenant Wallace on the highway. He knew pretty well where they were going, and good reasons, based on last night's card game, kept him from calling to them as they passed; other reasons, equally good, kept him from following them to Alm.

He walked slowly inside again. How bored he was! The others were enjoying pleasant company and conversation, while he sat alone in this big empty house, his wife and children away, and everyone else out working. Oh, how bored he was! They were all impudent, never giving him proper respect.

He could feel the key to the cupboard in his pocket, the key Gine had tried to hide. Why? Was she afraid that her husband would like to have a glass of brandy now that his grown-up son had come home? He was such a refined young man! Of course he had had a little drop at breakfast to settle his stomach, but he wasn't drunk, that he would swear to. "Ha—my heart! You needn't worry. You needn't feel ashamed of your husband, Gine!" And he wandered up and down between the parlor and the office, hating his wife and the whole world, feeling bored and ill-used and longing for company. Each time he turned in his pacing back and forth, he looked at the clock. He sweated in annoyance at the slowness of time. A feeling of faintness came over him as he listened to the sound of his own uneven footsteps echoing in the silent rooms. His arms and legs ached. It was unbearable.

The key to the cupboard was slipped into the lock; the beermug, the bottle of brandy, and a glass were put on the table. One had to strengthen oneself after being up all night, but surely Gine should have no reason to feel ashamed of him in front of their grown-up son.

The hours passed, and during the evening the parson got drunk. He fetched ink and paper and wrote a poisonous letter to the newspaper in Christiania about an unreasonable officer who conscripted poor cottagers and fathers of large families for military service just as they were in the middle of the spring ploughing and sowing season, even demanding they bring food for two weeks, and then when they came for their service, it was only to repair old uniforms. Why couldn't these officers wait until the spring work was done, or couldn't the work be done after the military service? It had always been apparent that his Majesty the King was always kind and thoughtful in his dealings with the heads of families. It was, moreover, quite curious that the conscripts always were farmers, not tailors——

The quill pen scratched painfully across the paper. This is what the major would get for his sarcasm. It would certainly bring an investigation of his conduct, and some real trouble, for the major general was keen on such things. It would serve the major right. Mr. Lind had several brandies and he felt grateful to the farmer, Hans Dahlbye, who had brought the matter to his attention. This fellow, Hans Dahlbye, was a lot better than the rumors one heard about him. In spite of all the trouble he caused Lind personally, he was a man who had some feeling for the common people.

When the letter was finished, the parson was very drunk. No, he didn't want anything to eat, he said, when the housemaid brought some supper. Then he dozed for a while before his wife returned from Alm.

The air in the room was close and stuffy with stale tobacco smoke and the smell of brandy. To Nicolai it was doubly depressing because the air outside was dewy and fresh. In the twilight he could distinctly see his father's tousled white hair and pale sallow face, that became grotesquely distorted as his thoughts and tongue struggled against drunkenness.

A deep feeling of shame swept over the boy. This drunkard, this decadent parson who went among his parishioners as an outcast, was his father. Vanity and frivolity and this uncultivated society had done this to his father, Nicolai thought. With aching regret he remembered his involvement with Laurentze, which would tie him to these same circles. He felt ashamed not only of his father but of himself, and the feeling of shame nearly suffocated him. He could stand it no longer.

"It's late, father. We'd better talk tomorrow."

"Tomorrow? No, the intimacy of a quiet night, my son—" the drunken man quavered and started to put his arm around the boy's shoulder.

Nicolai drew back. "You ought to go to bed, father."

The parson rose, his eyes flashing with anger: "You—you're ashamed of me. So you reject your own father, eh? Where have you and your mother been today? You've been with my enemies. And what's more, you took two horses right in the middle of the haying. You've betrayed me by being with those who speak ill of me. But one shouldn't hate one's own flesh and blood. Forgive your father, Nicolai, for he forgives you."

Lind spread his fingers over the newspapers on the table. He was very miserable. "Nicolai," he murmured, "you brought me messages and good wishes from Copenhagen, from persons of position and prestige. They gave you a warm welcome, because they remembered me with kindness. These greetings comforted me. I used to belong to that circle; they expected great things of me because, like them, I was a person of knowledge, education, and good taste. But I married and had to make a living; that took me far away from the places to which I was attached by my heart and nature. You see, I married and tried here and there to get a parish—oh, in Copenhagen you were proud to hear well-known men speak of me, but here you are ashamed of me.—Ha, ha, have you any debts, Nicolai? I had debts, which I paid, and now I have more debts. It is due to this large family of mine. Well, I spend something myself, I confess, but mostly it's my family. It's so long now since I married and I finally came here to live among this rag-tag bunch of storekeepers and majors and envious curates. Just look! See what I am going to put into the paper about that low creature, the major, who is always making fun of me. No, the letter is in the pocket of my coat out in the office. No, don't go, don't go get it now; leave it until later," he said as his son rose from his chair.

"Sit down and drink a toast to our dear friends in Copenhagen!" Lind continued, and he unsteadily poured more brandy from the bottle. "Skaal! You drink first, my boy, you are grown up now and can take a glass."

A cold chill swept over Nicolai; his father looked as though he had lost his senses. "No thanks, father, nothing for me. Please go to bed. You ought not to drink anymore today."

"I ought not, did you say, you—you," wheezed the drunken man. "You have no respect for your old father." He smiled maliciously and asked with deceptive gentleness: "Nicolai, tell me the truth: have you any debts? I have been looking at your elegant suit. I do know something about your finances. Tell me, did you come home because of your debts? You can confide in me."

When he got no answer, he leaned forward and said ingratiatingly: "I ask you this seriously; you should take your father into your confidence."

Nicolai was on pins and needles; he felt himself grow pale. Certainly he had debts, and he had expected to receive some money to pay them and to help with his studies. He had been thinking how to ask for the money—but to tell it now—

"Yes, father," he said finally. "I have some debts. I hoped for some money from you to pay them. I'll also need money to continue my studies."

Mr. Lind sprang to his feet, pushing the table aside. The glasses and bottle fell to the floor with a crash. With outstretched arms he almost flung himself on the boy. "You wicked son!" he screamed. "You fine gentleman! You highway robber, who intend to steal the last little bit of property left to your poor father! You—you—and you are ashamed of being my son!" With clenched fists he tried to hit Nicolai over the head, but he protected himself by covering his face with his arms, all the while conscious of his father's brandy-laden breath wheezing close to his face.

"Dear God! What is going on here? Oh, dear me! Let Nicolai alone, Lind." His mother appeared beside him half-dressed, trying to restrain his father.

The parson turned around: "There she is, too!" His voice failed him. For a minute he was too angry to speak, but then he screamed again: "You have betrayed me also! You went with this wicked boy to the house of my enemies! But I'll show you!" A steady stream of accusations against his wife and his son followed: she was squandering his property, and he wanted to ruin his good name and rob him of his last shilling.

Nicolai felt faint; he came to his senses only when he saw his father grab his mother by the shoulder and shake her so violently that she reeled helplessly. "Don't touch mother!" he cried out wildly.

In a second Lind turned on him, so furious that he was foaming at the mouth. "Get out of this house!" He would throw out this scoundrel of a prodigal son, this son who forgot his kind parents and had contempt for his father. He was never to cross the threshold of this house again. He had even led his mother into disobedience, perhaps even worse. Where had the money for new clothes for the boys come from? Did she think he was completely blind? It was theft, simple theft from the parish poor, committed just to deck out the brothers in the eyes of this squanderer who was trying to rob his father of his last shilling, earned by the sweat of his brow.

Nicolai stumbled about the room, trying to avoid his father's frenzied attacks. His father pursued him, now without his jacket, and swung at the boy and tried to hit him with his clenched fists.

"Go outside for awhile!" his mother cried. Nicolai ran through the front door into the yard. The door slammed after him, shutting out his father's wild accusations. For a long time he just stood listening, panting heavily, afraid that his mother was being hurt.

It was hardly half an hour before his mother appeared at the kitchen door; to him it had seemed hours. She was calm, but her eyes were red with weeping. Lind was in bed and was nearly asleep, she told him. Would he go up to his room now? Nicolai shook his head but whispered to her not to lock the door; he would wait outside until he calmed down.

He wiped his face and tried to fasten his waistcoat buttons. Some of them were missing. His father must have ripped them off when he grabbed him by the collar. He looked up. A maid in her nightcap peeped out of a bedroom window and saw him. He couldn't bear to be looked at; turning quickly, he walked down the road to the church. Without thinking he opened the gate and went through the churchyard. Leaving the gravel paths he walked between the graves. They were only low mounds, some with small wooden crosses, some without any mark at all. Here and there were large stone slabs with engraved figures and epitaphs. He stumbled against them without noticing where he was going and finally reached the far corner of the churchyard where the highway passed alongside the cemetery wall. With a hopeless sigh he threw himself down on the grass by the wall and lay gazing up at the sky with his arms under his head.

What was it all about, what had happened? The events of the whole day passed before him: first the laughing, clumsy-looking group of young people waiting in the courtyard, then the scene between his parents this morning, the visit to the Orres at Alm, and his walk in the garden with Laurentze. It all passed before his eyes with startling clarity, until at last his thoughts stopped before the last and worst incident. He couldn't stand any more. His father was a degenerate clergyman despised by everyone, an insane drunkard who mistreated his wife and children. What had he done to deserve this? Hadn't he loved and longed for his home, and hadn't he always dreamed of his homecoming as a wonderful event, while he suffered great hardships in his struggle to get an education in Copenhagen with almost no assistance from his family? After a while, self-pity and a feeling of righteous indignation helped to calm his inner turmoil. Exhaustion overwhelmed him.

A jackdaw flew screaming out of the black opening of the church belfry. Others followed, flapping their wings. They woke Nicolai, who, chilled to the bone, got up and sat on the edge of the wall. Above him towered a wide-spreading maple tree, and in its thick leaves the wind rustled quietly. The short summer night would soon come to an end.

What was it? What was going on? Why was he out here?

Laurentze!—His dreams from the first ray of dawn as the boat approached the Norwegian coast, the girl dressed in white at the midsummer-night bonfire, the longing for his lovely homeland—everything combined into a ridiculous self-delusion, which had been shattered by the happenings of the day and his meeting with the big blond girl that he had become engaged to.

God and the fates certainly could be cruel. For years the dreams about this girl had been his most precious possession. Those in their graves didn't imagine things, did they? That was better perhaps!—He shuddered. He was sitting in the suicides' corner of the churchyard. They were buried in the most remote corner of the church's consecrated soil, and the gravedigger hardly let them remain there in peace either, for he used to throw piles of twigs and trash in this corner to hide the small mounds.

Suddenly the sound of trotting horses came from the highway. He ducked down behind the wall, so he wouldn't be seen. It was two carioles, one behind the other, and they seemed in a hurry. In the first sat a big man in a dark traveling cloak, with his hat pulled down over his forehead. His chin rested wearily against his breast; his face was flushed and heavy. Behind in a second cariole was a still fatter, but shorter, man. He was swaying a bit unsteadily in his seat.

Nicolai knew them. The first was the councillor, Judge Weydahl; the second was Attorney Höegh. Yes, he recalled that Lieutenant Wallace had said that they were to hear a case this morning and had wondered how they would make out after the party at Emilienberg that night.

They were soon out of sight. So that was what the councillor was like now—apparently just the same as the other gentry of the district. Nicolai understood them all better now. Here they lived, a small group whose hearts and spirits

—weren't those his father's words?—because of their inclination and education were attached to Copenhagen or to their equals in station in other towns. Here they lived far apart, days and days of travel from even the nearest small town, without a chance to keep in contact with their former friends and acquaintances, who in the meantime had become "men of wealth and position." They were unable, even if they wished, to associate with the farmers—arrogant people, who, with a few exceptions such as the guest at Alm today, were willing to be flattered by being called landowners. They were obliged to be exiles in the district, even if they happened to be born there. Many had entered the civil service with such good intentions and then their spirits had just been dulled from lack of encouragement and having to live out their lives far from their own world, in the midst of people disgusting to them. Similarly, the material side of their culture was worn away by incessant clashes with the stubborn lower classes. Obliged to create some sort of social life of their own in the time that was left from their regular work and farming, they had to meet in such a provincial atmosphere that their social life encouraged the loss of their own virtues while it took on the vices of the farmers. The only one who had escaped the general corruption was Mr. Orre, the district tradesman, whose family had been worn out by generations of want and who now tried to restore himself by means of sugared water and republican principles.

Perhaps a strong enough man could stand this: to perform his duties during office hours in spite of having to choose between drinking and gambling at night, or be forced into the narrow sterile daydreaming existence of contemplating the past during those hours of the day when he was not sleeping or working. A weak man like his father apparently could not. What about himself?

No, never, never. Nicolai swore he would not tie himself to this district and be obliged to give up everything he valued. Yet if he married Laurentze? That wouldn't necessarily tie him to the district. Marry and pay debts; have children and make more debts (his father had said). And in all probability that would be his fate as well. He would have to try to get into the civil service in a rural district, for Laurentze would never fit into city life. It didn't make any difference whether he became the local bigwig in a coastal parish or spent a lifetime fighting the farmers in the Uplands; it would all be the same in the end. The poor girl, he murmured, she was too much of a little innocent from the country. He didn't even try to imagine what made him shudder when he thought of a lifetime spent with her. He just pitied her, for she had probably waited for him for years and relied on him to return and marry her.

Annoyed, he picked blades of grass from the edge of the churchyard wall and bit them thoughtfully. This affair with Laurentze, wasn't it just a stupid, childish attachment that he didn't need to worry about if he could wriggle out of it? She would just cry a little unhappily if he ran away. After all, he couldn't be asked to ruin his whole future just for a childhood dream and a twenty-minute talk in a country garden.

It was better to run away from the whole affair, from Laurentze, from this district, from Norway; better to go to a new land as so many had done before him, to become rich, to live well, to throw all these small worries overboard.—What had happened to his father, the major, the attorney, and all the others here, must not happen to him. He ought to run away and to do it immediately. Thank God, he still had enough money for the return trip to Copenhagen, and if he ran out of money, there was always the possibility that he could borrow some in Christiania. He would be of no comfort to his mother and brothers under the present circumstances, but he would certainly not forget them.

He would go back, say good-bye to his mother before his father woke up, and get one of the servants to drive him to the nearest coach stop.

The rustling of the wind in the top of the maple tree had died away. Behind the forests to the east, the quivering air of the dawn was colored by the sunrise. A cold blue shadow crept across the white-washed walls of the church, and high above its spire hung a lonely cloud whose edges were already tinged with red. A glowing radiance suffused its leaden grayness. Below the western ridges the lake lay quiet and greenish. From somewhere in the fields came the echoing sound of someone sharpening a scythe. Nicolai could not see this energetic fellow, but it was apparently someone who had no time to lose and would do his mowing even while the dew was still on the grass.

Some hours later a cart drove out of the parsonage courtyard. In the morning sun the dust swirled up between the cart wheels. Nicolai sat on the seat beside the driver. He turned and waved his hat to a woman dressed in black who stood looking after him with dry grief-stricken eyes.

* * *

Nicolai Lind never came back to his old home or to the district. But about 1850 a knighted diplomat and privy councillor, Nicolai von Lind, died in the capital of one of the smaller German states. He had kept his promise to help his mother and brothers, even though he never visited them.

Those who knew him best said that he had made his mark in the world not because of any extraordinary gifts or talents but because of his unflagging capacity for hard work, and his easy and gracious manners based on good taste and consideration and especially because of his marriage to a Holstein countess. He had been a homeless adventurer of the blandest type. He had avoided meeting with any of his countrymen.

The Perjurers

SPRING was coming. The snow had melted early and hedges and bushes were green in those places which caught the sun.

In the garden at Gihle, Palmström was pruning the branches of an apple tree that he was going to graft. He worked carefully and his crooked bony fingers held the bough tenderly. The old man had planted that tree as well as all of the other bushes and trees in the garden. It had been done out of sheer good will on his part and for his own pleasure; since the attorney didn't care about the garden and didn't pay him very much for his work, Palmström was allowed to do what he wished.

No one would have thought that respectable people lived at Gihle. The attorney had hardly touched or changed a thing since buying it from the farmer who had formerly lived there. The gray, unpainted buildings nestled in a little hollow. Long sloping hillsides which blocked out the view to the lake were divided into plowed fields on which the winter wheat had not yet sprouted. Behind the farm buildings lay the garden and a swampy area, and further up the hill were other farms, each with its own fields and woodlands. The highway ran right through the attorney's courtyard, passing the wooden well house with its tall pole and bucket.

The fields steamed under the hot spring sun as it shone through white wool-like clouds. Palmström wiped his sweaty forehead and rested for a moment. He watched amused as two innocent little wag-tails tripped along the edge of the flax bleaching pond by the fence. The water was a muddy brown and seemed to be very deep.

Palmström looked up as he heard someone knocking at the office window. It was the attorney beckoning him to come in. He wiped the sweat off his face again, grabbed his coat from the branch where he had hung it and went into the building.

He carefully wiped his shoes on the spruce leaves at the doorstep and opened the office door. The clerk was out so the attorney was alone; he sat relaxed and flabby at his high writing desk between the windows. His arms were crossed over his chest, and his good-natured pale blue eyes regarded Palmström steadily. The gardener stood respectfully by the door with his hat in his hand. The attorney pushed aside a pile of papers which lay before him. "Well, Palmström, so you're out doing your grafting these days, are you?"

Yes, he was. Palmström knew perfectly well that some people had the new-fangled idea that grafting was better done in the fall, but personally he'd trust to his own experience; the spring was the logical time of the year, for then in all creation the sap and juices of nature ran most freely, even in trees.

For some minutes the talk was about grafting and garden work and that Palmström deserved some payment for his labor. He couldn't quite get the meaning of all this, for the attorney usually didn't bother himself about these small matters or even offer to pay him before he was asked—then, of course, he got it immediately.

The attorney changed the subject. "By the way, Palmström, do you happen to know anything about the woods at Romstad?"

Well, Palmström was familiar with all the places in this

district, the location of those woods as well, even though he had to admit he hadn't been up there for quite a while. But wasn't the attorney himself the owner of these woods since he had taken them over from the estate of Lieutenant Juell?

Attorney Höegh got up from his chair and, hands in pockets, paced up and down the office. He didn't like the question. He sat down again and continued looking at Palmström; this time, however, there was something hard and sharp in his eyes as he spoke.

Certainly he was the owner of the Romstad woods and he hoped to keep them. He had to admit, however, that it hadn't been a very good bargain, because it looked now as though he would get into a legal squabble over the property. Had Palmström heard about that man from Hadeland who bought Hoff in Kverndal valley last year? A puritan and pious hypocrite who envied everyone and even begrudged himself and his servants their food. That fellow wanted more than rightfully belonged to him and liked to cause other people trouble with lawsuits. The fact was, and Höegh wanted Palmström to know the truth, that he had bought the Romstad woods firmly believing they reached up to the Lok Brook. You know where the brook runs into the Hoff river, but this—this stranger insists that the property straight down to Gjeitlok Brook half a mile further downhill, is his. Now—this summer, in fact—there would be a local inspection and a claim made about it. Because of that it would be necessary to find someone who was acquainted with the boundaries in that particular area willing to give testimony regarding them. Besides, he had deeds for the boundaries being at the Lok Brook.

Palmström looked down at the floor; a cunning smile hovered around the corners of his mouth. Of course, he would be glad to do anything he could; he would ask everyone he could think of who might be able to be a good witness for such a fine person and good patron as the attorney. He broke into Swedish in his enthusiasm and then bowing, stood there with his tattooed right hand over his heart.

They were both silent for some minutes. The attorney looked at his papers and kept turning them over and over absent-mindedly. Palmström waited. At length he rather hesitatingly mentioned something about payment for the gardening.

The attorney took a silver daler from his purse and put it on the desk. "Here you are for the present," he said. Then pounding the desk: "But if you can find two good witnesses for the local inspection—you get what I mean—to testify that the boundary is at the Lok Brook, you shall have full payment for your little jobs around the garden and fifty dalers to boot. How's that?"

Palmström put the coin in his pocket, mumbled his effusive thanks as he bowed humbly, and backed out of the room. The smile had frozen on his face. Attorney Höegh, without speaking, turned back to his desk and became absorbed in his papers again.

The office was on the north side of the house and not a single ray of sun ever found its way there. The air was stale and damp and filled with the musty smell of the old papers that filled the shelves from top to bottom of the walls. Attorney Höegh had lived in the district for a number of years. The furniture was sparse and cheap: a few plain leather-covered chairs for visitors, a double desk painted green with a high chair before each side, and in a corner a wide oak cabinet with iron-studded doors. The room was untidy. It smelled unhealthy and was covered with dust. The attorney's wife had seven children and a big household, so she really couldn't be blamed for not keeping the office clean.

The attorney sat bent over his papers reading the same words over and over again, not turning the pages; he merely saw the words without understanding what they meant. He couldn't get the Romstad woods out of his mind.

It was an awkward situation, not easy to handle, and he was not at all happy to be mixed up in it. It was all due to Councillor Weydahl. Didn't he have enough without trying to grab those woods, but at any rate his motives had been the best. There wasn't much lumber business in the district even though there was considerable timber. People in this district seemed to think it was more suitable for the poorer farmers in the upper valleys to engage in this risky business —those who didn't have their good income safely assured from ordinary farming and growing grain. On the other hand, if the woods were not too expensive and transportation not too far and difficult and the timber could bring quite a profit, it didn't matter whether the owner lived in this region or up in the hills.

The councillor had reasoned like that when he had suggested that the attorney go halves with him in buying the Romstad woods. And it wasn't at all expensive if it really reached to the Lok Brook. The attorney had had some doubts about that himself. He remembered Lieutenant Juell, the poor fellow, never used to think it was that size. But Weydahl had assured him rather abruptly that the boundary between Romstad and Hoff was the Lok Brook— and from that he had understood that that's the way it was. The judge would have had to get approval from the finance department if he himself had wanted to buy allodial property, and that is why the attorney was put down as the purchaser. What the hell was this hypocritical stranger from Hoff to him? If the fellow was right, he'd have to prove it!

This psalm-singing farmer was the only one in the whole

district who had been willing to keep that shameless vagabond of a preacher, Hans Nielsen Hauge, and now he was mule-headed enough to start a lawsuit against HIM! And there it was. There wasn't much to lose but still he felt uncomfortable. He wasn't single like the councillor; he had a wife and seven children to support.

Earlier Weydahl had hinted that it would be a good thing to have witnesses. The attorney had understood this, and for that reason he had talked to Palmström whom he had seen giving evidence for Hans Dahlbye in one of that notorious, rich farmer's many conflicts with the law. Höegh, being at that time attorney for the defense for the accused, had shuddered when he heard Palmström and another man take their oaths, because he knew they were false. Yet Hans Dahlbye was acquitted, and later on he had openly boasted that the whole thing had only cost him ten dalers. The attorney suddenly found himself turning red, and he felt as though he would choke. Certainly he had a few things on his conscience; but this—Now he and Hans Dahlbye were in the same class, and he himself was the one to pay Palmström the most.

He pounded the desk so hard that his ink pot and quills danced: "God save me, but the councillor is a scoundrel!"

He had said it aloud; frightened, he looked around the room quickly and then turned again to his papers and began to work at them painstakingly.

In a way, Attorney Höegh and Judge Weydahl were friends. Neither of them could be called talkative; in fact, the councillor hardly spoke an unnecessary word. They were both big, strong men and rather resembled each other in their physical appearance. The attorney, however, was shorter and heavier and seemed to be more outgoing and amiable. The councillor gave the appearance of being too stern and reserved, in spite of his straightforwardness. Strangers were apt to think his melancholy the result of a great grief, and many people would think of the sorry affair of his wife's death, when they spoke of his manners. Those who had known him before, however, looked for the key to his character in his life before that occurrence.

What was very well known about him was that he was an excellent farmer and had made a model farm of his land. Farmers from all over came to see the improvements he had introduced. They adopted many of them, and Magistrate Winterfeldt had sent reports that were forwarded to Copenhagen regarding the great service the councillor had rendered to farming in East Norway. He had brought in English plows, introduced new methods of ditching, and was able to make stall-feeding of horses on a large scale practical. He had even experimented with the new and useful root called the potato, but he found the soil in this part of the country too heavy to grow it successfully.

People were rather surprised at first that the councillor could afford the quite considerable amounts of money he spent on his passion for farming. It was well known that he had no money of his own, and that since he and his wife had had no children, he had inherited nothing from her. Soon people stopped talking about this, however, because it was apparent that his farming was very profitable. Since he had received permission many times from the Exchequer to buy small farms near his residence, it wasn't long before he had quite an estate to manage. After a while people said that the councillor had probably always been rich anyway, and so, as the years went by, this came to be accepted as the truth.

The only one who really knew anything about the councillor's private affairs was the attorney. He was himself an experienced farmer and had not only helped the councillor with advice and practical assistance when the judge was first getting started, but had even lent him money when Weydahl was short of cash. The borrower had always been scrupulous in putting up securities for the loan; now there was no longer any need for such loans, as the councillor's affairs were going along very satisfactorily, indeed. Interest poured in from their mutual and slightly risky speculations, and the attorney piled up quite a lot of money for his seven unprovided-for children, as he used to put it.

They had been greatly attracted to each other from the first time they met and, working together, they soon became friends. Less strong than the councillor, the attorney usually gave in to the more dominant personality of the other. He became the go-between and the councillor's deputy, using his own name when the councillor, as district judge, had to be kept out of things; as a matter of fact, sometimes their deals were rather questionable. On these occasions Attorney Höegh had always felt uneasy, but had soon been reassured by the other.

Weydahl wasn't at all avaricious. On the contrary, he was generous and hospitable, and it was difficult to see who would benefit from his work in the long run. Sometimes he said he hardly knew who would inherit his property, as he had only very distant relations.

It was both chance and the councillor's never-ending desire to keep adding more and more to his estate, his continual quest for more wealth and power within this little nook of the world where fate had decreed he play a role, which had led to the attorney becoming involved in the matter of the woods at Romstad. Little by little Höegh realized that in all probability the councillor knew all about the old boundary of the pastures. He himself had never doubted that it was at the Gjeitlok Brook. He would perhaps give in and drop the whole case, if it were not for this damned hypocrite of a stranger who was causing all the trouble.

* * *

A sudden storm had passed over the woods about noon. Then it had abated and wisps of fringed cloud drifted in the blue sky. Sometimes they covered the sun, and again it shone brightly, lighting up the gloomy dark pine woods. The Gjeitlok Brook dashed noisily down to the river in small, foamy waterfalls until it slackened its pace and finally came to rest in a long quiet river bed bordered by a narrow road. A makeshift bridge had been made by placing tree-trunks across the brook. The road was wide enough to drive on, and the ruts in the road winding through the terrain had been made rough by nature and traffic. Someone had tried to do a little mending at the worst places and had straightened it by felling trees or rolling stones into the boggiest hollows.

On the slope beyond the rushing water, was the Lon hut, a lonesome cottage in a little cleared space in the Romstad woods. The place had originally been cleared about twenty-five years earlier by Finnish immigrants who sometimes settled in the deep forests of the district. They would burn down the trees and build their small dwellings; a barn and a house all under one turf roof, as was common in the mountain districts where there was a shortage of timber. The cottage was surrounded by a small, miserable piece of land protected from the forest by a fence of split sticks. Close by stood some giant weeping birches, their branches of new leaves slowly turning with the wind.

The twin brothers, Bernt and Mons, lived at the Lon hut.

They were tailors, middle-aged bachelors, who worked at home, seldom going around to the households of the district as the other country craftsmen did. Most of their customers were servants and poor people, and thus had no accommodations for them; then, too, they had a cow and a pig which had to be taken care of. If it was necessary for them to leave the cottage, they were obliged to ask their nearest neighbor, "Two-child" Mari, if she would take care of their animals for awhile. She always did so most willingly, for she was left quite alone now, since her two children were grown up and had become tramps and beggars. But sometimes it happened that she was out herself, for she was in great demand as a fortuneteller and sorceress.

The brothers' hut was more roomy than one would suppose from the outside, for it contained a fairly large kitchen, as well as a smaller room.

Today they had a visitor, but they kept on working, sewing at a table near the one small kitchen window. The light shone dimly through the green panes of the little leaded opening. They were very much alike, both small, with smooth round faces, shiny reddish skin, thin black hair and dull brown eyes. They breathed noisily with their mouths half open, and when they talked, their voices sounded sleepy and brittle.

The stranger dried his clothes in front of the fire, since he had been caught in the rain as he came through the woods. It was Palmström. On a tray beside him lay a number of small, glistening mountain trout which he was carefully cleaning and salting, while at the same time he kept an eye on the kettle of coffee, boiling on the fire. The Swede had brought the coffee beans with him to make it.

He told them he had caught the fish in Bear Lake and intended to give them to the attorney as a gift. He wouldn't take money for them, because the attorney was such a good, kind man who really appreciated it when one did some little thing for him. And the trout in the Gihle tarn had disappeared since they stocked it with carp. It was the same with them as with animals; sheep and swine, for instance, would not graze in the same pastures.

Since the coffee was ready and poured into mugs, the sewing things were put away. While they were drinking their coffee Palmström told them about the inquiry and about this Hadelander and hypocrite from Hoff, who had the temerity to start a lawsuit against the attorney whom he kept praising to the skies. The twins echoed his words in stupid surprise that anyone would dare to contradict the great people of the district in this way.

He asked their opinion as to the boundary. They hesitated to answer; Bernt looked at Mons and Mons at Bernt. But when Palmström asked them if the Lon hut belonged to the wood pastures of Romstad, they certainly knew that, yes indeed, but Lieutenant Juell had never asked either labor or rent for it. Palmström told them that now the attorney owned the place and could claim the rent. They knew that too and seemed to become uneasy at their guest's remarks.

After awhile Mons asked Palmström if he had by any chance brought his leeching instruments; he had. The brothers whispered to each other for a moment or two, and then Mons asked if the Swede would be kind enough to bleed him; it was fourteen months now since the last time, and he felt that he needed it because he felt so gouty and congested. There must be some unhealthy blood in him somewhere; only he had no money—.

Oh yes, Palmström would be glad to. As for payment, he had bought some material from Orre's for a vest; if they wanted to, they could make it up for him some day.

Mons rolled his sleeve up to his shoulder and sat down on a chair in the middle of the room. Bernt put an earthen dish on the floor, and the Swede took a leather purse from his pocket, in which he carried some small plain polished steel objects with a long woolen ribbon wound around it. He took this and tied it tightly around the bare arm; then after washing the arm carefully below the ribbon, he probed around until he found a vein and cut it with his steel. The blood spurted out, and they all gazed fixedly at the thin red stream that ran down into the dish.

No one spoke until Mons thought he had been bled enough. He felt better already and not so congested.

The wound was bandaged and they pulled their benches to the table. Bernt set it with flatbread, butter, bacon and sour milk. They had supper together and Palmström again brought up the subject of the inquiry about the wood pastures. He didn't think the case would be easy to win, even though the records were in the attorney's favor. There would, of course, be an inquiry and local evidence would be heard. He would say this much: if two witnesses gave evidence that the Lok Brook was on the soil of Romstad, they would get twenty rix-dalers cash; yes, he knew that for sure.

Bernt thought that it might be a little difficult to make an oath on that. Mons only listened to them, pale and faint, with a feverish glow on his cheeks. Twenty rix-dalers was a lot of money for a poor man to have; if one had that much it might be possible to have two cows in the byre. He wouldn't meet their eyes when the others looked at him.

The Swede then started to tell them an amusing story concerning a gentleman from Lenvik in Sweden. It was about just such an inquiry. The witnesses had put dirt from their landlord's fields in the bottom of their shoes and then made an oath that they were standing on his earth. In that way they kept a clear conscience because there wasn't any doubt that they did. Palmström roared with laughter at his own joke and suggested to the twin brothers that they be just as clever if they really wanted to earn twenty rix-dalers. They too tried half-heartedly to laugh.

In a short time Palmström noted it was too late to go home that night, so he asked if he could sleep there. Of course he could, and though they offered him the bed in the little chamber, he preferred to sleep in the byre in the hay. He didn't want to put them to any trouble.

He stayed awake for a long time, muttering curses, and spitting in the hay. These idiot twins, they couldn't be too stupid and crackbrained to take an oath—.

When Palmström left at dawn, Mons went with him for a way, and before they parted, they struck a bargain: the brothers would take an oath that they were standing on the soil of Romstad at the Lok Brook, provided the twenty dalers were handed to them the night before. They had better not break their promise, Palmström warned, because then the attorney would eject them from house and home.

* * *

On a clear quiet morning in September, the brothers crossed over the log bridge. They were dressed in their Sunday clothes, for they had been asked to go to the local inquiry. They walked a little awkwardly, as people do who wear shoes that hurt them. "Two-child" Mari had agreed to look after the cow and pig if they didn't return by supper-time. They trudged uphill, through the woods where autumn had already colored the clumps of birches and maples, which were a pleasant contrast to the monotonous firs.

A local examination of the circumstantial evidence was made during the day, and the brothers were obliged to walk around with the group. Finally the concluding testimony and oath-taking took place in a little clearing on the mountainside above the Lok Brook.

The setting sun on the northwest ridges looked like a sparkling fire between the trees. Its oblique golden rays of light, shining between the thin-trunked pines and sparse dry grass of the clearing, nearly blinded the clerk who wrote in the register on a big flat stone at one corner of the open space. Dark shadows had already settled in the bottom of the valley, and in a short time they crept uphill, turning out the lights of the day, until as far as the eye could see there was only heavy dark blue forest.

The dusk increased rapidly and with it the evening cold.

The councillor looked tall and impressive beside the recording clerk; he had been on the go since early morning. The attorney and the jurors, all worn out, sat on the ground nearby. When witnesses were called to give their oaths, they rose, not without difficulty, to hear the judge read the explanation of oath-giving from the code of laws. He read distinctly and firmly. As he spoke the fearful words about temporal and eternal damnation of the perjurer, it sounded like a threatening prophecy in the desert.

The witnesses for the stranger from Hoff were first to be called. For the most part they were tenants and servants gathered around their master, who sat humbly on the stump of a tree with his hands folded. His lips moved in silent prayer for those who advanced to the stone to testify. Some of them were so shaken by the serious words that they changed statements they had already given. In the end none were able to give any information that they had not learned second hand, and even that they gave with hesitancy and uncertainty. The judge had a great deal of trouble getting their statements and evasions properly recorded and at the same time making them vague enough so that the witness would agree to them.

At last Bernt and Mons were called. By this time the councillor seemed tired of talking, so that while he read for them the explanation of oath-giving, his voice turned hoarse, and even though he cleared it and went on, he spoke lower and indistinctly. Even so the brothers were scared. Their answers were confused, and they seemed completely bewildered. Noting this, the councillor tried to simplify the questions for them, and looking at them steadily and with authority asked if they did or did not stand on Romstad soil. Then they both answered quickly that they certainly did; they stood on the very earth of Romstad. They had given that same reply all day, and now they swore to God they did.

The court rose, the case was adjourned, and the verdict was to be given in a fortnight. The jurors signed the register, happy to get away. One certainly couldn't get much sleep, whenever one was a juror, *that* they could swear to, having climbed around the mountains for hours, like shepherd boys with no time to eat or drink.

All there shook hands and said goodbye, respectfully bidding farewell to those who represented the law, even though they were to go back together to Hoff where they had left their horses. The two from the Lon hut left immediately to take a short-cut through the woods. The stranger had said good evening to them very kindly, but the attorney paid no attention to them whatever. He was too busy offering brandy from his pocket flask and kept murmuring about all the trouble—and that he really doubted if the Romstad woods were worth it.

The brothers walked home. At first they hurried, then slackened their pace, as it was rather difficult to see the path in the darkness. They often stumbled over roots and stones, and Bernt winced with pain; his feet were sore. Mons clenched his teeth and would not give in, even though he nearly fell. They did not talk, and each kept to his own side of the road as though they were afraid of each other.

The road ran beside the river; the valley, a narrow one, was formed by steep hills on each side. Above their heads stretched the high, dark blue autumn sky where a few pale stars twinkled.

Before they were halfway home, a full moon had risen. Suddenly Bernt stopped and untied his shoe strings. Mons hurried on past him, until suddenly he dashed through a clump of alder bushes and down to the river, which just here flowed quietly in broad eddies. He untied his shoe strings, sat down and took off his shoes. Then, one after the other, he shook them out over the water; dirt and gritty sand poured out of them. He also pulled off his stockings; they were stuck to his feet, had big holes in them and were stiff with dried blood. The dirt and sand which had been in his shoes had scraped all the skin off the soles of his feet.

He put both legs in the cold water and dabbled them up and down cautiously. The moonlight shone clearly on the water, and he could see big white sheets of foam float by.

Mons sobbed fretfully, not because of his sore feet, but because in spite of all he and Bernt had sworn falsely. How strange it had been; he had trembled all over when he came up to the councillor, who was reading out of the book. If it hadn't been that he felt the attorney's eyes following him, he would never have taken that oath, not he nor his brother. It was only a lame excuse and an invention of the devil to put earth in their shoes, and Palmström had been the devil's disciple by tempting them. He had felt this way all the time, but one didn't for some reason or other really realize it until too late.

What the councillor read had been horrid. Mons wondered if it could have been from the Bible or other holy scriptures. He was now all that had been described and his brother Bernt was just as bad.

He remembered the words only too well, because they had been repeated so many times when the witnesses for the Hadelander were sworn in. Now he was an unwilling, stiff-necked offender and sinner to be punished in hell for all eternity; he would be driven continually down the gulf of destruction where there was no redemption whatsoever, his life and soul lost and damned—and perhaps his mouth and tongue would turn black, if it was true what people said would happen to perjurers.

He pulled his legs out of the water and sat with his feet together and his chin between his knees. The sheets of white foam continued to drift past him. The hollow sound of a cataract was borne down the hillside on the night air. The forest seemed to howl, and the noise of water rippling against the banks of the river was one long roar, pounding through the whole valley, increasing and diminishing, but sounding endlessly.

—Did someone call him? He pressed his hands to his ears and kept mumbling over and over: "Our Lord Jesus Christ, on the day of judgment be a strict judge of me, and pray that for my sins I be damned to eternal pain and delivered into hell to be punished for all eternity." If he had learned it in the catechism when he was confirmed, he certainly would not have taken the oath he swore today. But he had not seen it in the catechism, he remembered, because he used to know all his lessons by heart; the curate had praised him for that. Oh—that he should behave like this!

A shadow passed by. He turned quickly in terror, hitting his elbow as he rose. It was only Bernt.

Mons put on his shoes and stockings in a hurry as his brother waited for him silently. "Did you wash your feet, Bernt?" Mons asked sheepishly. The other nodded.

They went on toward home. At each step the water splashed and oozed in Bernt's shoes, for he had washed them as well. After a while he stopped and groaned: "I can't take another step! I have cramps in my legs!"

Mons took hold of his shoulder. "Brother dear, try to walk a little farther; we are almost there." Bernt's face in the light of the moon looked like that of a dead man. Mons tried to help him, supported him underneath his arms, and dragged him along. Bernt hobbled along like a man on crutches and whispered: "You wanted it; it was you who wanted it. They can't put us in jail, can they? No one knows about it except the attorney, and he wanted it too, just as you did—"

They staggered along, and after they crossed the log bridge close to the Lon hut, Bernt revived a bit, but then Mons collapsed. Now he felt spasms in his legs. Lying down in the grass, he started to talk deliriously: "Our heavenly Father punishes us on our legs when we have sinned with our legs. He strikes us with lameness and sickness in our legs. Behold, we shall never again walk!" And he kept on raving in scriptural sentences and psalms. Bernt had no idea how his brother knew all this, and he was terribly frightened. They were both stricken with the same plague, and they had both committed the same sin. Was the judgment of God on them already?

Mons pointed to the hut and groaned: "There's no use buying a cow or calf; we won't be able to get any use out of them. It's no use—damned be all my property in this world; damned be my earth, my fields and pastures, my cattle, my beasts and my sheep and my cows and my swine, so that they shall never thrive and I shall never get any profit from them or their products; and after this day I shall never succeed, for I shall be damned in every effort, damned in life and soul!—"

Bernt tried to quiet him, and dropping on the heath beside his brother, pushed him down into the grass to stop his screaming. But the one stretched out on the ground went on spasmodically: "Poor cow, poor pig—" until the cramps were so painful they quieted him.

Side by side they crept up to the hut and in the door. They both fumbled for their flints and managed to light a fire on the hearth. "Two-child" Mari had left, but the night's milking was sitting in a pan on the table. They were thirsty and both drank of it in turn, down to the last drop.

Bernt threw himself on the kitchen bed, and Mons went on into the little chamber. They both fell asleep immediately and did not waken until noon; then Bernt got up; he wanted to see how Mons was, but he couldn't walk. He had to lean on a chair because his legs wouldn't hold him.

In the little room he saw his brother sitting up in bed and looking at his tongue in a small broken piece of an old mirror.

The Lon hut tailors lived on there for many years. They always did their sewing at home for they weren't able to get around to the farmers' houses because of their lameness. They hobbled about on crutches; since they couldn't walk they lost their cow and pig through lack of proper care of the animals. But they managed some way or other, for they didn't have to pay rent and they were able to keep on with their tailoring, and fortunately for them they both died before they needed parish help.—The Romstad woods up to the Lok Brook were awarded to the attorney.

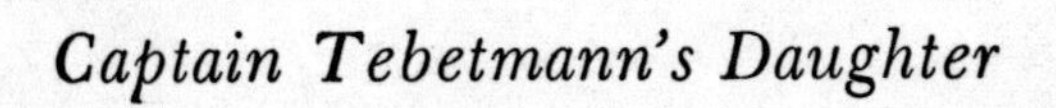

Captain Tebetmann's Daughter

I

CAPTAIN ALOYSIUS TEBETMANN lived a rather lonely life at Kjelsrud. The house was located on the outskirts of the district and away from the main roads, but that was not the chief reason he was left alone; nor was it because his wife was dead, since for years after her death there had been gaiety in the house.

The captain had had a son, a brilliant boy, who like his father had chosen a military career. He was a very promising young man and had already risen to the rank of lieutenant when suddenly he died of a fever.

The captain never recovered from this blow, and now physical infirmities were added to his grief. His eyesight deteriorated, and the gout became so bad that he spent most of his days sitting in a rocking chair with his legs carefully wrapped and propped in front of him. Because of his illness, the captain sent in his resignation, even though he wasn't required to do so. There was still peace and, at the moment, no danger of war for Denmark-Norway. Many of the overage and incapacitated officers kept their commissions and got their full pay for years after they were unfit for military service. Captain Tebetmann, however, said that a cripple was of no use to His Majesty's army, and so sent in his resignation. The papers were approved by all the authorities, and after a while he received his official letter of discharge with assurance of royal favor and the usual half pay.

The pension would have been enough, perhaps, if the money had kept its value, and if the good captain had had the slightest talent for economy. In addition to this lack, the soil on his farm was so poor that it cost almost as much to cultivate it as the year's crops were worth.

But there was no question about it. The pension just had to suffice for he had no other income, and an experience he had had as a young man made him terrified at the very thought of running into debt. The money ought to have been sufficient, but it never was. One day as he sat thinking about his problem, he suddenly tore his bushy white hair, frowned, and in a perfect frenzy with himself broke the stem of his favorite pipe. His thick little body shook, and every bone seemed to creak as he cursed furiously and tore at the shabby bank notes in his hand. Captain Tebetmann used only one curse, but he used it often. "Devil take me!" he shouted, and it echoed through the large rooms. "Devil take me!" he bellowed so loudly that the servants heard and fell silent in the kitchen. Over and over again he roared out his curse until at last he fell back in his rocking chair, suddenly having got the bright idea that if one did not buy any more than one could afford to pay for, the money would be enough. Devil take him if that were not the truth.

After he introduced this principle into the household, the standard of living at the farm fell so sharply that no one cared any longer to visit him, and the sick old captain was left lonely and forgotten. Once in a while, it was true, friends or acquaintances dropped by to see him if they happened to be in the neighborhood anyway or because they felt ashamed that they had not called on him for a long time.

The captain had never paid much attention to his daughter, for while his son lived he was occupied almost entirely with him and his future. Even after his son's death, the old man never seemed to notice his daughter very much, busy as he was with following the campaigns of Bonaparte on his map. The captain was passionately interested in military field operations. His own long military service had been limited entirely to peace-time drill, and when in 1788 he had been garrisoned at Fredrikssten, he had suffered the disappointment of his life. As for girls, he had never liked them, and because of that, his motherless daughter Henrikke was brought up among the servants.

She was very much like her father, small and stout, dark, with coarse hair and sunburned skin. Her mother had always called her her "little gypsy," and it was apparent that the blood of southerners ran in Henrikke's veins. She was noisy and boisterous, and her dark eyes were always laughing; yet her father very seldom scolded her for her bad manners, for when he did, she just laughed and behaved even worse than before, and if he cursed at her continual laughter, she just laughed more loudly and ran away.

A stranger could hardly tell from the language and clothing of young Miss Tebetmann that she was not an ordinary farmer's daughter, but there was something about her, something dauntless and imperious, that gave the impression she was accustomed to command. And indeed that was exactly what she did in the kitchen, in the barn, and in the cowhouse. She ordered about and bossed all the servants from the lame maid, who was actually the housekeeper, down to the kitchen boy. They obeyed her implicitly, since even when she was quiet and good-humored, they were afraid to annoy or anger her, for she had a strong will and a quick temper.

In the autumn of 1807, when Henrikke was nineteen years old, rumors reached the district that a large English fleet had anchored off Denmark and threatened Copenhagen. A few people believed it, but others shook their heads, refusing to accept such a fantastic story.

The older people had become accustomed to the war that for years had gone on between the powerful states of Europe. Bits of information about world affairs were rumored and spread throughout the countryside. News was awaited with eager interest. The fate of the various royal families and the changing boundaries of the kingdoms were talked about and discussed as neighbors sat snugly over a glass of punch, or as acquaintances met on the way to church. Factions formed—some people sympathized with England, some with France—and, if the drink was strong enough, both sides might get into heated arguments. Farmers fought one another at the Christmas parties and at funeral feasts, all for the sake of European politics, and at auctions and other social events, farm hands and cottagers often came to blows for the same reason. The young people grew up with constant awareness of their parents' talk of faraway battlefields, so, in their daydreams and play they were field marshals commanding armies. The children did not throw stones for fun and sport; they bombarded cities. And when they sailed their play boats on the spawning-ponds, fiery sea battles were in their minds.

Everyone felt quite sure, however, that the faraway war would never come to this secluded country of Norway. People felt quite sheltered and safe within the quiet of their native region.

Lieutenant Wallace was the first to bring rumors to the captain that the British fleet had anchored in Copenhagen harbor. He wasn't thanked for this bit of news, however. On the contrary, the old captain was very skeptical, for he imagined that people sometimes made fun of him by telling him strange stories. The British fleet in Copenhagen? Why would the British come to Copenhagen? Didn't King George have enough enemies already; besides, he needed Norwegian timber for his ships. And weren't Napoleon's armies in Germany ready to come to the aid of Denmark in case of trouble? Oh, no! Devil take him, blustered the captain. The lieutenant had better stop making a fool of him. It was just stupid stuff and silly nonsense. After all, Copenhagen had excellent forts, plenty of troops, and enough good guns to drive off any unwanted visitors. The Swedes had discovered that in the past, and the British—devil take them—had better be aware that they faced a bloody battle if they stormed the ramparts of Copenhagen. The lieutenant had better go home and go to bed and get rid of these feverish fancies. It would be better to think twice next time before he tried to convince sane and serious people of such silly things. And by the way, if these rumors happened to be, well, more than rumors, the lieutenant was glad perhaps, because then he might meet his relatives; perhaps he might even have the duty of guarding his high-ranking rich relatives, if it became necessary to intern British prisoners in this country.

The old captain should not have taunted the lieutenant in this way, because it offended him very much, for it was true that his father was an English naval officer who had made his fortune in Denmark. The lieutenant himself had started life under the most favorable circumstances and had had every chance to make a fine career, but his good looks had got him into all sorts of trouble. Then things were made even worse because he was rather stupid. His long-suffering family had finally arranged to have him leave Denmark and "exile" him to Norway. Here he could have lived quite a comfortable life, as his family gave him a generous allowance in addition to his army salary, but he was forever lamenting his ruined career; he thought he had been wronged and he did not understand how or why he had failed. Most of the time he was unhappy and bored, and in his boredom he seemed to devise every possible way to waste his money. In even the most casual reference to his past or to his family, he suspected a deliberate insult, and this time he flared up, even though he only partly understood what the captain said.

Angrily the lieutenant reminded the captain that he ought to remember that he was an old man, of whom one could not claim physical satisfaction for such insulting remarks; he ought to bear in mind that his old age protected him! Did the captain really accuse him of being a liar and a traitor to the king whose uniform he wore? And was he really insinuating that he just dropped in here like a beggar with some wild tale?

When Lieutenant Wallace lost his temper, he stuttered helplessly, and at such times he talked incoherent nonsense. In his anger he tried to spit out something, but each word brought twenty from the captain, who certainly was hard to convince. Finally the voice of the lieutenant was drowned in the captain's torrent of words. Henrikke, who was with them at the time, did not hesitate to enter the quarrel on the side of her father, and soon her broad provincial speech, the lieutenant's Danish, and the captain's rough drill-ground language mixed in a chorus of wrath that made the walls of the old house quiver. Finally the lieutenant left, slightly mollified by the captain's explanation, but with the bombastic assurance that his honor compelled him to return as soon as his message had been proved correct.

They didn't have to wait long for his return.

It was afternoon. The rain poured down, and the wind

tore through the old cherry-trees outside the entrance of Kjelsrud, slapping their stiff boughs against the windows with a sound that spoke of autumn.

The captain's gout had tormented him more than usual; he was cold and sick of the weather. He had lit the stove, and, there in the twilight, he sat in his rocking chair, his feet on a little footstool, a handkerchief over his face. He snored quietly. Henrikke sat by the stove roasting apples. Once in a while she tested the apples and turned them over. Then she sat gazing into the fiery-red eyes of the stove, as she listened to the wind howling in the chimney.

Meanwhile a man was urging his horse at a brisk trot uphill to the farm. He had turned up the collar of his cloak and pulled down his hat to keep out the heavy fog that was thick with rain. He could hardly see the fence posts along the road, which was in fact more like a rushing stream than a highway. He dismounted in the courtyard, tied his horse to the well, and went inside.

The two in the sitting room had not heard his knock. Henrikke, startled, jumped up at the sight of a person in a dark riding cloak standing in the doorway. She quickly opened the stove-door for light to see who it was.

Captain Tebetmann awoke and asked, yawning, "Who is that?"

"It is I," answered Lieutenant Wallace. "I guess you already know the truth of the message I brought on my last visit."

"I have read the Prince of Augustenborg's announcement of the blockade," the captain said irritably. "I apologize for not believing you. You may gloat over me if you choose."

"I don't want to gloat. I'm sorry to tell you that I have more important and distressing news."

"Really, really! Has the British king been forced at last to make a proper declaration of war? I wouldn't call that very distressing."

Wallace sat down uninvited and without taking off his cloak. "He has not. But Copenhagen has been bombarded, shamefully attacked without a declaration of war. The town is burning and has surrendered—and the Danish fleet is captured."

"Are you crazy, Lieutenant? Have you gone completely mad? Copenhagen conquered? You are lying, man," the captain shouted wildly and made a motion as if to hit him.

"I have just heard the news from Councillor Weydahl. As a matter of fact, I have come here directly from him, and he had just received the express from the major general." Wallace spoke hesitatingly, as if he asked forgiveness. He did not feel insulted this time.

"What about the King and the Crown Prince; are they prisoners or dead?"

"Fortunately they are perfectly safe, captain. They escaped to Jutland before the battle."

Captain Tebetmann fumbled for words: "Escaped! The Crown Prince fled, leaving Copenhagen to fare as best it could? Did you say 'fortunately'?" The captain continued sharply; "Did the Crown Prince flee?" Lieutenant Wallace did not answer. The captain pulled himself together and took his feet off the footstool.

"During the entire forty years I served the King, I had no opportunity to use my sword at his command. Now war is here, and I am a cripple—." His tongue seemed paralyzed. Almost sobbing he continued, and his words were thick and slurred. "And the capital of the kingdoms conquered and their future king dishonored!" He tried to get out of his chair, but his legs gave way under him and he stumbled.

"Devil take me!" he shouted as he fell with a thud to the floor and lay there motionless.

Henrikke, who had not caught the full meaning of their words, dropped to her knees beside her father and put her arms around his shoulders. "Father is dead," she whispered almost to herself and put his head in her lap.

"Oh no, Miss," the lieutenant said trying to comfort her as he, too, knelt on the floor beside the captain. He heard the old man breathe. "He has only lost consciousness. He has only fainted. That isn't dangerous."

A maid and the lame housekeeper, scared by the unusual sounds, came running from the kitchen. Very quickly the lieutenant told them what had happened. Then gently pushing Henrikke aside, he lifted the captain and put him back in his rocking chair.

"I think we'd better put him to bed," said the housekeeper. As the others carried the old man from the chair into his bedroom, Henrikke tenderly steadied his head which had fallen backward helplessly.

The maid ran for candles. Watching the housekeeper unfasten the captain's shirt, Lieutenant Wallace noticed that she was gaunt and very pale, and that her forehead was shiny with sweat.

"Shall I go for the doctor?" he said.

"It's far," she answered as she turned to the maid and told her to send for Johanne, the cup-woman. She would be able to come right away and would be there in half an hour. She asked the lieutenant if he would be kind enough to stay for awhile and go for the doctor later if they needed him. The sick man lay groaning and muttering, though he did not regain consciousness.

Lieutenant Wallace went into the sitting room. He was still in his wet cloak, but now he took it off and threw it on the floor. The storm had not abated. Rain continued to fall in torrents, and the wind whistled against the house, causing the old timbers to creak and sigh. He was very tired after his fast ride through the rough weather, so he sat down by the stove, even though the fire had gone out.

The express riders from the major general had arrived at the councillor's house while they were at the dinner table. Judge Weydahl was entertaining quite a number of guests that day, for, as the people of the official class in the district saw signs of a war developing, they turned to the councillor for news; they assumed he would be the first to know about anything. The attorney and the parson had been there since the day before; Major Brager had come and the sheriff had come up to the house on the pretense of having some urgent business and was invited to stay for dinner.

The lieutenant distinctly saw in his mind's eye the blue, sealed envelope. It had been given to the councillor just as they were about to say "skaal" and drink their brandy. They had all noticed that the councillor had hesitated and then put the letter down. Wallace recalled how, later on, he had opened the letter and read it aloud to them all, but his eyes had seemed glued to the paper. A hubbub of confused questions followed, and the noise of scraping chairs filled the room. They had crowded around the councillor to have their own look at this fatal letter and to read it with their own eyes. They realized then the letter could not be misunderstood.

A few minutes later the party broke up. The dinner was left practically untouched on the table, for everyone hurried away to spread the news to his neighbors and friends. Lieutenant Wallace was overwhelmed. He simply had to talk to someone. He had to tell someone this news. It was then that he suddenly remembered his recent quarrel with

Captain Tebetmann, so he had his horse saddled and rode as quickly as he could.

At Alm he passed Mr. Orre who was taking his daily constitutional under his large umbrella. The lieutenant stopped, turned in the saddle, and shouted the news to him. Mr. Orre dropped his umbrella and started to wave wildly. The lieutenant couldn't hear what he said, so he just shouted: "It's true, it's positively true—upon my honor!" Then he galloped away.

Of course that haste had been unnecessary. Why hadn't he been more thoughtful and broken the news gently to the old captain? But he had been possessed by his information and, like a messenger of misfortune, had dashed up to him in a perfect frenzy. He felt ashamed.

In the quietness of the dark room, his thoughts darted about aimlessly until they focused on a clear, strong picture: the picture of conquered and burning Copenhagen. Was the lovely home of his parents with its pretty garden burned to the ground? His relatives and friends—were they alive? Those favorite places and streets of Copenhagen where he had known gaiety, joy, and even despair—were they now in ruins? His childhood home, the house of his loving parents, was captured and burned. A robber had forced his way in and plundered it, while he was far away. Lieutenant Wallace's spirit could not rise to such heights as to grieve over the fate of kingdoms and empires; he merely felt a genuine and deep sorrow for what concerned him. He who had been very proud of his English blood, was now a Dane with a Dane's hatred of the enemy who had invaded his peaceful country. He felt capable of murdering every Englishman who dared to come near him.

He tried to picture the battle scene—how the defense had been organized to withstand the attack—but he was not able to concentrate on it. He could only see the enemy's gun decks spreading death and destruction over the town; he saw the fire and smoke, the soldiers as they swarmed up the slopes to the ramparts, heroically defending their town. He would love to have been there holding back the enemy with his sword, its shining blade reflecting the red fire of the burning city.

Even in defeat one could reap glory and pardon—but after all he hadn't been in the battle. All of his old friends had been there; why not he? Wallace jumped up from his chair. He stamped up and down the floor in his heavy riding boots, completely forgetting that there was someone ill in the house. Never had his situation seemed more hopeless and distressing or his life more useless than it did now. Never before had he felt so bitterly about what he considered the injustice of his circumstances. "The Devil's to pay! The Devil's to pay!" he muttered. "Gun powder and blood, cannon balls, shooting, and stabbing with swords—the Devil's to pay, pay, pay!" and his voice became louder and louder, as if saying these meaningless words could overcome the dreadful thoughts which frightened and nearly overwhelmed him.

He was alone in the room for an hour or so, perhaps longer. The time passed quickly, but he grew more and more restless and unhappy. Just then Henrikke came in with a lighted candle in an iron candlestick which she put in the middle of the table. Berte, the housekeeper, came in also and said that the captain was feeling better. After the cupwoman had let his blood, he had become quiet and now he had fallen asleep. "Would the lieutenant care for supper?" No thanks, Berte was not to go to any trouble for him. He would go home now if he couldn't be of any further use.

Berte hesitated. Perhaps the cup-woman would want to send a message to the doctor later on—perhaps the lieutenant wouldn't mind staying awhile longer. She had seen to it that his horse was stabled.

As she left the room, Wallace sat down at the table and looked over at Henrikke, who had thrown herself on the sofa with her hands folded under her head. The candlelight revealed the chipped paint on the table, the broad shoulders and lean features of the lieutenant, and the figure of the resting girl. The rest of the room was in darkness. Even the row of white rococo chairs along the walls looked like shadows. The storm was beginning to lessen; the downpour had stopped; only the dying wind whistled lingeringly in the trees outside the windows.

Wallace became drowsy. His thoughts turned from Copenhagen and the rest of the uncomfortable pictures of the far-off battlefield to more pressing problems. Would the captain recover? Was it a real stroke, or was it just the fall that had knocked him unconscious? Poor Miss Henrikke—she was really quite pretty as she lay there on the sofa worrying about her father. And the housekeeper, what was the matter with her? Someone had told him something about the captain and his housekeeper, but he couldn't remember now who it was. Scandals and stories were told about everybody in the district; the devil himself couldn't remember them all. What was it now? Oh yes, the late Mrs. Tebetmann had been a very jealous woman and the maid Berte very pretty. One day when Mrs. Tebetmann was away visiting, the captain and Berte had been together. The captain's wife returned unexpectedly, and in order to save the captain, the maid had jumped out of the window. She broke her knee in the fall, but did not cry out, just crawled quietly over to the kitchen steps. She was found there hours later, late in the evening, in fact, and after that she had been lame. Yes, now he remembered. That was the story they told. And the lieutenant recalled that she had been greatly concerned about the captain today.

Poor Miss Henrikke! He saw her bite her lips to keep back the tears; she was very much upset and frightened. And, yes, very, very beautiful. He sat looking at her. Her hair was unpinned, and the long, heavy braids lay against her pale, tear-stained cheeks and fell below her breasts. Her dress was tight across her bosom. The little double chin was round and exquisitely shaped. Not so long ago in Copenhagen there had been a young, olive-skinned girl of whom she very much reminded him—.

The door was pushed open slightly, and a head on which perched a ribbon cap peeped in and nodded pleasantly. It was Johanne, the cup-woman. "Miss Henrikke, Miss Henrikke," she called. Henrikke jumped up quickly.

"Is Father worse?"

"No, child, he is much better. He is able to speak, and he wants to go to sleep now. You don't need to worry; he will soon be all right."

Henrikke sighed with relief; then, with a bright smile, she said, "I have been so frightened!"

Just to be on the safe side, the woman asked the lieutenant if he would kindly stop and tell the doctor to come to see the captain tomorrow. Then nodding again, she closed the door and disappeared.

Lieutenant Wallace got up to say goodby. Just as he was expressing his hope that the captain would have a quick recovery, Henrikke rushed over to the stove. She had suddenly remembered her apples. "I'm afraid they are too well done," she said with a wide smile that showed her strong white teeth. "Will you have one anyway?" And she went over to him with an apple in her hand.

He took it and thanked her.

II

Captain Tebetmann had had a slight stroke that night, and it was months before he recovered. It was Christmas-time before he could get from his bedroom to his rocking chair. The district physician, Dr. Müller, had been to see him a couple of times, but his visits were short. The doctor was always in a hurry to be gone, for he felt that Henrikke never treated him properly. She did not seem to realize that a doctor who took all the trouble of coming uphill to that out-of-the-way place to see a patient ought to have some refreshment, a hot drink at least, especially in the cold weather.

The curate, Mr. Vamberg, had also been to see the old man while he was ill. In honor of these visits the captain changed his shirt. He also received the Holy Communion just to be on the safe side in case his departure from this world was as near at hand as it seemed to be from the expression in the eyes of the curate as he prayed over him.

For about a week after these visits, the captain always felt melancholy and solemn. He promised himself very seriously that he would stop his bad habit of cursing and swearing. He really did give up his one and only curse, and when he felt it coming on, he would try to swallow it and then it would explode into a kind of angry grunt.

Better for him than either the doctor or the curate, however, was Lieutenant Wallace, who had a strange feeling of guilt for the captain's illness. These guilty feelings were not, of course, enough to make the lieutenant ride all the way up to Kjelsrud as often as he did. His impression that Henrikke was really a very pretty girl had turned into something much stronger. He had fallen in love.

From his bedroom the captain listened to the lieutenant's efforts to get some music out of the feeble, old, untuned piano in the sitting room. He even heard him sing sentimental love songs to Henrikke, and the old captain wondered. Wallace was surely not a very good catch, but could the girl expect anything better? She would have to marry someday, and it was going to be difficult to make a good marriage around Kjelsrud. Wallace had his salary—not very much, to be sure—but he also received generous help from his family; and that, in addition to what she would get when Kjelsrud was sold, would keep them. Or, if they should prefer to live here, they would at least have a home. Henrikke would be an economical and careful wife, for the captain had impressed on her that she should never buy more than she could pay for. He supposed that with a sensible wife the money would last Lieutenant Wallace a little while. After all, the eccentric lieutenant had seemed to be a little more sensible during the last year or so and lived pretty decently now. People had been used to calling him all sorts of silly names, but they didn't do it much anymore. Eccentricities ought to be forgiven a man who counted British lords among his relatives.

The days and weeks passed. The captain improved steadily, and though he was often tempted, he did not break his promise to stop cursing and swearing.

Wallace courted Henrikke with her father's secret consent. The lieutenant couldn't keep anything to himself, however, so it wasn't long before he told everything to the attorney and even proudly told him he wrote poetry to his love. This information was too good for the attorney to keep, so he told his wife. Soon everyone knew, and people were saying that it was all settled, and that as soon as the captain was well his daughter and Lieutenant Henry Wallace were to be married. The major's wife, who thought a great deal about clothes, even obtained for herself a pair of gold-embroidered shoes when her husband went to Christiania to do some Christmas shopping. As far as she was concerned, the wedding could take place anytime now.

Every one agreed that this would be a good match. Henrikke alone did not understand what was going on. She was too inexperienced to realize that Wallace was seriously courting her.

When she was a small child, they had teased her at home by saying she had a suitor. But it was only Erik, the son of their nearest neighbor, whose farm was so close to Kjelsrud that it was called Little Kjelsrud. Henrikke was a few years younger than Erik, but they had played together all their lives, and he had been to Kjelsrud so often that he felt quite at home there. He was an only child and badly spoiled, and the captain had permitted the boy to come to his parties. The uniforms and the way of life of the soldiers he saw at Kjelsrud were so fascinating to the farmer's boy that he enlisted as soon as he was old enough. His mother cried, and his father was grieved, but Erik was determined to enlist and did it in spite of them. After a while he was promoted to the rank of trumpeter in the Dragoons, but it wasn't long before he realized there was a big difference between being an officer and being a common soldier, so he persuaded his father to buy him out of the army, and he went home to Little Kjelsrud. For a while the captain hired him to work on the farm, because conditions at Little Kjelsrud were such that not a shilling could be spared. Now no one could tease young Miss Tebetmann about having a sweetheart who was more or less a servant.

The shock and fear everyone felt at the beginning of war soon subsided. During the winter one almost became used to thinking in terms of bad news from the distant frontiers. As soon as he heard anything, Lieutenant Wallace brought the news to the captain at Kjelsrud. It gave him an excuse and concealed his real reason for going to the farm so frequently. War was going on, but here in the uplands very few felt any effect of it. Stories were told about the general scarcity of foods and real lack of bread at places on the west coast, and about the harassment of the privateers, but in this district everyone felt safe; high hills and the mountain wilderness separated them from the coast where the enemy made his raids.

The country tradesman raised his prices on imported goods, and some of them became almost impossible to get, but it didn't hurt the people, for the price of grain was sky-high, and consequently one emptied one's glass in a toast to the honorable ally of Denmark-Norway, the Emperor of France.

The king of Sweden had been with his army on the shores of the Sound and had scolded the British a little when they burned Copenhagen. He might talk as much as he pleased; they were not afraid of him anyway, and he certainly would not dare to attack Denmark-Norway. At least that's what they said at the gay parties in the region around Lake Mjösen during the Christmas season of 1807. They had never drunk more heartily, sung more loudly, or made more brave and eloquent speeches. It was a festive season. The boasting and the brandy turned the holiday gatherings into a wild debauch. Around the entire lakeshore, from the magistrates down to the cottagers, all possessed the hearts of heroes and the courage of lions—as long as no British man-of-war was to be seen on the waters of the lake.

So before people really believed it possible and fully realized what had happened, the Swedes came. This new enemy attacked from the east, and it was only Norwegian arms that prevented them from overrunning the fertile lake district. If the thin line of defense could be broken then this district would be the first to be invaded by the Swedes.

The officers got their orders to join the army, and they had to go even though they were still tired and sleepy from the Christmas festivities. Lieutenant Wallace was one of them. He had meant to ask the captain his important question when he paid his farewell visit to Kjelsrud before leaving for the army, but he decided not to, since he saw no sign of regret nor the slightest indication of sadness on the part of Miss Henrikke. He had hoped for that and looked forward to it, for after all he was a warrior departing for battle.

During the next few nights, as the soldiers had departed, from Kjelsrud one could see lights burning in the cottages and farmhouses all over the hills and down to the frozen lake. Even on the other side of the lake, under the snow-white ridges of the mountains, lights burned in the farmhouses. The people kept an anxious vigil over those who now were away from home fighting.

The captain was left alone. He limped about the place leaning on his stick, melancholy and peevish, as he thought about this damned war that he had longed for all his life and that had not come until now, when he had had to put up his sword in its scabbard. His daughter Henrikke was bored also. Lieutenant Wallace had flattered and amused her with his attentions, and now she missed him. The loneliness oppressed her; she became sad and morbid, and something wild and turbulent seemed hidden in her laughter.

At last the sun came and melted the snow, the ground thawed, and the earth turned green again, but it would be a long time before spring plowing was possible. The horses were kept busy supplying the troops, and only a few hands were left for spring work.

The men who did remain at home were called more and more often from their work to stand guard at mountain lookouts or to meet outside the church to train for the home guard. A fat captain set up his headquarters at Alm to organize the militia and train the troops. For the most part, however, he did nothing but make trouble, because he was a German, and no one understood what he said. He was unable to exert any authority; everyone called him "the paunch," but his real name was Bauck. The weapons he used in training the men turned out to be very primitive; the magistrate had distributed models of a lance with a speartip on it for those who had no guns, and the men got busy in the blacksmith shops making such spears, and they thought they would be excellent weapons for tickling the Swedes.

Rumors flew about the region. Stories were told of battles along the Swedish border. One rumor even had it that the Russians had conquered the Swedes in a great battle near Stockholm, and that this would end the war. But, of course, the people didn't dare trust such a tale. It was considered another wild story, for down south one had only to stop and listen to hear the violent roar of the cannons reverberating from the eastern hills. There apparently was no hope for the end of the war as yet.

The rumors took a long time reaching Captain Tebetmann up on the hill. Still, he kept fairly well informed because he not only subscribed to the newspapers, but from time to time he also heard from Lieutenant Wallace.

One afternoon an old man trudged up the hill to visit the captain. He said his wife was miserable and unhappy because they had had no word from their son, a soldier in the army. He thought perhaps the captain would know whether his son had been killed. Even though the captain knew nothing about the boy, still he pitied the man and talked to him kindly about the army and the positions of the troops.

After this, other visitors came with similar troubles, for the old man had told his neighbors that the captain was the man to go to for information. Tebetmann welcomed them all and was kind to everyone. He read them the news from the papers, and if some were especially worried, he promised to write the major or someone in authority to find out about the missing relatives. He always did as he said he would, and sometimes when his visitors returned there would be a letter with news for them. They accepted any news quietly and with humble thanks, no matter whether it brought joy or sadness; anything was better than uncertainty. Perhaps the worst thing the captain had to tell them was that their loved ones had been taken to the hospital. That kind of information the men hesitated to tell their wives.

During the spring of 1808, almost every day brought some visitors to Captain Tebetmann, inquiring about a relative or friend. When it became warm enough, he received them on the porch in the shade of the wild cherry trees. He sat there watching the trees turn green, then flower and fade, and all the time he was busy reading. He gave his visitors all sorts of information in order to make them less miserable. He remembered he had had a son himself, so he was patient with all of them.

The people of the district vied with each other to bring

him his mail, and once in a while a piece of mutton or a string of fresh fish was left secretly with Berte at the kitchen door. No one wanted to give it to the captain directly, since he always asked them if they themselves had all they needed.

The captain thought of almost nothing but the war. He identified himself with so many of the people involved in it that he lay awake at night loudly criticizing the tactics of the officers in command. In his dreams he was the commander of the army. For a time his peevishness and melancholy disappeared, for the old captain had a strange capacity for forgetting, and he was not aware of more than one thing at a time.

During these weeks, however, Berte, the housekeeper, had her own heartaches and became worried and sleepless. Her conscience bothered her, for she knew she was guilty of many sins against the captain's wife, the late Mrs. Tebetmann. She had tried to make up for them by taking care of the Mistress's motherless daughter; it was her anxiety concerning Henrikke that was causing her so much worry.

The old housekeeper didn't worry when the girl seemed to be sick and lonely; she just smiled and said one must trust in the Lord, and hope that Lieutenant Wallace would return. Henrikke couldn't keep any secrets from Berte, who had known the household so well these many years and knew from experience the hot-blooded daughter of the captain.

Berte did grow worried about her, however, by the time the north winds of spring raised small waves on the lake and swept away the last gray floes of ice, and the brown forests of birch turned light green, and one heard the cuckoo call from the distant ridges. With the coming of spring, young Miss Tebetmann became gay and sang from morning to night. The old housekeeper's eyes were red-rimmed with weeping, for they saw things they disliked seeing.

She had watched and spied and listened at doors, and then she had warned Henrikke to be careful. The answer she got from the girl hinted at Berte's own indiscretion and asked her to mind her own business. It was a hard and cruel answer, and it kept Berte from speaking to the captain about the affair.

If it had only been a person more suitable to her in rank who was causing all the trouble, but it was this boy from Little Kjelsrud.

Erik could not bear to part with his trumpet when he left the army. Every Sunday morning he took it with him to a little wooded hill nearby and there he played the calls and tunes he had been taught with such care; to him they were precious remnants of his lost ambitions. Henrikke would sit attentively by his side, listening; to her it was beautiful music.

On mornings such as these they talked freely together. Erik poked fun at her suitor, calling him "fool Wallace." Hurt and angry, she, too, ridiculed the lieutenant in self defense. When the boy did not stop teasing her, she beat him with her fists. Erik pretended to be amused by this, but it really angered him.

After quarreling and being cross and grumpy with each other for a while, they forgot their differences in passionate reconciliations, as young people will, for what so often starts in hate is apt to end in love. Soon they would be playing at sweethearts again, as in the old days but now with less innocence.

Erik was not handsome, but he was big and well-built. He had red hair and freckles, a prominent nose and sharp blue eyes. His mouth was large and mobile with strong white teeth. His hands and feet were unusually small, and his walk and carriage had a military bearing. At one time his family had been of some importance but had long since fallen on evil days.

Henrikke was fond of him probably because he was the only boy around, and the attentions of the lieutenant had unconsciously prepared the way for the trumpeter. It was now he who dominated her. She belonged to the gentry, to the class that had lured him as a boy but would make him suffer doubly when he, being an inferior, in time was to be expelled from their circle.

But at least, during that spring they were happy. The servants suspected what was going on, but neither Henrikke nor Erik cared. In fact, Henrikke cared about nothing, and Erik lived on her courage. When the maids whispered together and hinted to him in the kitchen, he understood very well what they were saying, but he just ignored them and putting his hands into his pockets, walked away without saying a word showing by his swagger that he was very happy to have a real lady for his sweetheart instead of one of them.

One afternoon when the captain had gone to take his usual nap, he had trouble going to sleep; it was too hot and the flies buzzed and hummed in his ears. In exasperation he got up and, still in his slippers, took his walking stick and went out on the doorstep to get some fresh air. The sun shone brightly from a perfectly clear blue sky; the shadow of the wild cherry trees hugged the wall. The dust-gray ribbon of road wound downhill between the fertile green fields and meadows which seemed to shimmer in the hot sun. A tiny breath of wind brought an aromatic scent from the forest of firs. The dark blue ridges on the other side of the lake were reflected in the quiet, shining surface, made to appear greenish from the midsummer rain from the mountains. There was every indication of a good year, and Captain Tebetmann was happy.

Even the war news was good, for the last bulletin said the enemy had retreated beyond his own borders, so that for the moment there were no Swedes on Norwegian soil. He wondered about Lieutenant Wallace. The major had written that he was in the hospital with a bullet wound and thus was at the mercy of the care and skill of the doctors, which from past experience the captain did not regard very highly. However, it had been reported that the lieutenant's wound was not very serious.

Suddenly he heard the voice of the lieutenant singing but, after a minute or two, he realized it was only his own daughter mimicking her absent friend. It seemed a mean thing to do, and he disliked it, especially as only this morning he had told her the lieutenant had been wounded. It was mean and cruel to make fun of a wounded soldier. Angrily, he limped off in the direction of the singing, ready to scold her for such behavior. The singing continued:

"Oh wonderful maiden
Oh wonderful doll
I found you 'mong thousands
I picked you 'mong all . . . ."

Tebetmann leaned across the fence, and saw his daughter sitting in Erik's lap. They were sitting a little too far away from the captain for him to reach them with his stick, so he threw it at Erik, who sat with his back towards him. They jumped up. Erik, scared out of his wits, stood rubbing his back and then ran home as fast as he could, leaving his sweetheart there alone.

Henrikke stood looking at her father, who leaned on the fence. He was coatless, and his shirt was open. His white hair was mussed and rumpled, and his face was flushed. She did not move.

"Bring me my stick, child!" he shouted.

Hesitatingly, and with a look of defiance, she said: "You are not going to beat me, Father?"

"Nonsense! Of course, I'm not!"

Cautiously she picked up the stick and gave it back to the captain. He swallowed his usual curse about ten times. "Climb over the fence, child," he commanded at last.

She obeyed. He pointed to the front door, and she went in. The captain followed her like a jailer.

Now the father became his daughter's jailer. He didn't scold her—the captain wasn't accustomed to say very much—he just saw to it that she was watched constantly either by himself or by Berte. He gave orders that Erik was no longer to be admitted to the house and hoped that Lieutenant Wallace would return soon, perhaps this fall.

But, as might be expected, a sick old soldier couldn't keep a determined young girl from her lover, especially if her love was made stronger through defiance. Moreover, Berte betrayed him, even though she hated to do it. She was afraid of her master and equally afraid of Henrikke, but most of all she was afraid of what would happen if both of them lost their tempers.

Henrikke and Erik thought up all sorts of ways to meet. If the captain and his daughter happened to be sitting on the porch or under the trees, suddenly the sound of a bell would come from the farthest field. Then she would say, "Look, Father. The cow is in the rye!"

"Go down and bring her back, child," he would answer, shading his eyes as he looked in the direction of the sound. He was too proud to admit that he didn't see any cows in the field. Henrikke was off like a flash, and the sound of the bell slowly jingled and tinkled over toward the meadow. When she returned home hot and breathless, it was obvious she had been chasing a strange creature.

Sometimes she was supposed to help Berte carry the lunch to the farm hands in the fields. They certainly started out together and returned home together, but didn't see much of each other between times.

As the August evenings grew darker, Berte heard faint rustling noises coming from Henrikke's second floor bedroom. She was sick and miserable about them, but too terrified to say a word. The captain had become less watchful, and the daughter was quick to take advantage of his increasing absorption in the war, which had broken out again.

One afternoon when Henrikke went to meet Erik in the woodshed things came to a crisis. He was sitting on the chopping block with elbows on his knees, as she tried to make him understand that now they just had to get married.

The lengthening shadows of a cloudy day found their way into the woodshed, and while he searched desperately for something to say, he looked out across the green grass of the farmyard. Some hens were crowding around a proud cock, which scratched and dug in the earth. In the background were the dark timbered walls of the house; by the front door, he saw the wild cherry tree full of shiny clusters of black fruit. After a while, he rather absent-mindedly murmured that she ought to speak to the captain.

Wouldn't he do that, she asked him. He shrank from her with a grimace of distaste. His eyes avoided hers. He preferred to look at the hens.

"A man usually proposes himself," she said, "but you are scared, I guess, like last time . . ."

She waited for an answer, but he said nothing. An ominous quiet seemed suddenly to fall between them. He just sat on the block lost in thought.

When she spoke again it seemed to him as though her voice came from far away: "All right. I'll do it myself, if you don't dare . . ."

She turned on her heel and went straight across the yard to the door, but stopped at the step and turning called: "If you happen to have the courage, wait for an answer!"

He started after her. The hens crowded around his feet. How impulsive she was! The answer would come in time.

"Devil take me!" the captain roared from the house. The cock flapped his wings, and the hens cackled, scared at the outburst. Erik hurried home.

* * *

Five weeks later the wedding took place at Kjelsrud. Berte had been the peacemaker between father and daughter. She had talked to the captain alone for hours and hours, in fact for nearly a whole night. Early next morning a letter was sent to the parson, and at the same time Erik was sent for. Captain Tebetmann told him that since he had been made a father-in-law without being asked, he on his part had sent out notice of the marriage bans without asking the bridegroom. Things were hard enough, and he didn't intend making them worse, so he would arrange for a proper wedding.

The captain invited all the best families in the district, but only his parents were invited by the bridegroom.

Both the major's and the attorney's wives said at first that this was a wedding they did not wish to go to, and Dr. Müller and his wife decided they wouldn't go either. However, when Attorney Höegh found out about it, he was extremely angry on behalf of the old captain and certainly told his wife a thing or two. Furthermore, he made the rounds of all the most influential people in the district and made them promise to appear at the wedding; among them was the councillor, who did not often go to big parties. After all her talk, the major's wife finally decided to go to the wedding, and after the ceremony was over and the grand dinner eaten at Kjelsrud, she danced in the gold-embroidered slippers that had been bought for the wedding of young Miss Tebetmann. Nothing could alter the fact, however, that the bridegroom was not Lieutenant Wallace, who was still in the hospital in Christiania where he had received the Danish Order of Dannebrog for his bravery during the war.

Later at the coffee table, when toasts were made to the bride and bridegroom, Henrikke looked around at all the men, dressed in their handsome uniforms, and then over to her husband and parents-in-law in their somber black clothes. Her thoughts flew to Lieutenant Wallace, and she wept.

Autumn Assizes

IT was about a month before Christmas, and late fall weather had come to a valley in the southern Uplands. At this part of the valley the lake was rather broad, about six miles wide. Level country on both sides was divided into rich plowland. Behind the fields the slopes swelled into small hills, which in turn nestled against the high ridges, far away to where the forests had been pushed back by the encroaching farms and fields.

It was evening, and silver-white fog covered the lake, shimmering under the full moon which hung high over the western hills. There was some snow on the fields, not very much, hardly more than white frost. The roads wound barren and black from one farm to another. Conditions for sleighing could scarcely have been worse. It had been such strange weather; as soon as the snow fell, it had been turned into slush by the rain. Now it seemed there was going to be a real winter after all, for the ground was frozen hard at last, so that the snow would probably remain.

Along the edges of the hills, there was the faint glow of northern lights, which once in a while flickered into a green-blue radiance, but as night came they were dimmed by the moonlight. The countryside was very quiet. In a few houses a light shone from one of the windows.

At the sheriff's, however, all the lights were on, and one would have supposed there was a big party going on there; and there was, in a way, for this was the third and last day of the autumn assizes. At the sheriff's there were really six big feasts a year: Christmas and the autumn assizes were the most important; then came the spring assizes and Easter, with Whitsuntide and the summer assizes being much less important.

In the kitchen, all alight, the coach boys and farm hands sat patiently waiting for their masters, while the maids ran to and fro cleaning up as they waited for the punch-water to boil at the fireplace.

The wife of the sheriff sat at the supper table in the brightly lit sitting room with the children and some of the neighbors, who had come to help her. They were finished for the day; the bottle of brandy was passed around, and the beer mugs were constantly replenished. It had been the occasion of the year, and now they were all sleepy and exhausted from the excitement and the rich food. The sheriff's wife was really happy and content, for everything seemed to have passed off successfully, in spite of the fact that she had had to manage by herself this time without the professional help of Mrs. Nannestad, who in other years had always taken charge of the cooking. Now, Mrs. Nannestad was dead.

The war had brought about many changes, especially in money matters, so that Mrs. Nannestad's pension had melted away. Nearly all were hard pressed financially, so social gatherings and parties in the district came to an end, and without work, she became ill and died. She had earned her living more or less as a professional cook, so people could not believe that she had died of starvation. But anyway, thank heaven, no fault could be found with the meat or fish dishes, and even the sauces had been excellent.

All the candles had been lit in the big parlor, because the magistrates were meeting there. Ordinarily it was a gloomy room for the dark timbered walls were relieved only by white muslin curtains at the row of five windows on the outer wall. It was too large a room for daily use, and so was saved for special occasions, such as this, and consequently was furnished rather haphazardly. The sheriff leaned against the fireplace; beside him on a small table was a tobacco box and the steaming punch-bowl. He stood cleaning his pipe. On his fat little body he wore a tight-fitting green tailcoat with gilt buttons, a striped waistcoat and black velvet breeches. The effort of blowing into his pipe, as he cleaned it, made his plump cheeks as red as his rugged little bottle nose. He kept chatting cordially all the while with the two modest clerks and a very young officer who also lounged against the wall. He always called the young officer Lieutenant Bangsberg, as though he did not know that he was his own nephew, Martin. The sheriff had been only a corporal before he succeeded to the office of his father-in-law, and it was a point of pride with him that one of his relatives had risen to a rank in the army that he himself had never dared dream of. It had been a continual pleasure to have the young man with him all during the assizes and to show him off. The lieutenant was now quartered in the neighborhood, for his detachment had drawn back to this region, which was quite far from the battlefields, in anticipation of the armistice which was soon to be arranged.

The people in the large room had separated into two groups. Bailiff Jespersen and Attorney Höegh and one of his colleagues from Christiania sat at one end with Judge Weydahl. They tried to pass the time by playing Boston, but it was a dull business. The councillor, a striking figure in his red uniform, dominated the group even though he sat listening patiently while the visiting attorney garrulously recounted news from Christiania. The stranger with his

West-Norwegian accent had been very much in evidence during the entire three days of the assizes, and now Attorney Höegh, who had become rather sleepy, was thoroughly tired of him. The bailiff had taken off his jacket and put on a comfortable gray sweater. He was weary and ill, and kept nervously brushing the thin white hair off his wrinkled and sweaty forehead. He sat staring into one of the dark corners of the gloomy room, as though his near-sighted little eyes saw something interesting there. He was so preoccupied that he scarcely heard the talk around him.

The other end of the room was divided by a painted green railing installed just for the court. On the far side the judge and the bailiff, together with their clerks, had worked at a big table during the whole business of the assizes. At present, five rich farmers sat there. Four of them had been summoned as jury, and, as was customary, they had been asked to stay for supper. Their conversation was quiet and discreet, in order not to disturb the magistrates. For the same reason they entertained themselves with a little harmless card playing rather than their usual serious gambling. The fifth man did not play and hardly touched the punch which they all had before them on the table. He talked a great deal, however, without bothering to lower his voice; on the contrary, there was an irritating quality to his sharp, high-pitched speech, as if he wished to attract the attention of everyone in the room. The elegantly dressed little man certainly did not look like a farmer. His suit was made of fine blue broadcloth and he wore black silk stockings and gilt buckles on his shoes. The expensive thread-lace edging of his shirt-frill was carefully ruffled. The dark hair, brushed neatly across his high, rugged forehead, accentuated the pallor of his face; he had a straight, thin nose and unusually white teeth, visible between his strong red lips, but a small receding chin. His brown eyes glistened, and the arching eyebrows moved spasmodically with a nervous tic. It was very easy to see that his small, nervous hands, toying constantly with anything before him, were not accustomed to physical work.

He turned continually to speak to a bald, pock-marked farmer at his table. The dissipated old man, who looked as though he had eaten and drunk too much and too well, answered him with a sleepy good humor as he played his cards. The other three tall, blond fellows with a certain racial similarity, a noble grandeur in their hard features, laughed too, as they picked up their glasses. The speaker, obviously flattered by their approval, put his hand into his waistcoat and looked quickly from the host, the clerks, and the officer over to the Boston players.

It gave the sheriff a funny feeling when their glances met. He and Hans Dahlbye were relatives, but to have him as a house guest at the same time that he entertained the magistrates, made him uneasy.

It was lucky that Magistrate Winterfeldt, who had honored the assizes by his presence, had left the day before this self-invited guest arrived. But certainly none should accuse Sheriff Erik Krogsti of being inhospitable, even to this man Dahlbye.

One of the Boston players laughed loudly, "No-no-no!" cried the bailiff. "I was wrong—I thought it was the knave!"

"Excuse me, Mr. Bailiff, but you know any card which has touched the board is considered to have been played," the stranger from the west said firmly. Attorney Höegh laughed heartily, "You have a very observant partner, Councillor!"

The bailiff scratched his head: "It's my eyesight that fails me, not my mind. You beat a blind and glassless bungler, Attorney Lehmann.—Heavens, Sheriff!" he sighed, "why haven't you mended my glasses? It seems to me you have had them for a couple of months at least."

Sheriff Krogsti was a versatile man, who was even able to mend the watches and eyeglasses of his friends. He stopped blowing his pipestem and came over to them waddling slightly on his little bandy legs.

"Please forgive me, your honor. I have already taken the liberty of telling you that I cannot mend your spectacle frames without soldering them, and because of the war, the metals for soldering are not obtainable, not even from Christiania."

"My poor eyes certainly suffer a great deal because of this war," the bailiff muttered.

"That is the way the whole region takes part in the suffering; that is, through one of its civil servants," Attorney Lehmann said with sarcasm.

"If you ask me, it has suffered enough." The old bailiff waited sulkily for Lehmann to lead.

"Didn't you just say something, Mr. Bailiff, about the rising price of corn, and that the war was turning the local population into profiteers. . . .?"

Old Bailiff Jespersen strained his eyes to look over his cards. "Oh yes, the price of corn has gone up, unfortunately for us who are not farmers, but . . . what card is that?" he asked, as he peered toward the lead card.

"Seven of diamonds has been played," the councillor replied.

"The deuce, if we civil servants haven't suffered enough anyway." The old bailiff got up angrily, and started to tell them a little about what his work had been like lately: the ordinary services had increased; nothing was normal any longer; this continual mixed-up problem with tax collection alone doubled the number of cases. On top of this were the increasing number of watches to be arranged, so that they could light the signal fires if the enemy came near the district. Then there were the horses and wagons to requisition, the guns and ammunition to be distributed to the farmers, and these damned Swedish immigrants to be dealt with—to be found and forced to give oaths of allegiance, which bound them about as much as a thread did a horse—and then there was the increasing number of gypsies, vagabonds, and beggars to cope with, who were everywhere on the roads and filling up the jails! In short, the civil servant was just like a louse between two fingernails—unhappy were those who issued the orders and unhappy were those who carried them out. Good Heavens! If only one didn't have the daily headache of providing bread and butter for one's family! Would Attorney Lehmann like to know what the bailiff's income had been for the last year? Hardly two hundred dalers, my friend, scarcely enough to pay wages and food! He doubted if any of the sheriffs in the district were in such a difficult position as he was. They were, after all, paid in barrels of grain and today grain was money. But poor wretches like himself had neither farm nor fortune!

Exhausted, the bailiff sank back in his chair and pulled his sweater around him as though he were chilly, yet the sweat stood out in great drops on his forehead and hollow cheeks. "One has got to do one's duty, sweat and toil to death," he said. "My God, how I long for one single night free of worries, even if it be in my grave!"

Suddenly everyone in the room, even the farmers fell

silent. They all knew and liked Bailiff Jespersen, this cursing, hot-blooded man from up north, and they knew he spoke the truth.

The councillor nodded slowly: "Yes, Jespersen, your health is certainly suffering because of your work."

"Skaal, Bailiff," Höegh added soothingly. "Someday these terrible times will be over, even for you."

Sheriff Krogsti stood looking at his superior until he felt his eyes grow wet. "It has been a strain for us who are old," he said, then stopped quickly, afraid he had taken too great liberty in referring to the bailiff as old.

Lehmann cleared his throat loudly several times. He felt annoyed to some extent and wanted to point out, as politely as he could, how little such districts as this had to complain of, even though the Swedish army was pressing in on them, for on the coast and in the cities whole populations were starving because of the blockade.

No one paid any attention to him. The bailiff, who had not listened to any of them, got up, glass in hand. In a rather confused and abrupt way, he thanked those of his friends who were present for all of the good years they had worked together, the good days, and, yes, even the evil days when they came, that they had shared. In the course of the years, he had become ill and feeble, and soon it would be his unwelcome duty to turn over his office to a younger and stronger man. Even his insignificant work for the state in these troubled and dangerous times demanded the services of a more efficient and active person.

These were probably his last assizes and he wanted to say now how many pleasant autumn assizes he had attended. The most pleasant were always—and he hoped he could say this without offending anyone—in the home of Sheriff Krogsti, who was a perfect host. And this was not all he wanted to say tonight. He especially wanted to thank the sheriff for the zeal with which he performed his duties and the knowledge and wisdom he had shown during the war. Sheriff Krogsti was the only one in the entire district who had some experience from another war, the one of 1788. He had learned then in a few weeks what had in these years of war been very useful to them both, and, "Devil, take me!" the civil authorities had had to obtain their information for themselves, even in matters of great importance. There had, of course, been no lack of help given by the Central Administration, and it had always had in mind the welfare of the kingdoms especially in regard to distributing hundreds of notices, placards, and announcements. He would like to say skaal to him that helped so faithfully when it was necessary for everyone to help himself, "Skaal to the sheriff, to Erik Krogsti!"

The sheriff was deeply moved. He stuttered, and his drillmaster's voice sounded like a dog barking. This was the greatest honor that had come to him in his thirty-seven years in the King's Service, including the three years as a private soldier. He wanted to go shake the bailiff's hand, but his short little legs would not move—he was so overcome by emotion—so the bailiff threw his arms about his shoulders and pressed him close in a friendly embrace.

The councillor and Höegh suddenly became engaged in an animated conversation about the possibilities of sufficient water for their mills this winter, and the farmers resumed their card playing. Hans Dahlbye was now shuffling and dealing the cards.

Attorney Lehmann, however, paced up and down in his creaking boots, head bent slightly and hands clasped behind his back. The humor of the scene seemed to him scarcely enough to compensate for its lack of dignity. It wasn't becoming in civil servants to lose their dignity in the presence of common farmers. He thoroughly disliked the atmosphere of the group since Magistrate Winterfeldt had left. He had kept them in check; the magistrate had been amiable, of course; he was an ornament to his profession and would never have approved of this joviality after court was over. This gave farmers the impression they were among equals. Take this pale fellow, for instance, Hans Dahlbye, to whom as yet he had not spoken a single word. Was it in good taste for him as a farmer to act and dress in a manner that would be more becoming to a well-off merchant?

Lehmann went over to the table for his glass and stopped for a moment to talk to young Lieutenant Bangsberg, whose correct behavior had made a good impression on him. He skaaled with him and, slyly calling attention to the sheriff and bailiff who had just toasted each other, said he was sure the lieutenant would not allow himself to rusticate in this damned backward region.

The lieutenant, blushing like a girl, replied, "I was born here and, when peace comes, I intend to settle down here in the district."

"Is that so? You have property here perhaps?"

"My father is a farmer and rather old; he wants me to take over."

Attorney Lehmann's geniality vanished and, after remarking that the sheriff made an excellent punch, the lieutenant said, "It isn't bad. A man as well acquainted with the wine merchants in town as my uncle, the sheriff, is, can still get good French brandy."

The clerks still stood quietly by the stove. They were the only ones of the whole group who were conscious of their proper position, and even they had been drinking more than usual. Attorney Lehmann approached the eldest and inquired rather abruptly: "That pale fellow over there playing cards with the farmers is Mr. Dahlbye, isn't he?"

The clerk replied quickly, whispering behind his hands: "Hans Dahlbye, yes, known also in Christiania, perhaps. I would say he had rather a bad reputation if he were not a relative of our host."

"Is he really?"

"Yes, a cousin of his mother's."

"Family relationships certainly go to great lengths in this region," the attorney said in a loud, pompous voice. "Why is he so well known?"

"The indictments and lawsuits against him will soon make a pile heavier than a man can carry, and it's not so easy to say what they are about," whispered the clerk looking around him cautiously. "He's always acquitted," he continued, "though once in awhile found guilty of small things that can be fixed with a fine."

"I see, I see. Hans Dahlbye is persecuted innocence, is that it? I can hardly believe it. It's true, isn't it, that the clergy are his favorite target for trickery and especially his own venerable parson?"

"Venerable? Hm, with your permission, Mr. Attorney, there is about the same degree of venerableness, quarreling and trickery on both sides." The clerk drew down the corners of his mouth with a cunning look and wrinkled his nose as though he smelled something bad. His companion laughed admiringly.

"Hm—is that so, is that so, my friends?" remarked the attorney coldly and, filling his glass from the punch-bowl, he moved away. The sheriff had replaced Lehmann at the Boston table and was being warmly praised by Attorney Höegh. Even Weydahl bowed to the sheriff in a friendly way and spoke kindly to him. "I think even the councillor joins in this, for there is certainly a faint smile on his serious face," thought Mr. Lehmann. He felt himself above all of them—the only intelligent and cultivated person in this rustic community. He looked at the whole business objectively, and leaning against the railing, he decided to watch this Hans Dahlbye more closely, a man who was described by the amiable magistrate Winterfeldt as an insolent and morally offensive farmer.

What stories were not told about this man? What kind of deeds, good and bad, were not credited to him? He was accused of so much, that it was hard to believe half of what was told of him. An atheist, and such a fanatical enemy of the church, that there was good reason to suppose that he had induced his henchmen to steal church property just to show his contempt for religion and its symbols. Then there were the tales of immoral conduct, including the fathering of several illegitimate children who were brought up according to the ridiculous principles of Rousseau, and consequently had little but a musical education. Perhaps, worst of all, was the fraternizing with the roaming bands that came from the Swedish border and spread over all of eastern Norway. A vengeful spirit, it was said, had led to the burning of property, attempts on the lives of fellow citizens, lying and black-marketing in grain and contact with enemy spies! And such a man was accepted by this group of magistrates of the district!

Hans Dahlbye stood this impudent and offensive scrutiny for a short time, but the nervous twitch of his eyebrows became more noticeable as he moved uneasily in his chair, to the evident satisfaction of his critic who was relishing his superiority. After a few minutes, Dahlbye turned, and looking the other squarely in the eye, said: "Do you want something?" Even the four other farmers looked angrily at Lehmann.

"Oh, no, I don't want anything. I have just heard you are the well-known Squire Hans Dahlbye."

"And who are you?"

"I am Attorney Bernt Eckhoudt Lehmann, at your service." It was said with an irritating cockiness.

"So that's your name. By the way, I am a farmer, just plain farmer."

For the second time that evening Lehmann encountered this strange pride of being a farmer. It irritated him. "One of the free Norwegian farmers of allodial succession, I presume," he smiled sarcastically.

"That's right, since my grandfather too owned his own farm. I assume yours didn't."

"Certainly not, no; he was an agent in Bergen." Lehmann was enjoying himself very much.

Hans Dahlbye turned to him and said sharply: "Who cares whether you're the son of a shopkeeper or a tailor—skaal, fellow!"

Lehmann suddenly felt no more desire to cross swords with this fellow. He walked across the room to join the Boston party, where his arrival was announced by the sound of his squeaking boots. Behind him he could hear Dahlbye ask, "Bangsberg, what did he call himself?" and then the farmers burst with laughter.

Shortly after this, the lieutenant said goodnight. Höegh took this occasion to toast the brave soldiers who defended the borders of their country against the enemy, and everyone gave a loud skaal. Lehmann suggested they sing the national anthem, so they all stood up, glasses held high. Höegh and the farmers, however, couldn't remember the words, so they just growled out the tune; the old bailiff tapped out the rhythm on the table with his fingers, but the councillor never moved his lips. Lehmann was the only one who sang. Finally he was joined by the lisping clerk, who by this time was so drunk that he could only follow shrilly out of tune, and the bailiff shouted: "Mr. Jensen, shut up, do shut up!" The evening ended in general hilarity, in the midst of which the clerks disappeared.

This patriotic attempt, however, had lifted their spirits as well as loosened their tongues. Toast followed toast: To the councillor, to the old bailiff, to the enterprising towns of Norway (this addressed to Lehmann), to the Norwegian farmer. On and on they went. Glasses began to shake in unsteady hands; punch was spilt on the tables and cards. The different groups seemed to melt together in the smoke-filled room. The magistrates and those at other tables left their seats and gathered round the large table where the farmers were drinking and skaaling. The toasts turned into stories and tales, and the national hymns soon changed to ditties and the choruses became stronger and louder and more raucous.

The door opened slightly; then it was pushed wide open, and in the doorway stood Madam Krogsti, the sheriff's wife. From behind her broad shoulders the maids peeped curiously at the jovial guests. Madam swelled with pride when she saw her husband, Erik, sitting with the bailiff's arm flung around his shoulders so familiarly.

The people, the whole room, in fact, seemed to move about Mr. Lehmann in a drunken, misty haze; he felt almost reconciled to the situation when suddenly, in the middle of a ditty, he stopped. Before him he saw a pale face with a sneering grimace. It was Hans Dahlbye who sat there smiling so coolly and maliciously at him. Lehmann tried to sit up in his chair and look a little more dignified. He asked the councillor if it wasn't time for them to break off and go to bed as they had to leave early in the morning.

Weydahl answered curtly that he was enjoying himself. He hadn't said very much but he had drunk heavily. He just sat there with his arms crossed and seemed to be listening to the singing and laughter from far away.

The group of women moved aside to let someone pass, and the sheriff looked up as he felt a tap on his shoulder. "Hello, Martin, my boy!" he said in a slurring voice, surprised at the sudden return of his nephew. "I guess you found your quarters pretty lonesome. Were you bored? Come, take a chair and skaal!" "Nothing of the sort," said Lieutenant Bangsberg. "When I went to my room I found a letter from town with information that I thought . . . I would bring to you right away."

The room became absolutely still. The voice of the officer quavered a little. He was obviously upset by the news he had to tell them.

"What's that?" said the councillor, suddenly paying attention.

Questions about the war, new battles, the government and Napoleon were flung at him. Embarrassed, the lieutenant leaned against the railing. "Secretary of State Falsen is dead," he said quickly in a low voice. Before any more questions could be asked, he continued: "He committed suicide. He drowned himself in the harbor after he left the theater one night. He was ill from overwork, upset, and afraid the war would be lost."

They all stood up, stunned; they looked at the lieutenant, excited and scared. No man had been more respected and dear to them since this terrible war had come with its problems and grief. Now the news about Enevold Falsen and his death brought to them sharply the real situation their country faced, and it sobered them.

The bailiff broke into loud sobs and hid his face in his hands. He had only met the dead man a few times and had never been close to him; but an incident, which had happened only a short time ago, now became an important happening and made him feel guilty. He saw himself as having embittered Mr. Falsen's last days. He told as best he could how the Administrative Council had ordered the bailiffs to raise a considerable amount of money for advance payments for military expenses. When the money could not be raised, the Administrative Council had blamed him for inefficiency, if not worse, in the tax-collecting. The old bailiff had then written a most disrespectful letter stating the accusations were unwarranted and unreasonable. Mr. Falsen had returned his letter with a note in his own handwriting saying that he considered it improper for a civil servant to send such a letter and for his acting superior, the Administrative Council, to accept it; therefore, he would consider it unwritten. In addition he had asked the bailiff to forgive any injustice that he might have done to him and begged him to remember that the members of the Council had an overwhelmingly difficult task to carry out.

"Have you ever heard of such a thing?" grieved the bailiff. "I feel like a dog, like a perfect beast, that I did not understand his difficulties, that I have hurt and offended a man who was head and shoulders above all of us, one who had the noblest heart and the keenest mind. The Devil take me!"

Councillor Weydahl took a step forward and raised his glass: "To the memory of Secretary of State Enevold de Falsen!" The words echoed in the large room. They drank in silence.

The voices of the drunken clerks talking to the serving maids drifted in from the hallway. They had not heard the news. Someone quieted them.

Attorney Lehmann, watching, felt something well inside him. These people were not pretending to be moved by this sad news; they were sincere. Yet Magistrate Winterfeldt had told him about their real indifference to the condition of their country. In his opinion, the farmers present tonight should feel guilty for their lack of patriotic spirit and eagerness to help. This, he decided, was just the time to take them to task about it while they were still in a receptive mood due to the death of Secretary Falsen.

He stepped forward, and in loud and eloquent terms described Enevold Falsen as a great patriot. He was quite carried away with himself as he began to point out to his audience the moral to be drawn from this great man and his devotion to his country. "Shall we not blush when we consider that our own negligence made his soul suffer?" At the same time he wanted to bring to their attention something that he had learned from an impeccable source, their lack of civic duty which was especially reprehensible because in these parts nature had blessed them so abundantly. Furthermore, he demanded that the people of this district make up for their past omissions. He corrected them with spirit and force and reminded them that the owners of the largest grain farms in this, the Norwegian granary, had very often not even pledged anything when they were asked for voluntary contributions for the feeding of the army. With no grain forthcoming, the gifts from the other classes, the military, the clergy, and the civil servants, even though they were almost more than they could afford, were of little consequence.

He painted a horrible picture of the results of the war

and the dreadful things that were happening in other parts of the country. Then he burst out with much pathos, "Even if it is your last drop of blood and your last daler, why don't you make these sacrifices?"

"Why don't we have peace?" someone put in dryly. Lehmann looked at the man angrily. Hans Dahlbye again; well, he needn't spare him. No one who was faithful to his King and valued his own honor would ask a question such as that. There wouldn't be peace until the King in his wisdom and the welfare of Denmark-Norway decreed it.

Dahlbye repeated sarcastically: "The wisdom of the Danish King and the welfare of Denmark would decree it!"

Now Lehmann went completely mad. Gesticulating wildly, sometimes shouting, sometimes hissing, he enumerated farmer Dahlbye's list of sins: This man, by both his official and private acts, had reaped nothing but shame and contempt; his continued immorality and atheism had brought him deserved punishment by his fellow citizens and by judicial authority. This person dared, even now in this place, to encourage disloyalty. He would say this not only because his shameless language made him suspect of being engaged in treacherous intrigues with the Swedes, of being one of the contemptible creatures of a mean enemy, bah!—

"The Danes and the Danish King's creatures always talk a good fight against the Swedes," Hans Dahlbye remarked scornfully. His white face had become even paler, his brown eyes sparkled dangerously and he had torn his fine shirt-frills to pieces without realizing it.

The two antagonists stood opposite each other with the table between them. In vain the bailiff and sheriff tried to quiet them. The farmers meanwhile gathered behind Dahlbye, but the councillor and Höegh had taken the lieutenant over to a window and were talking quietly about the particulars and exact circumstances of the statesman's death.

"Grain-profiteer! That's what you are!" shouted Lehmann. "You profit from the poor starving mountain farmers, taking their last daler from them."

"Very often they even offer me their family silver," answered Dahlbye.

"Grain-profiteer! You are a traitor, you and all your friends! Adulterer!"

Just then Hans Dahlbye grabbed up a long ruler that was on the table and started to hit the attorney over the head with it, but the sheriff grabbed his wrist just in time to ward off the blow. At the same moment Mr. Lehmann was swung around by his shoulder and Weydahl said, "I think it best that you come with me."

"You saw me attacked and insulted by this scoundrel! He is the one who has broken the peace of the assizes!" protested Lehmann. He followed the councillor willingly, however, through the scared group of women huddled together in the hallway and on into the councillor's room. The last glimpse he caught of the party was the stout, well-fed farmer swearing and clenching his fists at him angrily.

The room was in semi-darkness. The fire in the stove flared up spasmodically and cast flickering shadows. Mr. Lehmann, completely exhausted, sat on the edge of the bed silently watching the councillor as he paced up and down the room, occasionally kicking a chair out of the way in his irritation.

After a short time they heard footsteps on the stairs; then quiet reigned in the large room. Sheriff Krogsti came in with a candle and lit the two candles on the bedside tables;

Attorney Höegh and the old bailiff entered behind him. They were all stone sober.

"This was very embarrassing—too bad—too bad!" the sheriff kept saying. In a stunned sort of way he kept looking around him and not paying attention as to how he was holding his candle; he didn't notice the tallow dripping down on his velvet breeches.

"Never mind, Sheriff, you couldn't help it," said Weydahl, obviously upset himself. "Has Dahlbye gone?"

"He can't go home tonight."

"Oh no, that's true. Only let's be sure we don't meet tomorrow at breakfast. As I said, it's not your fault. Goodnight, Sheriff."

Krogsti took the hint and left the room. "Certainly this was very embarrassing," he whined as he walked out through the door.

The councillor threw himself into a rocking chair by the stove. Höegh and the bailiff sat down at the table; the latter blew out one of the candles because it shone in his eyes. Among the shadows of the four-poster, the thin arrogant profile of Lehmann was visible.

"The wretched rogue!" he said angrily. "I'll demand action be brought against him."

Jespersen and Höegh both started laughing uneasily as if to dispel the sinister atmosphere. "Devil take me, but you got away from him rather nicely," answered the old bailiff. "And yet," he added sorrowfully, "it was a sad and unfortunate thing to happen at such a time and place."

"I was completely in my rights," said Lehmann swelling with dignity.

"You were not!" the councillor's voice was harsh and rasping. "In the first place, you should have remembered where you were, Attorney—you had no right to insult a guest of Sheriff Krogsti in his own home; secondly, you ought to have been sure of the facts before you made any accusations."

"I venture to observe," Lehmann hastily replied, "that the private life of this Hans Dahlbye is well known to be quite scandalous, that. . . ."

"Oh, keep quiet about his private life! It has never harmed you or any of us, and besides it's no worse than many others. You've heard just as bad scandals as those of Hans Dahlbye among the best families in Christiania, haven't you? And yes, in other places as well. And as to his irreligious views, which you spoke of, we are a religious and pious people these days, aren't we?"

The councillor's scornful voice made the attorney feel absolutely weak. "Now, about this man Dahlbye," the councillor said. "I refer to the widespread rumors about his black-marketing grain and his supposed connections with the enemy and also of the opinion that Magistrate Winterfeldt expressed of him, and, mind you, none of us question his honesty or integrity."

The old bailiff let his watch strike and murmured something to Attorney Höegh, who yawned loudly.

"Of course we don't," the councillor continued. "But after all, it may be that the magistrate is not the best person in the world to judge Hans Dahlbye. Heavens, I could almost say if the magistrate had once in a while not been so proper and righteous, others wouldn't be so bad. Do you know what? I am tempted to say that people like Winterfeldt and you and the rest of us here are really responsible for Hans Dahlbye's behavior. Perhaps, just perhaps, if Winterfeldt had not been such a good and pious man, Hans Dahlbye would have become one."

It was obvious that the councillor was thinking about

something other than the immediate situation and about more than his words expressed. Something wild and gloomy seemed to take hold of him as he spoke. His words became mixed with colloquial expressions and the others listened to him, surprised.

"One doesn't imitate the virtues of one's enemy; one tries hard to be as unlike him as possible. The one who happens to get into a quarrel, to the death, with an able person will not himself be virtuous, for he hates his enemy with all his might, including his virtue. And fate might cause us to get into a quarrel with the good, you know."

Lehmann had regained his composure now and said impatiently, "This is a very strange explanation, but you do admit that I was correct in my estimate of his character."

"I do not!" was the harsh reply. "Use your common sense, Attorney! You don't know much about the Uplands, but sufficient at least to understand the situation. No man in these parts has the power and influence of Hans Dahlbye; you can be sure of that, and this will be more obvious, I regret to say, in the near future. Say what you want about the leading farmers of this district. Parson Lind, that ornament of the clergy, calls them 'culturally depraved and unnatural farmers,' Ha, ha! Credit them with vices as black as you want to blacken them, but they are not black-market profiteers, and such men would not be tolerated among them. Hans Dahlbye, his relatives and his friends, the leaders of the big farmers, have not proved to be avaricious, by Jove! We've had an army of suffering and starving people from near and far come to the district these days, because they have heard rumors that there is food here for empty stomachs. There have been beggars and vagabonds along with the decent ones. Poor people have come in droves, and without any distinction they have been fed at these farmers' tables, both during wartime with its scarcity as well as before the war. I'm sure no beggar has ever been turned away from Hans Dahlbye's house. If there has been, it is someone who has already been well fed in the kitchen of one of his personal enemies and, because of that, chased off by his servants. No one has been more willing to help or been more generous and open-hearted to the poor than the one you have just blamed for usury and profiteering. The talk about the family silver of the mountain farmers, this is pure nonsense and bragging. Just call an Uplander a damned sinner and he'll boast of it like the devil. Lehmann, you, like so many others in the towns, may have given twenty, thirty or even three hundred rix-dalers to help those in distress when you've been asked to by the high dignitaries or even from your own good-heartedness, and I'm not belittling it. Compared to Hans Dahlbye, however, it's not much. He's spent ten times as much. He used to be extremely wealthy, but he hardly bothers to find out what he has these days. He hasn't given just one gift at one single time; he has given away money everyday and he continues to do so. What's more, he gives without counting; unable to refuse anyone. He keeps open house for the poor and even for the rabble. For the rest, I am inclined to believe what they say about him: perjury, seduction and rape, arson, defiling churches—the whole lot—and even treason!"

Höegh coughed and got up as though he wanted to end the talk. Weydahl sat down in his chair so heavily that it creaked under him.

"These are certainly the strangest opinions I ever heard from a judge about conditions within his own jurisdiction," Mr. Lehmann remarked.

The bailiff said: "Many farmers have not subscribed very much for the voluntary contributions to the army but they have open-handedly supported the troops from their own districts. I know this because I've forwarded to them the letters of thanks from the officers."

"And I want to say," chimed in Attorney Höegh, "that as often as I have been prosecutor or defender in cases against Hans Dahlbye, I've very seldom found him worse than his opponent, and he was always better than his reputation."

"One is almost tempted to feel sympathetic towards this notorious farmer, who obviously plays the part of Robin Hood of the Uplands," Lehmann mocked. "I, at any rate, can't reconcile myself to his obstinate bad taste in the choice of his crimes and especially the strong suspicion that he has negotiations with the enemy."

The councillor leaned over to put a log in the stove. "You are as well read as you are witty, Attorney—you put me in a good humor, my boy!"

The words annoyed Lehmann, but he bit his lip and kept silent as old Bailiff Jespersen nodded warningly to him.

"What about going to bed?" Höegh said placatingly.

Weydahl sat back in his chair: "No, not just yet! I want to give young Mr. Lehmann some useful hints in return for his cleverness. He'll need them if he is ever favored with a good position in this region. You may be sure no one will forget the quarrel that took place tonight, for it cannot be smoothed over. If we, Mr. Bailiff, had just been newly appointed in the district we would not be forgiven for being present during the dispute." It sounded like a suppressed threat. "What you consider bad taste or willful obstinacy might in these remote regions far from towns, be considered normal. I am fairly sure education will help to change their taste, but as to their obstinacy and willfulness, I'm not so sure. Obstinacy, you know, flourishes where those who should correct it are regarded as representing the foreign administrators of an alien government. The people we are talking about don't meddle with the Swedes for money or profit. Some do, of course, those with the spirit of shopkeepers and other 'respected' people who slink, fawning around the civil servants, and use their connections with traitorous people as an excuse for smuggling and the like. No, these people having dealings with the Swedes in order to hurt and worry us, in a way, for fun. The Swedes are counter-poison against us."

"You refer to the hatred against the Danes; I don't believe in it," Attorney Lehmann said. "Most of us who are said to be so disliked are good native Norwegians, and Winterfeldt is even an Uplander, while Secretary of State Falsen, whom the farmers seemed to mourn so deeply, was of Danish birth. Besides, we are all subjects of the Danish-Norwegian State, the twin kingdoms!"

"Let me tell you something," the old bailiff said laughingly, "I have a groom who is married to one of Magistrate Winterfeldt's chambermaids. She wanted to teach their son the Lord's prayer according to the Bible; her husband listened to her awhile; then suddenly pounding the table with his fist, he cried: 'The devil fry you, Grethe, if you teach the child Danish!' What do you think of that? You catch the point, don't you? This has become a regular household saying around here since then."

"It's not that we are not Norwegians," the councillor broke in. "Yes, we are Norwegians; we are good Norwegians and citizens of all Norway, so that it makes very little difference to us where we were born. We have no real roots in any region. We are more loyal and faithful subjects than Hans Dahlbye and his companions, and we'll be able to prove this before long. But we would do well to realize that those who are landed proprietors in this district want to be the leaders in their own circles as their fathers were before them. Then we appear, carrying the book of laws in our hands and His Royal Majesty's ordinances respecting rank and precedence, like a halo round our heads. Furthermore, we demand taxes, obedience, and respect. They do pay the taxes after some grumbling. The obedience to the law, which we demand, is nearly always in conflict with their own traditional authority of custom and paternalism, but they submit, simply because they have to, yet they commit infringements of the law secretly and boast of every law they break. Never, however, have they bowed their necks under the decrees of rank and respect to us. This is their most sensitive point where we hurt more than their vanity; we offend also their old barbaric sense of honor. They won't give in and neither will we; consequently we have excluded and isolated them. So these very respectable farmers feel shut off, separated from society, not at home in the country where they have landed property, tied only to their families, perhaps to their friends in the district. We, with presumptuous confidence in our position, push them aside within their own land.

"I have spoken about responsibility: one of these days either we or our successors will reap the consequences of having provoked these people too long. We can only hope that someday they will be strong enough to take back their power. This will certainly shake the pillars of the state, but if they fail, the Norwegian nation will be destroyed. We should also hope that they do not rise against us too soon, because this will not only make us suffer, but may destroy our native country as well.

"When this takes place, you and I and Winterfeldt, as well as all of our colleagues, must bear the heavy burden of responsibility for what occurred and is going to happen . . . ."

Weydahl stopped abruptly. He leaned forward in his chair. Something seemed to prevent him from continuing.

"I should say that the councillor defends these stubborn farmers," observed Lehmann.

Weydahl looked at him: "Blood is thicker than water; I am myself of country stock—"

"Perhaps even His Honor the Councillor is one of the free Norwegian farmers of allodial succession," was the impertinent rejoinder.

"No, I am sorry to say, I am just the son of an ordinary sexton who has managed to push himself through and above the solid throngs of farmers—and this struggle has marked me," the councillor replied gently, almost mildly.

Höegh had been sitting, lost in silent admiration of the councillor. He had never seen his friend like this before, and he felt embarrassed and sorry for him. "Suppose we go to bed?" he suggested again. Lehmann and he shared the same room, and they went out together. The councillor seemed not to notice, for he paid no attention to them.

The old bailiff stood there hesitating. The gray coat hung loosely on his thin, feeble body. The sickly, wrinkled face showed his sorrow. He put out his hand: "Goodnight, Weydahl."

The councillor grasped it and held it for a minute: "Goodnight, Jespersen. Do you think . . . . do you believe . . . . there certainly were some dark spots in Enevold Falsen's life, events . . . . you know . . . . do you think, do you believe the memory of those, his conscience . . . . remorse . . . . drove him to death, even though he knew his fatherland needed his strength?" The words came haltingly and with difficulty. The old bailiff grasped the councillor's hand more firmly: "Perhaps, but I believe he worked and did his best for as long as he could. God doesn't ask more than that; so let us, as human beings, not ask more. Goodnight, Weydahl, and good-bye, in case we don't meet again. I leave before breakfast."

"Goodnight, Jespersen, farewell and thanks."

The councillor was left alone. The candle burned down and the hot tallow sizzled and smoked. He put it out and sat down again in the big chair in front of the stove. The flickering light of the fire fell on his feet and the large white hands resting on his knees. A log shifted; the light flared and lit up his anguished face. The lips were pursed tightly together, as though in pain, and his hair hung over his forehead untidily.

One question kept going around and around in his mind; it dug into his thoughts remorselessly and pried loose what was buried in his soul, wakened memories and forced old thoughts to come alive again. It pushed everything aside, destroyed every argument with which he tried to fight it. That for which he had worked became meaningless; his pride, the model farm he had created out of his property, became of no consequence; what he had accomplished in these parts seemed so little and so dearly bought, compared with the means he had used; his youthful ambitions and manhood dreams now appeared unworthy and small.

He didn't dare let the question take clear and definite form. He would defy it, ignore it, put it out of his heart and mind!

"It's late," he said aloud. Then, shaken by the sound of his own voice. "Best get to bed," he added, but continued to sit there, seemingly unable to move.

Yet the question rang in his ears. The combined tiredness and quietness robbed his defiance of strength and the query was there again: would you now be able to do the great thing? No. Could you have done it in the past? If you had not betrayed yourself and your ability, would you have been in a better position to help this country in its distress, helped it more than others? I don't know, couldn't know—he excused himself.

A hopeful thought relieved him of his heavy burden for a moment. You may still be helpful, you may know better than many others what is best to do, you ought to try, like Enevold Falsen.

A look of agony swept over his face: you no longer have the strength demanded for greatness; you no longer have even the pure will demanded for small chores; you are not capable of making peace between quarreling and fighting factions for they are likely to ask, "Who are you that you dare to rebuke us and give us advice?" And you cannot answer them.

He moaned with shame. His hands clenched the arm of the chair in pain.

Oh, the damned quiet of nights in this region! He lifted his head and listened. The sound of carriages came up the road. The sound of wheels rolling over frozen, uneven earth, of horses stamping under heavy loads, approaching.

The sounds grew louder and nearly shook the house. He got up from his chair, pushed the curtain aside, and with difficulty raised the ice-covered window. The moon hung low in the sky. Below him on the highroad, he saw wagon after wagon in a long row. Some had already passed by; half a hundred carriages stretched further on up the road. The horses and men cast long shadows on the frozen white fields. He knew what this was, but he called anyway, asking where they were going.

The nearest teamster stopped his horses. This made the whole column halt. Clouds of gray steam rose from the backs of the horses.

The driver called out that it was a transport column for the forts at the river Glommen. He cursed the bad driving conditions, evidently expecting more questions, but the man in the window asked nothing more. The marchers, the horses and the wagon train started again; load after load passed by; tired, steaming horses and tired men, who stumbled wearily beside the lorries.

At last they had all passed. The councillor shut the window, and sitting down on his bed, began to undress. This transport, this back-breaking work in the middle of a winter's night on bad roads, was all a part of war. Without it, there would be no possibility of getting so many people together for one undertaking. Perhaps it would be the war with its bloodletting that would weld the quarreling and fighting factions together in harmony.

Anne Cathrine Buhring

FAR away, over towards the Swedish border, a young girl sat sewing on the porch of a large old-fashioned house, built of brown-stained, weather-beaten timbers. The bodice of her checked linsey-woolsey dress was cut low, showing a full, round bosom below her long neck. She was slender and small-boned. Reddish blonde hair hung loosely on either side of her high, narrow forehead, and the thin white lips and too-small mouth gave her a pale and bloodless look, even though the chin was tiny and charmingly rounded. No amount of brushing or combing could smooth the curls at her temples or catch them all in the heavy knot on the back of her head. Her appearance, as she sat there pulling her needle in and out of the sewing so carefully, was of a child who had not been in the sunlight and fresh air for a long time and who, moreover, found her new task very difficult.

From the open door into the living room came a slow murmuring monologue. Sometimes the voice rose shrilly in excitement; at others it subsided to unintelligible whimpers. She paid no attention to the sound; she was used to it. Her father was playing solitaire and he always talked to himself when he played because, as the housekeeper, Miss Damman, said, he wasn't in his right mind.

Old Chamber Councillor Bühring had been playing solitaire for many, many years—longer, certainly than the girl on the porch could remember. They had been living here since she was five years old, in fact, ever since the time her mother died and the councillor had had a stroke and moved up here, having been forced to retire. They had lived here together, she and her father and Miss Damman, and every day he had played solitaire and talked to himself. She didn't understand much that he said and didn't pay too much attention to him either, for the housekeeper always said, "The poor chamber councillor is not quite well and doesn't think of what he is saying, so he often says things a young lady shouldn't hear."

The girl raised her head and looked down over the hill where the brittle grasses moved in the evening breeze. Down in the valley on the far field, soldiers were exercising; from the house on the hill they looked like swarms of ants.

Tonight no words of command floated up from the valley, for the wind was from the east. Further on beyond the field, the reflection of the sunset on the river gleamed through the yellow birches along the shore, and the green-brown ridges of the forest were set off against the afterglow in the sky.

A man with a tall shako on his head came suddenly over the ridge of the hill. The girl on the porch gave a jump when the man stood there in front of her, dressed in a red frock coat, light gray trousers, and high boots. A gilt sword hung by his side, and the brass buttons on his cuffs sparkled. With one hand he held the bridle of his horse and with the other saluted her, his hand to his shako. There was no greeting in return. The girl rushed into the entry, "Miss Damman! Stina! There is a soldier in the courtyard!"

"What? Why does the child scream so? Hm, everything is all right, since I drew the king of hearts—tell me, why does the child scream so?"

Next evening the old councillor sat on the sofa playing solitaire as usual. A lighted candle in a brass holder stood before him on the table. He was already fixed for the night in a red-flowered dressing gown, slippers, and nightcap pulled down so far on his head that it covered everything except the bristly white hair, which grew low on his neck. The eyelid hung loose and heavy on the paralyzed side of his sallow, wrinkled face. The trembling old hands dropped the cards on the table one by one, as he mouthed and muttered through his toothless jaws.

"Nine of spades—Oh yes, yes—jack of diamonds. No—won't go, five of hearts, hm—goes. Non—cela ne va pas—the ace, that's it—ça ira, ça ira. Hm, no, no—wait a minute, wait now," and he whimpered like a child.

His daughter, sitting on the other side of the table with her sewing, paid no attention to his talk. Tonight she had put a pink silk shawl around her shoulders, and every so often she dropped her sewing and gazed out of the uncurtained window into the blue twilight.

In the courtyard the soldier, tall and straight, marched back and forth, back and forth. Miss Damman, the housekeeper, was busily engaged in the kitchen, because four soldiers were now quartered at the farm.

"No, no, no—that's no good, no good—no, the queen of spades on the jack, that damned wench!—rien ne va plus—Oh no!" The old councillor, looking foolish and miserable, slapped the cards together helplessly and tried to get up from the sofa.

"Father, sit still, Miss Damman will come in a minute." Gently she pushed the pathetic old man back on the sofa, and going to the door, called: "Stina, father is sleepy and wants to go to bed."

Miss Damman came in, reddened by the heat of the kitchen; her footsteps made the house shake. "Oh dear me, I nearly forgot the councillor, poor man! When one has as much to do as I have—Come sir, come." She took his arm to help him up, and together they shuffled to the door. "I don't know what we're coming to. The maids have no morals anymore. So help me God, they aren't a bit ashamed; they're already flirting with the soldiers."

The young girl went out into the courtyard. She went over and stood in front of the soldier, looking at him searchingly. He stopped and saluted her smartly with his hand to his shako.

"Why do you keep saluting me? You have already done so half a dozen times today," she said. Her voice sounded deeper than usual and slightly husky.

The soldier, embarrassed, laughed instead of answering, and his hand fumbled up and down his thigh searching for a pocket to hide in.

"Are you going to war, soldier?"

"I guess I'm in the war right now, Miss, but by the way, my name is not soldier." He laughed a little, which hurt her feelings.

"Of course, I know that. I just called you 'soldier' because I didn't know whether you were a private or a commander, and one must address people by their proper rank or not at all, or at least so Miss Damman says. What's your name, then?"

He drew himself up stiffly at this rebuke and spoke the two words: "Iver Tollefsen," as if he were conveying a message.

"Won't you answer my questions properly, then? Are you going to war and fight the enemy, and are you a private or a commander?"

He understood what she meant but didn't find it necessary to explain the difference between a corporal and an officer. "I guess one is supposed to fight against one's enemies and not against friends in time of war. As for commanders, they are in charge of fortresses, and I don't see any walls around here except those over there—" and he pointed to the walls of the cow-barn.

Shrugging her shoulders she turned away. "But if you want to know, it is I who am in charge of all the soldiers on this farm," he added hastily.

She smiled mockingly. "Well since your army is quartered in our kitchen, you ought to see that it does not attack our maids—especially as you don't have a larger army to command!" Laughing loudly she walked slowly out of the courtyard.

"The Devil splinter me if I don't do just that, Miss!" he said angrily in a low voice.

With long angry strides he marched into the kitchen, and it wasn't long before she saw from her window that he had chased the three soldiers over to the stable and she could still hear him scolding them at bedtime.

* * *

The soldiers stayed at the farm about a week. Early each morning before the household was up, they rode down to the drill-ground and didn't return until dinnertime. The young girl and the soldier in his fine red uniform had soon been reconciled. The best of friends, they walked together every evening. His strides were firm and even, almost a march, while she picked her steps daintily, hopping beside him, all the while chattering away to him about the important happenings in her young life. She confided to her new friend that she had been confirmed last year, that Miss Damman had given her lessons because the school was so far away and the road so bad, that she was supposed to go to see her uncle who lived in Fredrikstad, only it was such a long way and would be such a tiresome and expensive trip.

Life was rather difficult these days, what with her father's half pay and everything so expensive because of the war and the money not being worth much anymore.

In the mornings as she dressed, she thought about the soldier, how handsome he was and strong as a bear. Then one day he didn't turn up at all, nor did he come in the evening for their walk. She didn't know he was on watch, and fearful, she lay awake and kept listening for the sound of his horse's hoofs in the courtyard. She couldn't hear any, and finally tired out, she started to cry. She was afraid to tell Miss Damman the real reason for her tears; instead she told her she had a pain in her chest—she was always too embarrassed to give the real reason why she was crying.

One Sunday afternoon Miss Damman joyfully told her that they were to get rid of their unwelcome guests. The next day all the soldiers quartered with them were to leave this district and march on.

"Even the commander?" The words slipped out before she could stop them. The girl turned pale and started to tremble.

"What do you mean? Are you . . . ," asked Miss Damman and stared at her in amazement.

Ashamed and desolate, the girl ran out of the room and down the hill. She threw herself on the grass and lay there weeping as though her heart would break, not noticing in her anguish that the sun had set beyond the ridges, and that the evening shadows were creeping along the valley and up to the woods.

The corporal meanwhile was walking on top of the hill in his fine regimental coat with his sabre clanking at his side. Suddenly he caught sight of the weeping figure in the meadow and ran over to her. She saw him come and wiped her eyes, but as she did not get up he sat down beside her.

"We march off tomorrow, Miss—"

"I have heard you do," she answered, gazing unsteadily at the dark red leaves of the aspen tree in front of them. They sat there silent for a long time. The girl, looking embarrassed, toyed with his sabre belt.

"We are going south; they say there will be a battle soon."

She dropped the sword belt and hid her face in her hands. Tears welled into her eyes again and trickled through her fingers.

"Why do you cry, Miss?" his voice sounded confused.

"Suppose somebody stabs you, warrior," she said tearfully and leaned trustingly against his shoulder. He took her in his arms cautiously as if lifting a bird and tried to comfort her. "That won't be so easy, dear Miss, I'll be all right."

She uncovered her face and threw her arms around his neck in distress.

"Oh, must you really leave, soldier?"

"I must go. A soldier in the King's service must do his duty. But I'll come back."

"Oh, if you only would! Do you mean it seriously?"

She pressed against him and trembled in his arms as he kissed her.

"You'll never leave me again? I'll marry you when you return," she said, kissing him again.

"Yes—perhaps," he sat there with his mouth half open. "If it—but the chamber councillor won't allow it, I guess."

She smiled gaily now: "Don't worry about that; father doesn't care about anything as long as Miss Damman is here with him. But you mustn't call me 'Miss' any longer. My name is Anne Cathrine. I will call you Iver; you call me Thrine."

"When the time comes, yes," he said, and in a momentary daydream, all the things that a corporal could become in times of war flashed through his mind—lieutenant, major, even Emperor of France. "If you will marry me, I certainly will come back for you, believe me, but not until the Swedes become more peaceful."

She wanted to know then from which district he came and something about his home. He described the region and said that his farm was just below the Herset Hills.

"What's the name of your farm?" The image of his cottage home with its little cabbage patch and his old mother puttering about, picking slugs off the cabbages in the summertime, appeared to Iver Tollefsen.

"Outlook," he answered slowly.

"Is it large?"

"It's not of the largest certainly."

"Are your houses finer than ours?"

He gazed up the hill for a moment: "There is a big red barn."

His heart grew lighter as she changed the subject and made him promise for sure, absolutely sure, that he would come back for her when the war was over, and that he would never, never marry anyone else. He promised and then swore to it, and between tears and laughter she kissed him. Suddenly she heard Miss Damman calling her from the house. Scrambling up she started to run up the hill, but he stopped her long enough to ask her not to tell the housekeeper anything about them until the war was over, when he would come back for her.

Next morning the dragoons rode away from the farm. Anne Cathrine stood on the porch in the dawn waving her pink shawl to the retreating figures. And Iver Tollefsen turned his horse and saluted her smartly with his hand to his shako.

* * *

The war lasted for another year, and the girl longed for her lover. The Swedes made peace—and she waited. Nothing ever happened at the chamber councillor's, either in peace or war. She never heard of her warrior, and no one she could ask about him came to the farm.

Then the Christmas after the peace, Miss Damman dropped dead on the kitchen floor. The old councillor was never happy or comfortable after that; he stopped playing solitaire, and when spring came, he too died.

Now Miss Bühring was all alone. The parson took care of her affairs and arranged to have her sent to her uncle in Fredrikstad. She, however, thought of her soldier and wept. Secretly she decided that on her way to Fredrikstad, she would find out once and for all whether he was alive or dead, so after she started her journey, she changed her route and boarded a coach going to the district Iver had told her was his home.

It was not surprising therefore that on a summer day a coach stopped near the Herset farms. The haymakers were surprised when the young lady alone in the coach asked for directions to the farm called "Outlook." As they told her they never heard of the place, they saw she wore a pink shawl around her shoulders and white satin shoes on her little feet. But she kept insisting it was close to the Herset Hills and had a big red barn. Then they smiled in amusement, as they realized what place she wanted, and showed her the way up to it, for she meant the cottage "Peep-Out." The coach rolled on.

It was Anne Cathrine Bühring. She had dressed in all of her finery: pink silk shawl and her mother's white satin slippers which she had also worn at her confirmation, all in the wonderful anticipation of seeing Iver.

Finally they reached the cottage. She jumped out and

looked around. Close to a tiny red barn was a low gray cottage. There was no one around, but she heard someone cutting firewood in the woodshed. She opened the door to the cottage and went into the room. An old woman sat by the fire, and Anne asked her if Iver Tollefsen was home. Yes, he was. The tall gaunt woman looked at her in astonishment and asked her to sit down while she went for him. In a few minutes a man, sweaty from cutting wood, unshaven, in shirt-sleeves and patched trousers, entered the room.

He was her warrior. She didn't notice that he was not in his beautiful uniform; he was the one she had longed for and waited for. He stood there strong and awkward. Half frightened of her, he kept rubbing his hands up and down his trousers in embarrassment, wishing he had his Sunday suit on. She just wanted to put her arms around his neck and thank him for being alive. She hesitated a minute and her blood ran cold with fear. Perhaps he didn't want her to come like this. She couldn't speak and felt unable to move.

He shuffled his feet and at a loss for words stammered out: "I thought perhaps—well, I knew this place wasn't the kind—and then things didn't turn out the way I thought they would in the war, and I didn't make more than corporal —and, well, I just didn't dare—can you forgive me for not coming!" he pleaded and reached for her hand.

"You don't wish that I hadn't come?" she said almost in a whisper.

"You can be sure, if you'll take me the way I am and live here as I do, then I will be so kind to you, so kind, do the very best I can—." He still didn't dare to look at her but then she grasped his hand, her head began to swim, and she leaned against him sobbing convulsively: "Please don't be cross with me for coming!"

Very timidly he held her tight and, stuttering a little, said again: "Don't talk like that—here I am and you see how I live. If you really love me—." He was in an agony of fear until she put her arms around his neck.

The old woman, Iver's mother, returned. With a good deal of embarrassment her son told how the whole thing had happened. She didn't say very much but shook hands with the young girl and then busied herself with starting the fire and making coffee. Every so often, however, her keen eyes looked searchingly at the young people.

That night when Anne Cathrine, tired from her journey, had gone to bed in the little room adjoining, the old woman sat down at her spinning wheel. This was a sure sign to Iver that his mother was going to question him, so he waited quietly. After a long silence she said, "I guess—well, perhaps you intend to marry the girl?" This might not be very easy, she went on, for he certainly couldn't take it for granted that her folks would permit it.

Iver's heart sank. They were going to get married anyway whether her relatives liked it or not. Dejectedly he asked her how he could manage to get their consent.

For a long time his mother sat there thinking. "Didn't you find Judge Weydahl's horses when they took the wrong track in the mountains coming back from summer pasture last fall? I guess he will remember that," she said thoughtfully. "You know if he can, he always helps those poor fellows who ask for it. You ought to go to him tomorrow."

Iver didn't answer. He didn't feel like going to the judge in this business. Sure, the councillor was kind and helpful—there was no doubt about that—but this was a matter of marriage and Iver had heard all sorts of gossip about the judge and the women of his household since Mrs. Weydahl's death.

One of the maids who had been there since the mistress died had been married to his groom, who had been given the lease of a farm in the far south of the district. Another maid had been married to a workman from town. In both cases the weddings were very hurried.

In spite of his qualms he went to the judge for help. The councillor wrote to the girl's uncle in Fredrikstad, and when his permission came, they got the marriage license, and Corporal Iver Tollefsen and Miss Anne Cathrine Bühring were married.

It happened that about a year later Anne Cathrine was sitting alone in the cottage, rocking the cradle and singing to her little baby. She had had to leave Iver and her mother-in-law in the fields harvesting while she came in to tend the child. Suddenly a huge gray-haired man stood in the doorway, said good day and asked for the corporal. She got up and curtsied, since she knew instinctively that this was one of the magistrates. She started to call her husband but the stranger stopped her. "Don't bother," he said. "I presume you are Mrs. Tollefsen?"

Yes, she was Iver's wife.

"And for sure he has a very pretty wife," said the stranger, "and money besides. Here is your inheritance which was sent to me to give you."

He pulled out his wallet and counted out a pile of bank notes on to the table, but he was looking at her rather than at the money as he counted. "There it is, three hundred and twenty rix-dalers. It makes the family pretty wealthy, I guess."

He walked toward her, all the while looking at her in such a way that Anne Cathrine was ready to sink through the floor with embarrassment. He walked up and touched the reddish blonde hair that curled unchecked around her face now that Miss Damman was no longer there to keep it smooth. "Yes," he repeated, "the corporal has got himself a very pretty wife."

Anne Cathrine, surprised and frightened almost to tears, stepped back, and as she did so, knocked against the cradle causing the baby to waken and cry.

"Good heavens!" he muttered under his breath, "you already have a squalling brat? Please remember me to Iver and give him the money." At the door he stopped and pointing to the child asked: "Is it baptized yet?"

No, it was to be baptized the next Sunday that services were held in the parish.

He hastily took a ten-daler bill from his pocket and put it on the cradle. "I guess I ought to give my sponsor's gift since I was, in a way, the best man," he said. Then he went out, climbed into his cariole, which he had left on the highway, slapped the reins over the horse and left.

When Iver came in for supper, he said he was indeed disappointed that he hadn't been there when Councillor Weydahl had honored them with his visit.

In the Councillor's Kitchen

IT was a few minutes to midnight. Out in the kitchen, Lars, the groom, had just put a fresh log on the embers and, leaning back against the high back of the settle, was idly wondering if it would catch fire. It burst into flame, and the warm glow lit up his thin elderly face with its gray stubby whiskers. Håken, the parson's coachman, sat across from him on a straight chair. He had propped his elbows on his knees and, head in hands, dozed off and on, his head bobbing up and down fitfully. His back was turned to the large kitchen table piled high with the half-empty dinner plates and dishes from the elaborate meal which had been served in the drawing room. Dishes, pots and pans were all piled up waiting to be washed. Miss Nannestad and the maids had hardly finished carrying out the dessert dishes before they had to start brewing punch and setting up card tables for the councillor and his friends. The washing-up would just have to wait until tomorrow.

The flames leapt up and the log split with a crash sending sparks over the hearth. Håken woke with a jerk at the sound and looked around him sleepily. The flames sent flickering shadows deep into the large gloomy room, touched the table, turned the glass and silver into live things, and even reached the wooden bed in the corner where Lesbet, the kitchen maid, lay snoring behind the bed curtains. She had thrown herself down there exhausted after three days and nights of continual work; the councillor's Christmas party for his friends had been going on that long.

Lars yawned loudly. Then he pulled a short dirty clay pipe and a quid of tobacco from his pocket and, cutting it rather absent-mindedly on the seat of his chair, filled his pipe.

Håken followed his movements with greedy eyes. It seemed to him they all lived very well here at the councillor's; they even had tobacco, in spite of its cost. The beginnings of an envious grudge evaporated, however, when the old man reluctantly handed him half an inch of it. Håken cleared his mouth and spat into the fire to get ready for the full enjoyment of this precious gift; for nowadays since war had come, it seldom happened between Christmas and Easter that a man got a quid in his jaw. As for smoking tobacco, he had even forgotten where his pipe was, it was such a long time since he had last used it. Neither spoke.

The door to the drawing room flew open, and Miss Nannestad, slim and quick, came rushing in with a punch bowl in her hands. After the death of her mother, Hans Orre had sent her to a sheriff on the west side of the lake to learn housekeeping, and now she was in charge of the councillor's household. There were many in the district who had had their own opinion about her taking that position. A hum of voices and laughter, carried on the smoke-filled air, floated after her from the other room. Then the door swung shut and the housemaid jumped up wide awake from her bed.

"Lesbet, quick—hurry up, run down in the cellar and get a quart measure full of punch-brandy! Is the water hot? They need one more bowl, and then I think that will be enough for tonight. I asked you, is there hot water in the pot?"

Lesbet didn't stop to answer. She went over and picked up the quart measure; Lars handed her a couple of lighted pine knots, and flinging open the cellar trap door, she disappeared into the black open hole with the burning torches in one hand and the quart measure in the other. Miss Nannestad lifted a big copper pot from the fire, touched it to see if it was hot, and then leaning over the hearth, turned the winch and swung the pot over the flames.

As she stood with one foot on the edge of the hearthstone she said to Håken: "The parson asked me to tell you there is no hurry to harness the horses because he doesn't intend to leave for another hour. The services will be in the annex church tomorrow."

"Oh yes," Lars muttered, "there has been a service there once already this Christmas."

"What! Are you still up, Lars?" Miss Nannestad broke in. "You might just as well go to bed—Wallace, the attorney, and Captain Bauck are all staying overnight."

Lars paid no attention to her, and just then Lesbet came up from the cellar. Miss Nannestad took the pot off the hook and carried it over to the table. The others sat listening to the clink-clink of her spoon as she stirred the brandy and hot water into the bowl. The pungent aroma of the hot punch filled the room.

"Is it cold outside, Håken?" she asked.

"If the lake isn't already frozen, it will be by morning," was the reply.

"Then I guess you would like something to warm your insides," and she poured him a cup of punch.

"Thanks so much." He took the quid out of his mouth and started to drink, but hesitated and looked at Lars.

"Go ahead and drink it, please. Lars will have his later. Would you like a drop, Lesbet?" Miss Nannestad asked the housemaid who had thrown herself on the bed again.

The tired girl emptied her glass with one gulp and went to sleep again. The two men drew closer to the fireplace, and the housekeeper carried the punch bowl into the drawing room.

The room fell silent. Only Lesbet's snoring and the sucking noises Lars made with his pipe broke the quiet. From time to time he spat into the glowing embers, but he didn't bother to talk to his companion, for he considered him just a youngster. Envy welled up again in Håken's soul. To be able to sit like this in a cheerful kitchen with a pipe full of tobacco and a cup of punch to warm one, this certainly never happened at the parsonage.

In his own mind he tried to calculate how much Lars would make in tips during the year. He figured about eight dalers silver a year, not bad! This was a good place to work. If only one could be in a house like this, it would certainly be different from the parsonage where there was hardly enough to eat, and it was mostly rancid pork and moldy cake. The parson's servants moped about with empty stomachs while their master drifted around from one to another of the rich people's houses, losing every penny at cards, and his wife sat home crying, and the children ran around barefoot in rags like beggars.

His thoughts were interrupted by the jingle of sleigh bells in the courtyard. The dog barked and Lars got up, stretching himself; "Who in hell is out at this time of night?"

He opened the entry door and hissed at the dog to be quiet: "Sh! Tyras, sh! Keep quiet, keep quiet, you beast! Sh!" The cold swept into the kitchen on a blast of frozen air.

"Why, hello, Hans, is that you?"

"Yes, it's time for us big shots to arrive, isn't it?" A man, enveloped in a big, shapeless wolfskin coat, heavy boots, and a cap pulled over his ears, entered the room.

"Good evening folks! Just as I expected, there are others waiting here too." He pulled off his coat and threw it on the bench; then trying unsuccessfully to kick off his boots, he turned to Lars for help. "Please help me, I can't seem to get them off by myself. My boss sent me to get Captain Bauck," he went on, mimicking his master, Mr. Orre, the country tradesman of Alm, "If perhaps the young captain would like to join me and come home before the flies come out—Did you get that, folks? And I don't think he meant the summer flies!"

Håken and Lars laughed, and Lesbet turned sleepily on the bed.

"Well, you go ask him yourself," Lars snickered. He had heard the housekeeper say the captain intended to stay until tomorrow.

Hans, however, meant to take Captain Bauck home with him, since the master had come to the servants' wing after bedtime and had particularly asked him to get the captain. He had told him to take a heavy cloak with him, for he supposed the captain had lost his own during the Christmas parties; it was a fortnight yesterday since Bauck had left Alm.

Miss Nannestad came into the kitchen and after talking with Hans returned to the party in the drawing room with Mr. Orre's message. Hans's errand was greeted with uproarious laughter from the party, and this in turn was drowned out by a deep bass shouting: "Skaal, Bauck, our dear friend! The good tradesman is searching for his lost sheep." Then bursting into song, it continued:

> "unyielding fate carries him away
> with force from our bleeding breast. . . ."

"Gracious Miss Hebe Nannestad, how could your lovely lips really manage to convey such sad tidings! Skaal, Bauck, our friend! We drink to your memory when you are so cruelly robbed of our company—skaal, friend! And of course the fifty dalers you won are most willingly given to you by the parson. Isn't that so, your reverence?" The shrill voice of the parson could be heard, and then they all roared with laughter again.

"Sounds as though Wallace is let loose," Hans commented.

The door to the drawing room opened and a round-faced, fat little man in a captain's uniform appeared. "Hans, my boy—so there you are! How Leben sie at Alm? He must wait ein Bischen, ja? I say wait for me, I will soon be there!"

"I guess we ought to go, Captain, remember the horse will be cold."

"Ach, put him a cloth on! The animal shall stand doch eine halbe Stunde, he he, verstehe?" the captain objected, waving his hands.

"The horse will be all right," the councillor shouted from the other room and, turning to Miss Nannestad, said, "Make some punch for the men in the kitchen! Attorney, it's your turn. Come Bauck—the cards are waiting!"

The fat little fellow tapped Hans on the shoulder placatingly: "The horse will be all right, my boy," and he waddled hastily back to the card game. Captain Bauck's assignment to organize the home guard had been canceled when the war with Sweden was over. He had been quartered at Alm, and whether or not the authorities had forgotten about him on purpose, at any rate he stayed on, courted Aunt Birgitte, and regularly signed for his pay, which was forwarded to him in bank notes that were worth less and less because of inflation. But because of Mr. Orre's generous hospitality, this didn't cause the captain much trouble.

"What are they doing in there?" Hans asked. "Oh, playing cards—poker, I guess," grunted Lars. "They've been at it for three days now. They are all playing and drinking except Wallace, who just watches them and drinks."

Hans went out in the courtyard to take care of the horse, while the housekeeper brought out the glasses and punch pitcher and told them to help themselves. They filled their glasses, said skaal, and after the first drink, sat down with their glasses before them, Hans and Lars on the bench beside the fire and Håken on the chair where he had been sitting. He was given a new quid while the others took out their pipes.

"Is there any news from the south?" Lars asked. As a sort of host, he now felt he should keep the conversation going.

Yes, there was some: that farmer Åseth had been to the store in a great hurry; he had been on his way to Röros with flour. Hans told this very quietly.

"Oh, did he? Åseth didn't spend much time celebrating Christmas this year, eh?"

Spitting into the fire, Håken ventured, "He probably intended to go past Röros?"

Neither of the older men would answer this directly. Lars did ask: "You were at the Grundset market up there this spring, weren't you Håken?" Oh yes, sure, he had been there.

Had he by any chance taken any of those Swedish propaganda pamphlets or brought any of them home?

Håken flushed and felt uncomfortable. Well, he had picked some up just as everyone else did.

"Perhaps," Hans put in. "If, however, he were that man Åseth, he would know better than to carry on this business, for"—and he pointed to the drawing room—"if the men in there got wind of it, the rogue would certainly end up in jail."

"For sure, farmer Åseth is a smooth one," said Lars as

he put another log on the fire. "He knows to keep on good terms with the authorities and fool them at the same time."

Håken looked around him cautiously; he had heard people say there was gunpowder in the flour bags Åseth loaded on his sledges during the war.

Hans only smiled tolerantly.

"Perhaps," Lars mused, "Perhaps he manufactured powder in his cellar? Where else would he get gunpowder? No, my boy, it was just plain flour, but he got sugar and coffee and English yarn and other good things, obtained across the border, that he brought back with him. They were bought for cash by people from other districts."

"But, the devil dance!" Hans cursed. "He would never touch all of the money that Åseth made, even if it were bins full, if he had to promise to do what that man had promised to do for money. You know what I mean, Håken; you read that pamphlet you picked up."

"Well, after all, you know, it was a foreigner who distributed those pamphlets, not Åseth; he hardly stopped at the market place that time. But really, so many strange things are happening these days, with the authorities one has today."

"You mean when one is in the parson's service?" Lars looked at him fiercely.

"After all," Hans said, "Åseth does not always get all he wants for his money. It just depended on the person he was dealing with. Last week, for instance, when the farmer was in the store he had bought something but had not had enough bills, and he asked them to charge it. Oh, you should have seen Mr. Orre then. He became sweet as a lark and gentle as a girl and said, bowing: "Oh, my dear Mr. Åseth, credit is a very delicate matter. I must say I prefer to sell for cash, and besides, you know the value of the money is changing so rapidly!' 'Well, I thought you might trust me for that much,' answered Åseth angrily, 'but I promise I'll pay you in silver.' Then old Mr. Orre, who kept bowing and scraping and getting sweeter all the time, answered: 'Oh, I'm sure everyone trusts you; only I must ask you to pay for everything in Danish currency. In fact, you know I sell nothing for Swedish money.' I wish you could have seen Åseth storm out of that store as red as a rooster."

They all laughed hilariously and touched their glasses together with a clink.

"Old Orre, let me tell you, is a good old guy." Hans stretched his legs out in front of him and glanced over at Håken rather provocatively. "I wouldn't change my master for yours, Håken."

Håken changed the subject. Did they think the mirage that had been seen recently in the neighboring district of Hadeland was real? The parson's wife had read about it in the paper. They said they had seen the whole French army with banners, cannons and dragoons, and some even said they caught a glimpse of the Emperor himself.

Lars didn't doubt it at all; such strange things happened these days that no one wondered at mirages or miracles. These things were nearly always omens of something that was going to happen, perhaps a new war with the Swedes. There were those who had known before the last war what would happen, for he had talked with one who knew that spring that the English would attack Copenhagen in the fall.

Hans asked who it was.

It was an uncle of Lars, and he was a man who never told a lie. He had been in the mountains with a couple of horses, and since he was busy at the farm, he wanted to return that night. As he walked along in the darkness and drizzling rain, suddenly there was a rustling movement all over the moor and it seemed as though every little bush was alive. He stopped and tried to figure out what it was all about, and then he saw a whole army of little men in gray uniforms with silver buttons.

"What kind of weapons did they carry?" Håken asked.

"They had bows and arrows, no guns, and some had swords in their hands. He thought it safest to keep as far away as possible, so he hid behind a rock and stayed there until the army had passed. They didn't pay any attention to him, just marched on as quickly as they could.

"When they were well out of sight, and only the echo of their footsteps reverberated through the mountains, he got up and started home again, all the while wondering what kind of people they were and what they were up to. A little farther on he met a tiny man in a uniform that was so bright it glittered like gold, and he had feathers on his hat. This was the commander. He stopped and wanted to know if my uncle had seen his army. When my uncle said yes, the little man wanted to know if he had been frightened of them. 'But did they let you pass?'

" 'They didn't speak to me,' my uncle answered, feeling that he need not be afraid of such tiny folks.

" 'Well, you may not have been afraid of them, but you certainly shall be of me.' And with that the little man brandished his sword, and as he did so, he grew taller than the firs. My uncle started running madly. Finally, exhausted, he looked over his shoulder to see if the wretch was still following him, but there was no one there.

"My uncle didn't get home until next morning and went right to bed and stayed there for a week, he was so exhausted. When he told what had happened to him, lots of people said that it was a warning that the people of the netherworld had started war and were marching toward Sweden."

The others had dozed off while Lars told his story, so that when he stopped the kitchen was quiet. Hans yawned and napped off and on; Håken leaned back in his chair and breathed with long whistling noises. The fire was almost out; only the embers glimmered, and there was no other light in the kitchen.

Softly and stealthily the entry door opened. A man entered. The dog, which had not made a sound, followed him in, sniffing; but the man pushed him back gently with his foot and brushed the snow off his boots with his mittens.

Those at the fire felt a cold blast on their backs and looked up sleepily.

"Is someone there?" asked Lars as he put a couple of pine knots in the embers.

The stranger said good evening and came over to them. The others got a shock. A Lapp was out tonight! He was an average sized man in a yellowish-gray suede suit with shining pewter buttons. Like most Lapps he wore a long coat, breeches tied with vari-colored braid around the knees, the tassels dangling down over his high worn boots. He didn't bother to take off his low blue frieze cap which was made wide at the top and edged with a red cord. His plump, brownish face was shiny and beardless. Black tufts of hair hung over his forehead and covered his ears. The little eyes catching the reflection of the fire glittered watchfully.

"Good evening, all of you who are in this room," he said in a kind of sing-song voice. "Don't you usually ask travelers to come in and take a seat by the fire in wintertime?" He spoke with an accent, and they could hardly understand his Norwegian.

Lars muttered something that was meant to be a welcome and added that he brought bad weather. He moved a little bit, however, to give him room by the fire, but Lesbet, wakened by the noise, got up in her stocking feet and brought him a chair.

"Thank you very much. These are certainly bashful boys; here is a pretty young girl alone in bed and three fellows just sitting around." He pushed the chair away and sat down on the pile of firewood next to Lars. "It takes a good fire to make me thaw out," and with that he threw fresh logs on. "But for sure, a good drink will help too," and he reached for the pitcher of punch and emptied it. "Some good people are living here, to judge by the punch; I hope they're not too good to give a poor traveler a bed for the night."

"This is the residence of the judge of the district, Councillor Weydahl," Lars informed him. The judge was pretty strict with people like him, but he needn't know the Lapp was here if he would leave very early in the morning. "But you'd better speak to the Miss."

"Could be, could be: the judge and the sheriff have the thing fixéd between them. One makes the arrests, and the other convicts," and the Lapp smiled knowingly with his head cocked to one side.

The other men were wide awake now. They felt ill at ease and worried as to what he might do, but they didn't want him to know it. This kind of fellow was likely to revenge himself by all sorts of sly devilish tricks, even magic, even at a distance. An ordinary man had better not make him angry or it might be disastrous for the cattle as well as people.

Lars was furious about the punch; it was certainly too good for that Lapp's black throat, he thought, as he bit off a big quid of tobacco and sat toying with the rest. Quick as a flash the quick supple fingers of the Lapp had snatched it out of his hand, bitten off a quid and put the rest in his pocket. Lars cursed to himself; this was his last piece of tobacco. He looked at the Lapp out of the corner of his eye and met the thief's cunning, triumphant look. He let the incident pass in silence. The Lapp teased the other by saying meekly: "Blessed is he who gives to the poor out of his abundance."

As the door to the drawing room opened, the Lapp leaned back into the shadow of the hearth. Miss Nannestad came out and asked Håken to harness the horse. He was pale and groggy after his fitful napping by the fire.

At the sight of the stranger, she stopped suddenly: "Who is that?"

The Lapp, looking very humble, got up and in a whimpering voice said: "Just a poor traveler who asks for lodging for the night, honorable lady!"

Uncertainly she replied: "God help you if the councillor sees you; he isn't kind to people in clothes like yours. But there is a bed in the servants' kitchen; you may sleep there. Go now, and leave the first thing in the morning."

"Can't I stay here and get a little warm first?"

She looked toward the drawing room: "No, go right away; the councillor will be angry if he sees you here. Lars, please take him over there quickly. Please. I have to help them put their fur coats on. Hurry now! Do you hear?"

He came up to her whining softy. "Does the good lady send a poor traveler out of the room without letting him sit for even a moment by the fire?"

"I guess you're warm enough from our punch," Lars grunted; he had become brave now that the housekeeper was there. She meanwhile was on pins and needles. She knew quite well how bitterly the councillor disliked vagabonds, and she knew too that he was drunk and would come in to the kitchen any minute.

"Do as I tell you quickly! Get out of here, will you!"

The Lapp made a horrid face and bent over as though to kiss her hand: "Not so proud, not so proud, my dear young lady!"

She stepped back and stamping her foot cried, "Get away, you nasty fellow! Get out this minute, this very minute, or I will have you arrested. This is the judge's house and if he knew you were here he'd take care of you, believe me! There is a lot of difference between decent travelers and Lapp riff-raff like yourself."

His bright, evil eyes measured her from head to foot. Their wicked gleam seemed almost to swallow her up, and at last she saw nothing but his eyes. She turned white as a sheet and hid her face in her hands.

"He, he—you a miss but no virgin, you'll drive me out into the cold winter night, will you? You wait, just wait, you'll be colder than I am within a year. Decent people! Be decent yourself, you pregnant bitch!" She sank to the floor moaning. He leaned over her and hissed something in her ear.

Hans and Lars were going to jump on him, but the Lapp slipped away and was out of the kitchen before they could catch him. The dog barked loudly and then suddenly it gave a long miserable howl.

Miss Nannestad with Lesbet's help soon recovered her composure. The Lapp hadn't made much noise, but still she wondered if they had heard anything in the drawing room. Evidently not, for as she listened she could hear loud talking going on as before. The attorney was singing a ditty, and the parson was scolding the cards drunkenly.

"Harness the horses for the parson," she said to the men

who stood there amazed at her fainting spell and seemed already to have forgotten the Lapp. She returned to the drawing room, and Lesbet noticed she had swallowed her tears and was calm again.

After the parson and the captain left, Lars saw by the moonlight that there was something black lying in the snow. It was the dog—dead—killed by a stab in the neck.

Something strange happened to Håken on his way home. The parson slept during the short drive to the parsonage. Håken was driving along when suddenly a man jumped from behind a tree onto the sleigh and hung on to him for dear life. "Heigh ho! Now the Lapp and the devil are going to get a ride on the parson's sleigh," the man shouted in the driver's ear. Håken shook with fear, but the parson slept, dead drunk. The sleigh bells jingled merrily as the sledge flew over the road, and the snow spattered up from the horses' hoofs. The Lapp hung on until they passed the church and then, whispering to Håken that he intended to preach the sermon there tonight, he was gone.

The Sermon

IT was a Sunday morning and the parson, Mr. Lind, was on his way to the annex church. The road was rather steep and wound through a thicket of firs which were bent almost to the ground with snow. The parson held the reins and Håken, the driver, still very sleepy, sat on the back seat. They plodded slowly up and up until finally the sleigh reached the top of the hill where the forest ended. There on both sides were sloping meadows and broad fields. The snow-covered land gleamed and glittered in the morning sun. Only the tops of the rail fences and the blue shadows they cast were visible above the snow. Here and there one could see clumps of birches with rime-frosted branches. Hugging the gentle slopes of the hills were sturdy dark houses surrounded by big farm yards and cow-barns. From every chimney smoke spiraled softly into the calm air; against the pale, clear, frozen sky loomed the serrated ridges with their forests of firs. One could easily see that this region, the parish of the annex church was one of the richest parts of the district.

The parson looked straight ahead, for up the valley he noticed a sleigh moving slowly along, the faint tinkle of the sleigh bells drifting back to him. Now he could even see the back of the man in the sledge and recognized the cap he wore. It was Sheriff Krogsti. He cracked his whip urging his horse to catch up to him and the sleigh shot forward down the hill.

The sheriff reined in his horse to the right side of the road to let them pass, but the parson slackened his speed as he came abreast of him.

"Good morning, Sheriff! Are you too on your way to the annex church this morning?"

The sheriff turned half way around in his seat. Between the fur collar and the earflaps of the shaggy fur cap one could see his serious, weather-beaten face half hidden by big horn-rimmed spectacles.

"Good morning, Mr. Lind, Whoa! Whoa! Will you stop, horse! I am, but I'm sorry to say I don't intend to go to church. I am busy every day of the week, including Sundays. This time I am on my way to question some scoundrels farther north. Such people, as a rule, can be found at home on Sunday morning; they aren't likely to be found, I am afraid, among those who go to church. Ha, ha!"

"No one could be more conscientious than you, Sheriff; it is necessary, of course. Not long ago"—the parson took care not to say yesterday—"there was even such a fellow at the councillor's and he gave the maids a bad scare. I happened to be there that night, and, believe me or not, on my way home the scoundrel was bold enough to jump on the back of my sleigh. He certainly got off in a hurry; I hardly caught a glimpse of him. I guess he realized he had made a mistake —that it was not the sleigh of an ordinary farmer."

Håken didn't move a muscle as he listened to his own story of last night's events told by the parson in this way.

"I never heard of such a devilish thing! Hm-hm, I beg your pardon. This rabble is getting pretty bold, Mr. Lind, but I am not going to let them get away with it, as far as. . . ."

"I am sure you do your best, Sheriff. Am I late, by the way?" the parson interrupted.

"Just a minute, I'll take a look." The sheriff fumbled in

the pocket of his sheepskin for his watch, but before he managed to get it out, the other had cracked his whip, the horse set off at a full gallop, and the sheriff was left sitting alone staring after the sleigh. The sheriff put his watch back in his pocket, thoughtfully wiped a drip off his nose with the back of his mitten and said, smilingly, to himself: "The parson looked as though he hadn't left the councillor's until this morning."

The horse trotted on. Today the caretakers of justice need not hurry, for at the moment the villains were asleep; they never sinned on Sundays.

Close to the church was the house of the parish clerk where the parson always stayed when he held services at the annex. In the kitchen the clerk's wife sold coffee to the parishioners for two pennies a cup. The business had not paid lately, for fewer and fewer went to church. The parson was accustomed to put on his robe in the parlor because it was too cold in the church, and here he could also meet with those who might want to speak to him about their problems before the sermon started.

At the church every farm of any size had its own stall where the farmer could leave his carriage or sleigh during the sermon. The stables were simple wooden sheds built in rows and open on the side facing the church. Today there were not many present for the service, since only half a dozen horses were in the shed.

The bell had already rung for the first time when the parson arrived. The fat little parish clerk, Mr. Hågensen, was waiting for him in the doorway. He quickly snatched the suitcase containing the robe and collar from Håken, the driver, and respectfully followed his superior into the parlor. The room was small and stiflingly hot from the glowing stove. Even though the sleigh ride had helped to refresh him, the parson was feeling very unwell after a week of carousing and the pungent smell of the coffee brought him by the clerk's wife made him feel sick and faint.

"No thanks. . . ." He didn't really want any. Was there no one waiting for him? Well, he really didn't expect there was any urgent business. Now, if Mr. Hågensen would help him to dress?

The clerk timidly reminded him of the eleven people who had said they wished to have communion today.

Communion? Was communion to be held today? He certainly had not remembered. He supposed there was neither wine nor bread. "Will you please look in the traveling bag and see if Gine had by chance remembered. . . . No? Then, that's that!" The parson threw on his robe angrily.

Did the clerk happen to have some wine in the house? No, of course not. Couldn't communion be postponed to the next Sunday they had services?

Mr. Hågensen begged him to remember that there were some parishioners from far away—miles away, in fact.

"What the. . . ." The parson thought uneasily of the gossipy curate and the coming visit of the bishop. There would be enough silly talk and sufficient misunderstanding and inconvenient explanations without this. If he could only figure out some way or other—perhaps Mr. Hågensen could think of something?

The clerk blew his nose self-consciously. If the parson approved, no one would ever notice the difference between his wife's red currant juice and the communion wine.

Mr. Lind thought for a minute. . . . This was certainly running a risk. On the other hand, necessity knows no law.

"You see, Mr. Hågensen, the Lord's supper is not rigidly

prescribed and the kind of wine is not specifically stated in the Scriptures. The unleavened bread on the other hand. . . .?"

"With your permission, Sir, there is no leaven in the so-called flat bread, and it might be broken into small pieces."

As the problem seemed to have been solved, a picture of the last evening's party flashed through the tired, confused mind of the parson. He tittered nervously, "Well then, my dear Hågensen, we are not finessed! But, of course," and he took the clerk's arm familiarly, "we enlightened people can talk this kind of thing over privately, but it wouldn't do to tell it to the common people. It would just create unnecessary annoyance among the simple-minded. Besides, on my honor, there is nothing wrong in it. You just bring what is necessary."

The clerk blew his nose again and hurried away to get a bottle of his wife's currant juice and a piece of flatbread. Meanwhile the parson finished buttoning up his robe.

"It is perfectly all right. Let me taste it just to be sure . . . it is rather sour; you might put some powdered sugar in it. Please be so kind as to give me a hand with this collar. Thank you! Good, you bring what we need to the church, I trust your discretion. . . ."

The church bells rang out over the sparkling white, Sunday-quiet landscape, as the parson crossed the yard to the house of God. They were silent for just a little while, then they began tolling again to gather the people of the district. The little group of parishioners waiting for the bells to stop ringing now moved toward the church and went in.

As he mounted to the pulpit, Mr. Lind suddenly felt the drop of juice he had tasted. It burned his throat and tasted disgustingly sour. His hands were damp, yes, really wet, and he felt the most irritating itching in his finger tips. The sparse gray hair was flattened to his skull with sweat, and there were unaccustomed red spots on his hollow cheeks.

It seemed to him as though the dirty stone walls of the church moved, and when he looked down at the fifty or so people in the congregation, locked in their family pews like their horses stabled outside, he felt as though he would faint. He decided he had gone rather far last night at the councillor's.

At last he wet his lips with the tip of his tongue and, in a low, quivering voice, read the gospel of the day. It was about Jesus as a child teaching in the Temple. On the spur of the moment, he couldn't think of a thing to say about the text, just rambled along about the self-satisfied and learned pharisees versus this child's simplicity. He stopped and coughed and forgot what he was saying, but he knew he had to continue talking for some minutes.

With a great effort he pulled himself together and suddenly he recalled his ordination sermon in Copenhagen many many years ago, and before he knew it, he started repeating that one in a loud, serious voice. Its subject was the importance of the ministry.

The congregation was startled; they were not used to hearing the parson express himself so fluently. They listened to him with deep attention while he discussed the duties and responsibilities of the pastor, his need to enrich the life of his parish by developing the heart as well as the reason.

At this point Mr. Lind lost the thread of his sermon and suddenly stopped. Jörn Mæhlum, the rich farmer to whom he had owed the price of six barrels of barley for the last three years, was sitting close to the pulpit and seemed to be laughing. Yes, it was three years ago now since he had lost his entire barley crop to Mr. Korslund, the tradesman from across the lake, at a game of cards. The concluding prayer was murmured almost unintelligibly. His mouth was dry and parched and he felt miserable and faint as he left the pulpit.

The chalice shook in his hand as he served communion, and the loud discordant singing tortured him. Of course, it was partly his own fault. The clerk struck up the music for words according to the Evangelical-Lutheran psalm book that he himself had introduced into the parish:

> Jesus' word has made me able
> to meet him at his supper table.
> Here I am, remembering thee,
> As you are remembering me.

In a pew all by themselves, however, were two very deaf old maids from the farthermost part of the district. They had brought their large old-fashioned leather-bound psalm book by Kingo with them and had just found the psalm they knew the late parson, Mr. Adler, always used for communion:

> To the holy supper in His name
> I now intend to go
> for my soul's comfort today to gain,
> to have an end to sin and pain.
> But oh, I know
> I am loath to go
> Deep into sin and misery
> that make my life in vain.

The verses of their song were longer than the others and they paused a little before each new one, while the parish clerk hurried tirelessly through his, so when he was at the fifth verse, the two old maids were just starting in a loud voice on their third and last stanza. Finally they finished, yet, noticing that those around them still held their books in front of them and that their lips were moving, they thought for awhile, then started all over again, so after the others had long since stopped singing, the two old maids repeated:

But oh, I know
I am loath to go
Deep into sin and misery
that make my life in vain.

After the service the parson sat alone in the vestry. He was exhausted after the exertions of the morning. His heart pounded and mists seemed to pass in front of his eyes; his body trembled and shook, and there was a constant ringing in his ears. Before him on the table was the half empty bottle of currant juice and the communion chalice in which there was still a drop left. With shaking hands he poured it out, dried the holy cup on his robe and, filling it again with juice from the bottle, drank it down with great gulps. The cold, sour drink steadied him for a few minutes. It made his stomach rumble and left a disgusting taste in his mouth. He was afraid he was going to be sick. It certainly didn't agree with him.

Just then the clerk came in and asked the parson if he was ready for dinner.

"Thank you very much, Mr. Hågensen, and please remember me to your wife, but I don't want anything to eat. I am going home right away, for I am afraid I caught a cold in my stomach driving over here this morning. Listen, Mr. Hågensen, would it be possible to get me a small glass of brandy?"

Oh, no trouble at all, if his own homemade corn brandy would do. So the parson hurriedly followed the clerk out of the church. Those still standing in the churchyard took off their caps and the two as they passed nodded silently to their greeting.

Miss Nannestad

SPRING came suddenly and with it the usual hectic preparations for the plowing season.

Snow still covered the fields and meadows of the councillor's farm even though the slopes bordering the lake were sun-baked. The earth under the maple trees was half frozen ice and mud with rivulets trickling down from the hills. By the sides of the road, however, last season's brown grass was already visible where the snow had melted. Between the stony shore and the thin melting ice of the lake was a widening strip of blue water on which ducks, looking like little black spots, were swimming.

Behind the cow-barn the councillor stood watching the farm hands cart the dung out. He had wrapped a scarf around his neck and pulled the brim of his hat down low to protect himself from the chilly wind that made the twigs and the straw fly about. The rest of his body, which lately had become a little too heavy for his legs, was enveloped in a coat of homespun which reached to his boot tops. These days the councillor was accustomed to lean on a silver-headed cane when he walked.

He was cross and upset. That damned Swede, Palmström, whom for very good reasons he had put up with and endured for a long time, now had done the incredibly stupid trick of stealing some fine linen from Major Brager's wife. It couldn't be any one but Palmström. The very impudence of the theft pointed to his brazen shamelessness. And besides he had been noticed poking his nose into things around the major's farm at Emilienberg, and at night of all times. He was beginning to be a little too smart. It looked as though the old bird was going to get caught this time, especially since the sheriff had not hesitated to express his suspicion of Palmström openly.

The boys who were busy shoveling the dung out of the cellar of the gloomy old brick cow-barn caught an occasional quick glimpse of the judge. He certainly did look cross, so they tried to do their best. One sledge after another came up the hill from the fields, backed up against the doors of the cellar, was loaded with manure and went down to the meadows again. The runners scraped and squeaked over the half-frozen ground.

"Whoa you—will you whoa!" A redheaded, overgrown youngster, whose voice was just changing, was shouting at his strapping young horse which wouldn't back up to the cellar doors. "Hey you—come, come!" The young boy was pretty rough with the curb bit.

"Don't you know how to drive, Jens?" the councillor reprimanded him. "You have to handle the horse properly."

"This horse is a devil," the boy answered quickly. "He is so hard-mouthed that—" and he pulled the bridle too roughly again. The horse reared, the dirty brown slush spattered around, and the horse's hind leg got out of the shafts.

"Get over here—hurry, get the horse over here," thundered the councillor.

The boy obeyed sullenly.

"Why, you sloven, you've even harnessed the horse wrong!" the councillor scolded and slapped the boy angrily on the back with his walking stick.

"Look at the hame—it is crooked, do you want to break the horse's back? Unharness him right away!"

Jens just loosened and lifted the hame a little. "This harness is a damned wreck," he grumbled.

"I said, unharness that horse!" The boy obeyed reluctantly, taking his time. The councillor was boiling mad. With one hand he grabbed the bridle of the horse and with the other he caught the boy by the nape of the neck and shook him. The boy, swinging to and fro helplessly, screamed with pain and terror: "Au!—ah, ah!"

"This will be a lesson to you—to treat a poor dumb animal as you have!" And with that the councillor forced the bit into Jens' mouth, twisted the reins around his hand and pulled, all the while thumping the boy on the back with the knob of his stick. "This will teach you! Do you think this is any better treatment for the horse than for you, you young devil?"

He loosened his grip and the boy staggered back half strangled and whimpering. When he pulled himself together sobbing, he sneaked off wiping the blood from the corners of his mouth.

The men in the cellar, who had stopped working, now made a great show of being busy and those drivers who had watched from halfway down the hill hurriedly resumed their work.

The councillor patted the horse which was heaving and shiny with sweat. "They bullied you, didn't they, Blakken? There, there!"

The dinner bell clanged. "Hey Mathias—you!" he called. "Stable this horse and be sure it's treated very well, will you?"

The dinner bells on the other farms joined in; they were

wont to sound off right after Judge Weydahl's. The sound carried far and wide.

After dinner the councillor went out again to supervise the cleaning out of the dung cellars. He was always very careful about the treatment of the manure because he considered it the single most important item in the whole area of agriculture, in the catechism of farming, as he used to say. He felt better now. Perhaps he could figure out a way to let Palmström off easily. The trials were likely to be inconvenient for quite a few people—but after this the old rogue had better be very careful.

The weather had changed, and the wind blew biting cold. The shadows of the maple trees were now long and blue on the snow. By the few rays of light that slanted in through the doors of the dung-cellar, the councillor standing outside could keep an eye on Jens who was pitching the dung out of the barn onto the carts. He was not to be allowed to handle a horse for some time. The young rascal needed a good lesson once in a while if he was ever to grow up to be a real man.

Suddenly Jens dropped his pitchfork and began pushing the dung aside with the toe of his boot. "Look what I've found!" he shouted excitedly.

"What is it, my boy?" asked the councillor.

"It can't be a calf—I think . . . oh no, it couldn't be—yes, I guess it is—the body of a baby—"

"The body of a child?" The councillor splashed through the muddy puddles and peered in through the low door. The two men who were inside with the boy went over to him and carefully picked up the thing which showed white and shiny in the dim light. They carried it outside. It was the corpse of a child.

They laid it on the snow and then wiped it off with a grain

bag which Jens had fetched. The men stood looking at it in silence. It was the corpse of a newborn babe; there wasn't any doubt about that and the blue mark around its neck was evidence enough as to how it had died.

As one of the sledge drivers came up the hill, the councillor cleared his throat and said: "We'll have to look into this. Take it into the coach house and lock the door!" He turned and walked away. There was a strange expression on his face, and his teeth were tightly clenched.

The men with the corpse wrapped in the bag followed him. Jens trailed along behind with a malicious smile on his face.

There had to be an inquest which meant an examination. In the big kitchen at the councillor's, all the women of the household and cottages, ten or twelve in all, had been gathered together. They knew why they were there, and some of the young girls were bashful and frightened for fear someone would think them guilty. The older ones seemed less nervous: they could not possibly be suspected owing to their age!

The councillor, silent and gloomy, sat at the head of the table. He had asked Miss Nannestad to assist him in the examination, so she went from one woman to another, opened their dresses and examined their breasts to see if there was milk in them. She was very, very pale and went about her task without saying a word. The councillor watched closely as she went from one to the other.

A kettle of coffee hanging over the open fire on the hearth had been forgotten and boiled over, running steaming and whistling down into the glowing embers. A shriveled old farm woman, who couldn't bear to see good coffee wasted, ran over to the fire, and lifting the pot off, said it would be a shame to have it wasted. Her words cut the silence like a knife, but no one paid the slightest attention.

Now it was her turn. She laughed, her toothless gums showing, "Ha, ha, Miss, are you even going to examine me? He, he," and she tried to move away, but the councillor made an impatient motion, whereupon she herself unhooked her dress, but she was furious and ashamed.

The ordeal was ended and the culprit not discovered. The councillor gave a sign for them all to go. Then, quick as a flash, the old woman rushed up to Miss Nannestad. "If all of us have to go through this, she has got to be examined too," and grabbing at Julie's bodice with her claw-like fingers, she tore it open.

Julie Nannestad screamed, reeled and fell backward against the table. Her shift was wet in front under her breasts.

"There you are, you pig!" the old farm woman shouted hoarsely—

The strange rigid look swept over the face of the councillor again. He took Julie by the hand and led her through the dining room, where the table was still covered with their dinner dishes, and on into her room. It was the same bedroom that she and her mother had shared while they took care of the house before the new judge had arrived—the man who had been the greatest and strongest man in her whole life.

She threw herself on the bed. The councillor went to the window and stood there gazing out over the lake.

Behind the mountains on the other side the sunset was a flaming fire. The shadows cast by the ridges spread darkness over the ice, but the open water along the shore was dyed blood-red. The bedroom was aflame with the fiery radiance of the setting sun.

"Weydahl—help me! Help me, Weydahl!" Then she sat up and stared at him silent but terror-stricken.

"I shall have to send for the sheriff. I can't help you much now."

"Oh, help me—help me!" she begged over and over again, and buried her head in the pillows.

"I will do what I can, but I am afraid it can't be much.—Julie, you should have told me this before—before, then I might have been able to help you."

"But I did tell you, councillor," she whispered.

He remembered then. She had said something about her condition one night when she had been sad and dreary. And yes, now he remembered the deep, lead-gray circles under her eyes.—"You only mentioned it once, and I thought perhaps you were mistaken, since you—"

Sobbing, she lifted her head and stared at him bewildered, and he opened the window quickly as though he wanted some fresh air.

All this time he had been standing with his back toward her, unwilling to meet her eyes. Now he turned and looked at her gravely. "I shall have to send for the sheriff, but—" his voice sounded vague. "I don't need to have anyone watching you tonight. I will lock the door, I guess you would rather be alone—I shall have to send for the sheriff tomorrow morning. It's too late tonight."

He closed the window and stood fumbling for a long time with one of the locks, because his hand trembled so. She buried her head deeper in the pillows as she heard him go out and lock the door. Motionless she lay there while the last rays of the sunset and twilight in turn skulked into the bedroom.

The neighbors waited in vain for the councillor's supper

bell to ring that night. It hung silent. Finally one of them dared to ring his own, but it sounded unsteady and hesitant. The others waited a little longer; then they too started ringing.

That night supper was about an hour late in the entire district.

The night was black for there was no moon. In the morning there was a light drizzle falling on the lake, the fields and the forests. The maple trees stretched their naked branches into the veil of gray mist. The window in Miss Nannestad's bedroom stood wide open. Julie had run away. They searched for her, and in the shallow open water off the shore, found her. They all understood that her relentless will had not deserted her in this last struggle.

Famine

I

THE wild joy of skylarks singing filled the air. It crowded the heavens and came floating down in a shower of cheerful sounds from the clear blue skies. Even though it was rather early, the morning heat had already spread its hazy veil, dimming the bright colors of the midsummer day. The western ridges, turned a dark violet in the sun, were reflected in the shimmering green water of the lake. This was the kind of weather which forced crops to grow in the fields and meadows. In many places, however, the fields lay fallow with only a crop of weeds on them trying in vain by their bold show of flowers to hide the rich black soil. Where the fields had been planted, the seed had come up sparsely in small strips with large, barren spots between. Apparently the people had had very little seed this spring.

Palmström and Mr. Nyeberg, the organ player, were standing in the shadow of the church wall. They were talking to Lars, the gravedigger, who was smoothing the bottom of a newly dug grave. Mr. Nyeberg had become very thin, and his hump jutted sharply out between his shoulder blades. His pale face was listless and dull and he seemed to be chilly in spite of the fact that it was a very hot day.

"Piping hot today," Palmström said.

Lars heaved his shovel full of gravel onto the edge of the grave, pulled himself up panting heavily and took his hat off his old bald head. He had scarcely any eyelashes, so his weak eyes, afraid of the light, hid under drooping eyelids. His nose was flat and small, and a pattern of fine blue-red veins branched out from its tip all over his plump cheeks; a long white mustache covered his mouth.

"Only the devil knows why people are so busy dying in the summertime," he said. "It makes a lot of trouble for those of us who have to get them into the earth. My son and and I have nearly killed ourselves in this heat."

Nyeberg tried hard to smile: "Maybe you know what those people are going to live on who do not die this summer. At any rate, Lars, you make money." He looked around the churchyard; there were many mounds of fresh earth, and six black holes yawned silently, graves still empty.

Yes, he made money all right. The trouble was that the people from whom he made it were in such a damned hurry.

"This, I guess, is what the parson thinks," said Palmström. "They are in too much of a hurry, so he delays the funeral ceremony until he can bury a lot of them at one time."

"Well, he did twenty last Thursday," the gravedigger told them and started working again. The two sat down on a gravestone and talked quietly. They were going to call on Mr. Lind, the parson, and ask him if Mr. Nyeberg could have some help from the parish grain storage. This store of grain was usually controlled by the parson of a district for use in emergencies. The gravedigger continued digging and scraping down in the grave and throwing the dirt and gravel up on the sides. He soon stopped again, however, and they heard the familiar gurgle of liquid from a bottle being drunk by the man down in the hole.

Nyeberg sighed, "Quite a lot of brandy for the diggers and bell-ringers these days," he said loudly.

Lars stuck his head over the edge of the grave again:

"Still, there are plenty of those who ask me to ring the bells who have no brandy. They can't afford it, so they say."

Nyeberg wondered greedily if the brandy he had down there was any good.

The gravedigger disappeared for a little while. Then popping up again he asked: "Would the organist care for a little drink?"

"Thanks a lot!" Nyeberg grasped the bottle offered to him, leaned back and took a long swig. "Wait!" Palmström shouted.

"Does the Swede want some, too?" Lars asked.

The organ player took the bottle from his mouth; there was something in the bottom that rattled, he shook it: "What's in there?"

The digger's eyes became just slits. "Help yourself, Swede, if you want some—"

"What's in the bottle?" Palmström held it up to the light with some misgivings.

"Oh, that little thing isn't at all dangerous. Just a splinter of bone put in the brandy to ward off sickness." Frankly he thought Nyeberg really needed it.

The organ player, when he heard this, half fainted as he sank down on the stone again. He could hardly breathe, and cold sweat stood out on his forehead. "You blasted brute!" he scolded. Palmström gave a big laugh: "Damn you, I don't want your brandy; that's for sure, even if it is my last chance to ever taste some!" The digger with a dry cackle resumed his digging.

A little boy came running through the churchyard gate shouting: "Grandpa! Grandpa! There's someone here from Nerlien farm, and the funeral procession is already passing the councillor-farm." A stoop-shouldered man in his Sunday suit with his jacket over his arm was with the boy.

Lars pulled himself out of the grave. "Well, they'll be here any minute, then."

"Who is dead up at Nerlien?" Palmström asked. The man answered that it was oldest son and the daughter.

"Oh, no! Really! Two of the children at once? That's too bad. I guess this must be a terrible blow to old Gudbrand," Palmström said compassionately. "Nyeberg, we had better hurry to see the parson, he will probably have the funeral immediately, since these people are rich farmers."

The gravedigger went over to the church door, put a large odd-looking key in the keyhole and turned it. The lock made a rasping sound and the hinges squeaked as he flung open the heavy iron doors. The stranger, close behind him, curiously peered into the large gloomy nave. Carved wood galleries prevented most of the light that came from the small windows in the massive walls to come through to the nave, and big pillars cast long shadows.

They climbed the circular stairway to the bell tower. The rickety old steps were worn completely smooth, and the men held tightly to the stout rope that hung down the center in place of a railing. The old man, familiar with the stairs, went up quickly but the stranger from Nerlien had to watch his every step. At the top they crept along the low loft, bent almost double; then coming to a ladder they climbed cautiously as it creaked under their weight. At length they came to a tower room at the top of the church, and here the bells hung.

Here, too, it was dark and gloomy, but when Lars flung open the shutters the daylight streamed in bright and hot. Far below them lay peaceful farmlands in the sunny summer day, large farms and wide tilled fields where the haymakers were already busy. One could see the Swede and the organ player, almost like toys, walking through the parson's farmyard. To the east stretched mile after mile of forest, with the lake becoming a deeper green as it narrowed to a thin ribbon northward, but turning rather bluish and broader to the south; to the west dark ridges blotted out the view.

The man from Nerlien put down his coat and, taking a glass and bottle from his pocket, offered Lars a glass of brandy; then he too emptied one. Would they have another drink now? They quickly agreed and then threw the bottle in a corner where there was already quite a heap of broken glass and brandy bottles.

"Are there any others to be buried today?" the man asked.

"Seven today, but three were cottage people," Lars answered. He could already see the carriages from Nerlien coming.

They seized the ropes and pulled; at first the bell just moved, swinging; then it boomed and rang deafeningly in the little tower room; chiming and ringing their sound floated far, far away through the window openings.

The bell tolled and rang, tolled and rang—not much rest for it that day—it kept on ringing as one after another of the funeral processions went into the church, until the seventh and last for that day had made his last journey. One after another of the families of the dead came up to Lars in the bell tower to help toll the bell, and even those from the cottages brought him brandy for this service. Lars survived these gifts because, ever since he was a young man, he had been doing this, and so he was pretty well used to the digger's brandy. It didn't seem to bother him at all; still, there had never been as many funerals as there were these days. At night his son had to help him down from the tower, as he didn't trust his father to get down those steps alone. And still the bell chimed and tolled. Its powerful voice sounded all over the land: Hunger makes the stomach empty, and sickness blows—Norway starves! Every church bell in every parish told the same story that summer. There were some districts in which they had been through six such summers, but in these parts it was the first year of real famine.

Up to now they had managed one way or another, and they had even, for a time, been very well off, indeed. Extra crops had been sold to good advantage and never before had the farmers been as keen and less open to bartering in the markets as when the war blocked the import of grain from Denmark, and they could fix their own prices, free of Danish competition.

When the crops were scarce they kept on selling for money was hard to resist. Most of the farmers were accustomed to keep one year's crop in their corn bins; but gradually the stabburs were emptied and people did not save enough. Every spring there was less seed to plant; farmers now got high prices for their grain, and they just trusted hopefully that they might increase next year's crop or, better still, that the war would not last forever.

Magistrate Winterfeldt made every parson responsible for establishing a grain storage by voluntary contributions from the parishioners, but it was useless. In some places the farmers were very resentful; they wouldn't dance to the tune of the magistrates and parsons, at least more than was required by law, and they could hardly be expected to have grain for sale when they didn't grow enough for themselves. Besides, the cottagers and poor people who were starving always asked the nearest well-to-do farmer for help, and they were never refused.

In some places people joined together and were willing to contribute voluntarily to a common grain reserve, if they were allowed to cut timber in the King's forest, but refused to give away corn otherwise. In one district they said they would make a bargain with the authorities: they were willing to build a grain storage and fill it, if they were given the right to distill their own brandy—enough for their households. The parsons threw up their arms,—and reported to the authorities their efforts had been futile.

The spring of 1812 came around. By the time the fields were planted the grain bins were completely empty. In a few places perhaps, there were a couple of barrels kept in case of emergency, until the year's crop could be brought to the mills.

It was a rainy summer so there was little hay, but the farmers consoled themselves with the prospects of a good crop of rye; it looked really fine and promising. But one night in mid-August a fog covered the region. To those uphill it looked as though the lake had turned into an immense ocean, washing over the undulating fields, so that only the hills rose above it like islands. Just after midnight the fog suddenly rose and disappeared and there was a clear sky. At sunrise next morning steam rose from the lake, and now came frost.

When people started their daily work in the early morning, they were greeted by damp, icy cold air and noticed that the land was white with the first frost of the season. They hurried to the fields, breaking off spikes of grain here and there to examine them thoroughly. When they pinched the seed, a tiny shiny drop came out. They knew what it meant and pinched other spikes; the frost had touched each one. The day became hotter, but people continued to walk up and down their fields examining the grain. The night had not spared even a tiny piece of land.

The crop was badly damaged, but that wasn't all. Rain

followed the cold, so that the grain didn't dry out, and at last snow came, and the rye was still in the fields unharvested.

By this time some people started to look for the small books and pamphlets which had been distributed to the common people by some of their concerned and worried fellow citizens. These books had been laughed at and thrown away without a glance, even though they contained valuable information on how to use damaged food and how to prepare herbs and roots when grain was scarce. People who knew how to do such things were not too badly off. In the past they had added to the flour to make it go farther, but now such methods would not suffice.

Threshing that year was done more carefully than ever before. In the barns desperate hands and arms turned the crank that hammered the rod up and down, as if they hoped to bring food out of this mouldy, half rotted straw.

One night, just before Christmas, Matjas, one of the councillor's cottagers, very carefully swept together on the barn floor the grain crop he had raised on his cottage farm. He swept it up carefully with a broom and took the chaff as well as the grain. Then, just to be sure there was nothing left, he lit a torch and looked around. It was a paper bag full. He lifted and weighed it with one hand and then, carrying it out to the farmyard, gazed thoughtfully up to the sky: "Dear Lord in Heaven," he said, "as long as you have taken all the rest you might as well have this little bagful also!" And with that he threw the bag up in the air so that its contents were completely scattered to the winds. Then he went into the kitchen and asked his wife to make old-fashioned cream porridge with their last bit of flour.

Of course, Matjas, who worked for the councillor, would hardly starve to death. At the councillor's everyone was helped whether he belonged to the household staff or not. Naturally the upper classes and the big farmers able to do so helped people in their neighborhood. But at some places one could get help no matter where he came from, and no one ever asked for help in vain from either the councillor or Hans Dahlbye.

For a long time Mr. Dahlbye lived as he always had, and many wondered where the man got all the things he gave away and wasted, but at Eastertime it was rumored that he had gone to town and sold his family silver for rye and that he was killing his cattle just for meat. It seemed as though disaster just egged Hans Dahlbye on to lavish recklessness for which he certainly was not thanked. No one seemed to feel any gratitude towards those who didn't value their own charity.

At the councillor's things were managed differently. All through the winter there had been lots of activity in the kitchen. At first one only found cottagers and widows and children and cripples there; especially at twilight they sat in a row along the kitchen walls with their small bags and tin pails hidden under the chairs and benches. Everyone got grain according to his circumstances and number to support. No one got very much but enough to feed them for a short time if they added some ground bark, reindeer moss and other things to it. After a while others joined the group, people of some means who had certainly never considered themselves poor, but their silver dalers were of no use to them these days, since grain could not be bought at any price. It came to the point where even rich farmers put their knapsacks on their backs and walked over to their neighbors to borrow some flour for a dish of porridge or a loaf of bread. But the neighbor, more often than not, was in exactly the same position, so he slunk shame-faced down to the councillor or to someone else whom he normally would never have thought of borrowing from, and asked for assistance; not for himself, mind you, but for those at home who were waiting for him.

What Judge Weydahl gave directly did not perhaps reach very many, but he had devised different ways and means of helping. He had persuaded some men to make the long trip right up to the faraway valley of Romsdal to buy fish. He talked others who had some money into joining with country tradesman Orre and himself in buying grain through Mr. Orre's connections in Christiania and in the south. This was brought in as soon as the roads were passable and distributed to those who needed it most. But it wasn't free. Those who had farm land had to pledge to pay it back in kind. Now when these transports stopped for the night the loads had to be watched carefully for there were plenty of people up to tricks with the grain bags. For a barrel of rye a man could be robbed on the road, and for a half bushel of barley a burglar would break into a grain bin.

Those who suffered most were the increasing number of vagabonds, gypsies, and tramps and those who had taken to the roads for lack of food. Some of them lost their lives in the snow drifts. These were in a way luckier perhaps than their companions who dragged themselves along hunting for something to eat. Before the famine, beggars had been fairly safe at the farms, even though there had always been warnings that it was against the law to feed and house tramps without reporting it to the authorities. But now, no one minded catching them and bringing them to the local authorities. The farmer now acted towards the beggar as a dog gnawing its bone acts toward another that looks as though he might snatch it. The sheriffs complained of their great number of prisoners for they could neither house nor feed them. Then the government had a bright new idea. It exchanged the prisoners' ration into a certain amount of maintenance in cash; thus the authorities rid themselves of their problem and left it to the person himself to do the rest. However, one couldn't cook or bake with banknotes or copper coins. All too often those who were jailed were confused or insane boys who roamed about forsaken by their parents.

During this dark cold winter when misery and want were rampant, the plague came to the district. For a long time it had been sneaking about up in the mountain valleys, especially to the east near the Swedish border, where it was said to have been left behind by the army in 1808 and 1809. At first there was a frightful mortality among the children. The food seemed to cause a flux that weakened and tormented them to death. Dr. Müller talked quite a lot about "unhealthful food substitutes." Later a contagious disease which only the adults seemed to catch swept from one farm to another, leaving its dead, so there were no parties or Christmas festivities anywhere this year. Even in the homes of the very rich, where hunger was not known and scarcity had barely put its foot in the door, the big rooms were all silent, and the women of the house walked quietly and in stocking feet, for disease and death were not to be locked out.

Yet everyone of good family had to be buried properly, and those who survived would never dream of disgracing the dead by scrimping on his funeral. Even those who were extremely poor gathered together what they could to provide for a proper funeral feast for their relatives. "Thanks, I am quite well," said one man when he was asked about his health. "You see, I was invited to three funeral feasts this week."

As if all this misery and grief were not enough, a plague struck the cattle, causing horses to die in the stables and cows in the cow-barns.

When the days became a little lighter the children ran out in the melting snow and gathered the willow buds off the trees, not only because they were sweet and tasted good, but because they helped to fill their stomachs. Conditions for plowing and planting were rather bad, however. Everywhere horses and hands, as well as grain and seed, were needed. Yet everyone worked to the best of his ability; so did the authorities, and now grain storage houses were being built. With the coming of spring, courage came also, and somehow or other the necessary work was done. The hoped-for weather conditions came, so they could look forward to the best possible yield of the scanty seed they had been able to set aside for sowing. Strangers coming to the district realized how dreadful the suffering had been even up here. They thought that things would have been better here than in other districts. Sensible people knew that it would take a very long time, indeed, for this region to regain its former wealth.

To stave off hunger while the grain grew and ripened was pretty difficult. Nor would disease and death release their hold on the people or leave the farms, so the church bells tolled and chimed all through the summer: Hunger hollows and sickness blows—famine in Norway!

II

The grain storage house was located in that part of the district where those people lived who might need it most. It was just an ordinary barn that had been repaired and made watertight. There had been quite a little celebration when it was opened, and those present became emotional when the parson, Mr. Lind, at the first distribution had talked about the mercy of God, the zeal of the authorities, and their wise and thoughtful King.

Nothing further happened at the storage barn; no more grain was distributed, in spite of the announcement that another distribution would take place a fortnight after the first one. As a matter of fact, the magazine was situated near the parish chapel, and this had caused a disagreement between the parson and his curate as to which one controlled it.

Certainly the curate would not give one little bit of his rights to his superior, so each of the two clergymen put his lock on the door and both complained of the other to Magistrate Winterfeldt, who was of the opinion that this was a matter of principle and should be considered carefully. The settlement should be postponed until all statements were taken on both sides and a survey conducted to see how such things were handled in other districts where the same circumstances existed. Consequently the distribution of grain was stopped temporarily.

Mr. Lind told all of this to Palmström and the organ player when they asked him for grain. He was so angry that his white hair seemed to stand on end as he hissed and whined in his annoyance. Not half a barrel, no, not a quart of rye could he give out. There wasn't any possibility of such a thing until this jealous curate, this pharisaical Mr. Vamberg, was severely reprimanded and forced to stop his insubordination to his superior and cease creating dissension in the parish. They could certainly take it from him and tell anyone they chose. Of course, it wasn't necessary to repeat his exact words; he had been straightforward and candid to the organ player since he was a man associated with the church, and he relied on his discretion. The parson evidently felt some qualms about the whole business, because the curate in his wickedness sometimes appealed to the bishop about these matters under dispute, which were sometimes nothing more than distortions of his own frankness.

Mr. Nyeberg was crushed by the refusal of grain. His wife was ill, and they had a child to feed and no food in the house, since they had planted their little piece of land with their last bit of grain and trusted that somehow they would get by until harvest time. The little hunchback became more despondent and weak with every step on their way home from the parson's. Palmström felt very sorry for him as they parted. He was quite used to seeing what happened to such hungry fellows these days.

The Swede strolled along by himself for awhile. Then he threw himself on the grass by the side of the road to think. He breathed on his tattooed hand and rubbed it against his waistcoat to polish the strange colored lines. He looked, as he lay there propped against a stone with his hat pulled down over his eyes, as though he were asleep, but he was wide awake and completely absorbed in his thoughts. From under the brim of his hat he looked absent-mindedly at the other side of the dusty road over which the slanting pole fence made a network of shadowy stripes. Uphill he noticed a field of half-ripened rye like a border against an approaching mass of lead-gray thunderclouds. In the forest behind him a thrush chattered and trilled, and a woodpecker drummed unceasingly on the hollow trunk of a tree. The day was very hot and sultry.

It was really too bad about the organ player, Palmström mused. He had known Peder Nyeberg ever since he had come to this district, and then Peder had been just a boy. In spite of having no education, Nyeberg was certainly one of the few cultured gentlemen that he had met in Norway. This was surely due to the fact that he himself had helped to educate the boy and instilled in him enlightened ideas. They had lent each other and talked about every book and pamphlet either one had come across. In fact, they had shared hours of peace and companionship in his little hut up the hill, talking about and discussing the things they had read. Palmström prided himself on never having encouraged his pupil to break the law, not even the most unreasonable ones that everyone ignored. He had really been like a father to the lad; he had shared with him everything he had, his knowledge as well as his brandy, his life's experience as well as material things. No one could ever accuse Nyeberg of being the receiver of stolen goods, for Peder had always been very careful not to ask or know how the various things he was given had been acquired.

As he grew older, he had shown how grateful he was for Palmström's care and interest, and he became very useful to the Swede and his acquaintances, for he could write and was often employed to assist at the Civil Service offices, and there he got very interesting bits of information. He certainly was a very agreeable person and Palmström valued the connection.

Not, of course, that Nyeberg had done all this for nothing. Palmström had paid seven silver rix-dalers for the material for Nyeberg's wife's wedding dress, and before they were married he had given her a present of bleached linen for household things. Well, to be sure, it hadn't cost him much, since Major Brager's wife had woven and bleached it, but since no one knew it, it didn't alter the kind intentions.

The question that had to be decided now was whether he was going to let Peder Nyeberg and his wife and child starve to death on watery gruel and porridge made of bark and reindeer moss. Even the moss had to be carried down from the mountain on his own hunched back. It nearly broke the Swede's heart to listen to Nyeberg's troubles, but, by Jove, he himself was just barely making ends meet, his own provisions would only last for two more days! What could he do? The grain storage? What the hell was the use of having a grain storage if they couldn't get any grain out of it? Palmström brushed the lines of his tattooed hand again, licked and polished them. Certainly he wasn't interested in either clergymen or their quarrels; he couldn't care less; to finish off two of them in one blow would suit him splendidly. But people were pretty hard and merciless these days; the ordinary farmer was so greedy he didn't even pay any attention to black magic these days, and all the rest of the people were sullen and cross. Even Hans Dahlbye had hinted that he couldn't afford to give more than one meal to those who were not his fellow parishioners, and that was the man who prided himself on his firmness in making no exceptions for anyone. It wouldn't be of any use to ask him for help until his mood changed. The attorney at Gihle had turned the whole business over to his wife these days, and she surely watched things closely and managed very neatly. Yes, and Mr. Orre was as slippery as an eel and never gave anything except to those he liked, and neither he nor Nyeberg were among Mr. Orre's favorites, he guessed.

To hell with being humble and curry favor from the bigwigs! The grain in the storage bin belonged to the State, even though the authorities had become pretty particular about investigating and arresting people, thanks mostly to the councillor, for this strange man was as angry as a bull these days and didn't hesitate to put the sheriff on the trail of even the most inconsequential things. What a lot of senseless drinking and carrying on he had been doing since his housekeeper committed suicide last year. He didn't seem to care about anything anymore; he had no patience. Of course, Palmström couldn't really expect any of him, for the councillor had warned him pretty sharply after that trick he had played with the bleached linen at Major Brager's house. But what was he going to do about the organ player, his wife, and child and moss porridge?

A dog barked near him. The woodpecker screamed angrily, flew across the field and disappeared in the direction of the dark clouds which had been approaching the sun, whose rays made the clouds gleam along their edges.

A stranger came whistling up the road. He was a giant of a man with a fat round face which beamed ruddy and complacent. He wore a broad-brimmed straw hat, a shirt with red stripes, and a pair of long wool trousers which were pretty ragged and torn around the ankles. On his feet he wore a pair of rough, homemade birch-bark shoes; a bundle on the end of a stick bobbed up and down on his shoulder. A curly-haired poodle danced along after him wagging its tail.

Palmström jumped up: "Well, if it isn't dear brother Petter Wibom, walking around like a cavalier in pantaloons —and with a dog!"

"If it isn't my good fellow Palmström," came the answer in Swedish. "How are you these damned days? A little thinner about the cheeks, eh?" They were very pleased to see each other and shook hands cordially and went on speaking Swedish. The big tramp was in a good humor. The clever dog, named Caro, had followed him all the way down from Trondheim from some pine barren where he had rested for a few hours. He had been very friendly and was certainly an amusing companion. His last lodging had been at the horse-gelders at Kluftsveen, where the food was terrible, but today he had had a wonderful meal at Kjelsrud.

He said he had asked very politely at Kjelsrud for a brandy and something to eat and Erik, the husband, had himself poured him a tiny one. This was very much against the wishes of his pregnant wife, who stood near by looking at him with glittering black eyes, urging her husband not to be afraid of tramps. The dinner table was set with all sorts of delicious foods, such as butter, cheese, meat, pork and bread, and the uninvited guest had sat down and eaten without being asked to. Then Erik Kjelsrud tried to throw him out but Wibom made a nasty face at him, grabbed the farmer's knife and told the man he should send him on his way with a "skaal" in a big glass of brandy. This the farmer did, and let Wibom eat in peace. But then that old witch of a wife of his came back, threw the glasses on the floor, kicked up the dickens of a row with her husband, opened the door and told the tramp to get the hell out of there. He had said his blessing and slunk off, properly fed up with that outfit, for he hadn't wanted to get any further involved with that woman. She wasn't any ordinary peasant girl; wasn't she the daughter of the late Captain Tebetmann? For sure, he wouldn't want to be in farmer Erik's shoes; he certainly had found his master. The two friends laughed heartily over the story. They had both heard that the household at Kjelsrud wasn't a peaceful one since the old captain had sailed off. Ho! Ho! Oh yes, Wibom remembered, Devil take him, what a good-hearted old buzzard he used to be.

Clouds covered the sun, and a cool wind rustled through the pines of the nearby forest and sent the grain waving in the adjacent rye field. The cheery chatter of the thrush changed to an anxious whining kind of whistle.

A long flash of lightning made a jagged strip through the clouds. The two men stopped talking and waited, startled. Then the thunder crashed around them, and the field echoed it. The rain started and made the trees rustle; thousands of drops made black spots in the gray dust of the road.

"It would be nice to be snugly under cover," said the big tramp, giving himself a shake.

"Come on; it's just a mile up to my cabin," Palmström shouted as he started to walk fast, his coat tails flapping against his legs. "Besides, I have something to talk to you about!"

* * *

In the cool summer night that followed the rain, the little lake in the faint glimmer of the pale sky reflected the edges of the forest which surrounded it like a mirror. In the rushes growing by the side of the brook, a little poodle splashed and growled at the water creatures.

Somebody was in the grain storage. Two men carried out bags and put them on a pack horse. The poodle, bored at last with chasing those stupid frogs, shook himself and ran into the grain barn. The men shut the door as soon as they were finished with their business, prodded the horse to a run and, in their hurry, didn't miss the dog.

Next morning a miller a little further down the millstream heard a dog bark and wail, and noticing that the sounds came from the direction of the grain storage, he walked up that way and discovered that the building had been broken into and the dog locked up in it. He didn't let the dog out, but sent the miller boy immediately for the sheriff.

A few days later both Palmström and Wibom were in jail. Someone had seen them the night of the robbery going up the hill with the dog and a horse they had taken from the curate's pastures.

The rumors that Palmström had been caught spread quickly around the district and caused a sensation. For nearly twenty years this Swede had been going about, suspected of the worst and always involved in the meanest deals, but he had always been protected by the fact that people were afraid of him, so that no one dared to turn him in for the punishment he deserved.

They were afraid of him because he himself seemed to have no fear of God, the devil, or the magistrates. There had been an air of secrecy and deviltry about him, and he had been able to treat the common people any way he felt like. They came to recognize that he was well educated, yet his companions were horse-gelders, tramps and Lapps—in fact, all kinds of people whose main business was against the law. Such people certainly were of some use to him. Too, his profane mockery of the church and religion made people think he was in league with those forces which decent people had better not mention if they were interested in the salvation of their souls. There seemed to be no doubt at all that he made use of black magic. He had always made friends with the rich people and received from them both work and protection when he needed it. But apparently they now felt he was beyond helping, and the force of his magic was gone. Perhaps the time of his contract with the Devil had lapsed.

The homeless tramps and strangers, however, who lived their whole lives wandering over the country, roaming through the forests in the summertime, begging their food and lodging in the winter—if they did not live by stealing—these people were really terror-stricken, because Palmström had been a leader among them, assisting them by word and deed.

After a while, when people became brave enough to talk openly about his many misdeeds, their hatred for him and thirst for revenge grew. One by one, reports of his scurvy tricks and crimes continued to grow until there was certainly a good number of counts against him.

His trial in court took a long time because of the number and complexity of charges against him. The prisoners were tried individually. At first Palmström was as bold as brass and was very eloquent in his own defense. In spite of the warnings of his lawyer, Attorney Höegh, he insisted on saying that certain unscrupulous and lying people were trying to "frame" him because he was a foreigner, and that they were trying to cover up their own crimes by blaming him, that he was just a victim of their spite and envy. He asked all his respectable neighbors to forgive him if he had made trouble for them. It was certainly not unusual to err, and he was very grateful for all the kindness he had received in the years he had lived here, here where he wanted to remain until he died. To the evil ones, however, he owed no thanks and hoped they would reform. He was innocent and trusted in God and the protection of the law under the government of the good Danish King; that was the right of every accused citizen. The new bailiff, who had succeeded old Mr. Jespersen, was so infuriated by Palmström's impudent speech that he swore he would see this obstinate old man properly punished and given a good long time to repent; at the same time he would be a good example to others who might be inclined to play similar tricks.

An unexpected development in the case came about when the councillor, Mr. Weydahl, gave Palmström to understand that his friend Mr. Wibom had confessed to his part in the crime, and that the organ player, in order not to have his home searched, had handed over to the police one of the bags of grain the Swede had given him. At the next session of the court the prisoner said his conscience had been bothering him. He had by then been in jail for several weeks with a log tied to his feet, and the handcuffs had made his wrists rather sore.

He had hoped for and expected help, if not to be freed at least to escape, but everyone had failed and betrayed him, from his protector Hans Dahlbye, down to the organ player, his friend. Only their secret letters warning him not to be indiscreet had reached him, and, yes, they had managed to smuggle him a little food. Well, Palmström decided to make a clean breast this time and started with the organ player whom he wanted prosecuted for having harbored stolen goods; he went on and on, making serious charges against so many respectable people that it looked as though the whole case would cause such a holocaust of righteousness that everyone in the whole district would be involved in public disgrace and disaster. First he wanted to bring in Hans Dahlbye as a sacrifice to the angry authorities.

Two more court sessions were held. Mr. Dahlbye fought like a lion. Evidence from both parties was given, and Mr. Weydahl was sure there had been perjury on both sides. This was turning out to be very dangerous, indeed. One afternoon the councillor went over to see the accused. He talked to the prisoner for a long time, and afterwards Palmström withdrew all his charges. The only one who had been so seriously accused that charges could not be dropped was Hans Dahlbye, and legal proceedings were going to be taken against him.

Within a short time Palmström received the verdict which he accepted without comment. Some people thought he had gotten off too easily—only five years in jail and banishment forever from the King's realms.

Quite a crowd had gathered to take a look at him the morning he was sent in to town to jail. As he sat on the cart, he raised his arms to heaven and made a last speech. His hat fell off and his long ragged white hair hung down on his shoulders. His eyes gleamed wildly. He called on heaven to proclaim his innocence and prophesied that the judge's mouth which had sentenced him so unjustly should never again sentence anyone. The crowd just laughed at him, even though he nearly made them shudder. They didn't fear even Palmström's black magic any longer, for after all he hadn't been able to get himself out of the sheriff's clutches, had he?

Ingratitude is the only reward in this world, thought the old man as the cart bumped and jolted through the laughing and curious crowd. He remembered now; it was a night in spring—just seven years and five months ago, in fact—that he had robbed the church in Hans Dahlbye's parish, just to irritate the parson and show his contempt of the clergy. Dahlbye hadn't been there; he had merely pointed out the fact that there were valuable pieces of gold and silver kept there and rather easy to get. His nephew, however, just a boy at the time, had climbed up to the window sill on a chair and had handed the things out the window to the Swede and his companion. They got the baptismal font, the velvet cloth, the wafer box, and even the candlesticks. "But this," the lad had said, "I intend to keep for a souvenir," and he had put the golden chalice in his pocket before he jumped down.

III

In the fall of the year it was rumored around that the councillor was very ill and probably would not live very long. Dr. Müller had been to see him and found the judge so weak and exhausted from pain that he hadn't even had the strength to scold Lars for sending for him. He could hardly speak for he had a tumor at the base of his tongue. He had used to be so taciturn that the members of his household didn't particularly notice that for quite a while now he hadn't spoken at all. He had just murmured when he needed to speak to the clerks and often he had been seen to put his hand to his throat as though he had a pain there. On the day that the councillor didn't get out of bed at all, Lars sent for the doctor.

After a good bit of opposition, the patient finally gave in and allowed Dr. Müller to cut away the tumor; otherwise he would have suffocated. But as the doctor said, the operation was not very successful, as it left the councillor without the power of speech and unable to take any food except liquids.

Was Palmström's prophecy going to be fulfilled after all? Everyone believed that such was the case although no one felt that the Swede was innocent. The rich people would not admit to harboring such thoughts, but at the same time their smiles were a little cautious. The common people, however, had no doubt that the councillor was the victim of the Swede's curse. If it was not directly from the prisoner, at least it was from one of his gang, for they had no doubt that many would seek revenge for him. People broodingly discussed black magic and sorcery which were so dangerous to everyone. Apparently those tramps and outlaws who had made the Devil their lord and master felt that this was their remedy and means of getting back at respectable people.

The councillor's servants became obsessed with fear of black magic and became anxious and afraid in the dark. The dairymaid was afraid to be alone in the cow-barn, and the cottagemen now waited for each other before they would go home at night. The kitchen maid, who had taken over the duties as housekeeper since Miss Nannestad died, decided to move over to the servants' wing with the other servant girl. Their pretext was that they might disturb the councillor by the noise of their coming and going. Soon no one was left in the main building except the councillor and those who took care of him during his illness. Of course, there were the clerks who went back and forth to the office but they didn't live at the councillor's.

There were whispers of ghosts in the building, and the servants wondered why they hadn't been seen before. As long as the councillor was well, these apparitions seemed to be subdued, yet it had always been said that there were two, if not three, ghosts that were supposed to haunt the place from olden times.

Had anyone met a ghost? Had any ever been seen? No one could say, yet everyone felt there might be one there.

Weydahl dozed the days away. He no longer spoke and made himself understood by gestures and signs. If he wasn't understood right away, he became upset and angry and then he would try to speak, but he couldn't, for his voice was gone. All that was left was a gargling sound which couldn't be understood, and to make even that caused his mouth to be twisted with pain.

He had the curtains at his four-poster bed taken away, for he couldn't bear to be closed in behind them. Strangely enough, he wanted someone to sit beside him all the time, and the candles had to burn all night long.

Since he had no relatives to take care of him, and no women ever came to his bedside, old Lars and Matjas took turns caring for him. He had been a good master to them, and they certainly would not forsake him now. Their clumsy rough hands handled the emaciated body tenderly as they propped him against the pillows and helped him to drink when he gave a sign. Before long he was quite helpless and weak as a child. Both Mr. Lind and the curate had visited him to see if he needed any spiritual help; the councillor, however, became simply furious when he heard about their visits and rather rudely refused to see either of them. Finally Matjas told them frankly on their next visits that the councillor was too weak to receive visitors. This offended the parson very much, and the curate, Mr. Vamberg, felt rather hurt. However, they both swallowed their pride and said they would not come again unless especially asked for, but begged Matjas to send for them before it was too late.

One afternoon in the late twilight, Attorney Höegh drove down the maple-lined road in his cariole. Yellow and brown leaves already covered the ground. Puddles were covered with a layer of ice, so that the cart wheels made a cracking, crunching sound. At every step along the way, the horse must have wondered at his master's unusual quietness and gentleness. On the western ridges, the red rays of the sunset were still visible, their eery light shining through a tiny split in the dark skies.

Mr. Höegh was taken up to the patient, who, strangely enough, brightened at the sight of his visitor; it made the attorney feel ill to see the change that had taken place in Mr. Weydahl. The skin was stretched tightly across his high cheekbones. His chin was covered with a rough gray beard, and approaching death was already in the eyes that gazed out from their deep hollows.

Höegh sat down by the bed. He had grown stiff and old himself and was much too heavy. He talked at random for awhile but seemed distracted and thoughtful. Lars sitting in the corner sensed that the attorney had something on his mind he wished to speak about but could not do so now that he saw how ill the councillor appeared to be.

Weydahl listened a while and then wrote something on a piece of paper and handed it to the attorney who, after looking at it, said: "No, no, not for me, by all means—and it will not be good for you." But the councillor had made up his mind and nodded yes, so Höegh asked Lars to bring a pitcher of punch and some glasses.

Lars was gone for about half an hour, since he had had to send for a maid to make the brew. He placed the tray near the bed when he returned; as he did so, the attorney leaned over and grasping the hand of the councillor said sadly: "How can I thank you, Weydahl—isn't there something I can do for you?"

The councillor could only gurgle as he always did when he tried to speak. He shook his head and made a sign to pour the punch; then they clinked their glasses in a silent toast. The fingers with which Weydahl grasped his glass were bony and dry like those of a skeleton. The men did not speak again. Once in a while their eyes met; when this happened those of the attorney slipped aside.

They drank together several times, but the hot punch seared the throat of the sick man, and he coughed silently and seemed in great pain, so after a while Höegh left. He sighed and looked very depressed as he climbed into his cariole. Lars who had run after him with his whip, which he had forgotten, was taken aback when he received a whole silver daler for a tip.

The same night there was a heavy snowfall, which seemed rather strange to Lars since this was the first such fall of the year. Lifting the curtain, he saw by the light from the room the white flakes whirling close to the window. Beyond the radiance of light it was a dark, dark night—not a sound, not a glimmer of life.

At midnight it was Matjas' turn to watch in the sick room. Lars went over to the servants' wing, since Matjas had told his wife to go to bed in the kitchen in case he should need her.

The patient was very restless. He tossed and turned in his bed. He breathed with difficulty, panting and with small grunts, as if his breath was caught in his throat.

It may have been because Matjas had emptied the punch mug and the drink made him fall asleep that he did not waken when very early in the morning the councillor got out of bed. Putting on a robe he took from a rack, Weydahl then opened a drawer and, taking a key from it, picked up one of the candles and walked out of the room. With firm steps he went up the stairs to his office.

There he put the candle on a desk, unlocked one of the cabinets and rummaged around looking for something. After a while he picked up a bundle of papers; then he lifted a register from the shelf where the mortgages were filed. The book was so heavy he could hardly move it. By the light of the candle he read something here and there in the record and then tore out some of the pages.

Holding them and the other papers in his hand he left the room, forgetting the candle which he left on the desk. Fumbling along the dark hallway he accidentally pushed open the door of the room occupied by his late wife. The shock sent him reeling across the hall where he leaned against the wall for a moment. It was years now since he had opened that door. His last bit of strength deserted him, and he nearly fainted.

In the drawing room a clock struck the hour, and the deep sounds of the strokes resounded through the big house.

After a moment he pulled himself together and went downstairs.

Matjas jumped up from his sleep to see the councillor lying in great pain on top of the bed. On the floor beside it lay the robe, just where he had thrown it. Weydahl beckoned him to come close and then pointed to a bundle of papers on the table and from them to the stove. Matjas couldn't figure out what he was trying to say. The councillor made gurgling noises in his throat and clutching the papers stuck them into the candle flame. Then Matjas realized what he wanted, he grabbed the papers and threw them into the stove and left the door open so the councillor could see they had been entirely destroyed. Then he helped the councillor to be comfortable in bed and covered him up. The hours passed, and again Matjas fell asleep. The sick man seemed to be resting, for he breathed more easily.

At daybreak Matjas wakened again. A deep stillness seemed to hang over the room. Matjas went over to the bed. The councillor lay there with his arms crossed on his breast. He did not move when the other touched him. He was dead. Matjas tried to close his eyes but they jutted out, round and glassy, and the eyelids pulled back up and refused to shut.

Matjas wakened his wife who was asleep in the kitchen bed. "The councillor is dead," he said as she raised herself sleepily on her elbows.

"Oh, he is, he is—" she whimpered, "he has gone through his last struggle, then—even he has—"

"I ought to send for someone," Matjas said uncertainly, only he didn't know whom.

After a while his wife remarked: "I guess, well, perhaps you should go tell the attorney."

"I'll ask Lars," Matjas said and left the kitchen.

As he waded through the big drifts of snow in the courtyard he heard sounds indicating that someone was already at work in the cow-barn, and he wondered why there was a light in the office.

A new day was breaking. The lake lay there dark and quiet, leaden-looking, but the surrounding snow-covered hills glittered as the flush of a wintry dawn rose above the forests.